MARSTON MEADOWS

John Fuller

CW01499221

Chatto & Windus
LONDON

1 3 5 7 9 10 8 6 4 2

Chatto & Windus, an imprint of Vintage, is part of the
Penguin Random House group of companies

Vintage, Penguin Random House UK, One Embassy Gardens,
8 Viaduct Gardens, London SW11 7BW

penguin.co.uk/vintage
global.penguinrandomhouse.com

First published by Chatto & Windus in 2025

Typeset in 11/14pt Minion Pro by Six Red Marbles UK, Thetford, Norfolk
Printed and bound in Great Britain by Clays Ltd, Elcograf S.p.A.

The authorised representative in the EEA is Penguin Random House Ireland,
Morrison Chambers, 32 Nassau Street, Dublin D02 YH68

A CIP catalogue record for this book is available from the British Library

ISBN 9781784746544

Penguin Random House is committed to a sustainable future
for our business, our readers and our planet. This book is made
from Forest Stewardship Council® certified paper.

MARSTON MEADOWS

POETRY

Fairground Music
The Tree That Walked
Cannibals and Missionaries
Epistles to Several Persons
The Mountain in the Sea
Lies and Secrets
The Illusionists
Waiting for the Music
The Beautiful Inventions
Selected Poems 1954 to 1982
Partingtime Hall
(with James Fenton)
The Grey Among the Green
The Mechanical Body
Stones and Fires
Collected Poems
Now and for a Time

Ghosts
The Space of Joy
Song & Dance
Pebble & I
Writing the Picture
(with David Hurn)
Dream Hunter
(with Nicola LeFanu)
New Selected Poems 1983–2008
The Dice Cup
Gravel in My Shoe
AWOL (with Andrew
Wynn Owen)
The Bone Flowers
Double Dactyls
Asleep & Awake
How Many Children?

FICTION

Flying to Nowhere
The Adventures of
Speedfall
Tell It Me Again
The Burning Boys
Look Twice

The Worm and the Star
A Skin Diary
The Memoirs of Laetitia Horsepole
Flawed Angel
The Clock in the Forest
Loser

CRITICISM

The Sonnet
W. H. Auden: a Commentary

Who is Ozymandias? And Other
Puzzles in Poetry

FOR CHILDREN

Herod Do Your Worst
Squeaking Crust
The Spider Monkey Uncle King
The Last Bid

The Extraordinary Wool Mill and
Other Stories
Come Aboard and Sail Away
You're Having Me On!
Up and Down the Chimney

AS EDITOR

The Chatto Book of Love Poetry
The Dramatic Works of
John Gay
The Oxford Book of Sonnets

W. H. Auden: Poems Selected
by John Fuller
Alexander Pope: Poems Selected
by John Fuller

Contents

III

I

Marston Meadows

A Corona for Prue

1.

Come, then, we'll walk (what else is there to do?)
Down to the goosey river, where the weir
Sprawls like our dreams and seethes throughout the year
Into the secret fields. Just me and you
Tracking the shape and startled peekaboo
Of a lost roe deer (surprised to find us near
But fixed in curiosity, not fear).
These are the meadows, and our rendezvous.

It seems an age since the retreat of March,
Its caution and alarm. Then we were shocked
By graphs in April and the great delay
Through weeks that reached like columns of an arch
That rises into mist, our vision locked
In the uncertainties of dangerous May.

2.

In the uncertainties of dangerous May
Arrives this sense of yielding and of stasis.
It's the new sun that does it. It outfaces
All of our nightmares with its brilliant day.
It wins its endless quarrel with the grey,
Touching with colour all the roses' faces.
It brings the beetles from their hiding-places
And all the beasts into their sexual play.

And now the joggers splutter round the Parks
Like frantic surgeons. Sounds of silence bring
Some kinds of paranoia: far away
Meaningless bells, unusual meadowlarks,
With all the threats and terror of the Spring,
And Summer coming into disarray.

3.

And Summer coming into disarray
Reminds us of our earlier expectations,
With all the flowers stalwart at their stations
And blossom heavy on the branch's sway;
Magnolia's cold flames that straightaway,
It seems, curdle the lawns; the celebrations
Of lilac and wistaria; the patience
Of irises that line the waterway.

All come and go as always, and short June
Yields to that month that we possess, that knot
We tied a diamond time ago, the new
Life that we made, early but not too soon,
Now more than ever sharply aware of what
We see before us underneath the blue.

4.

We see before us underneath the blue
A civil landscape more or less undefiled,
Peaceful, with seated cows, but hardly wild.

We tread a fluid map the centuries grew.
Each ancient boundary's a parvenu:
Villages suburbs, old mills reconciled
With the cool walks of Addison and Wilde
Where knowledge has its hopeful vistas, too.

And all the time a steady watercourse,
That brims and floods when opportunity
Allows, confines the paths we wander through.
We need no maps (they never show a horse
Or darkening cloud) and only hope to see
The ancient green world that we thought we knew.

5.

The ancient green world that we thought we knew
Seems always fresh. We are the audience
With privileged private seats at an immense
Performance in rehearsal, always new
And yet familiar. It's nature who
Produces this perennial, intense
Theatre of burgeoning magnificence,
This symphony of green, this pulsing zoo.

That world is both itself and what we are
And always have been since the earliest slime
Began to stir, or Yahweh moulded clay.
It rightly tells us mind is molecular
And we are bodies. Yes, and every time
It moves us still, whatever we may say.

6.

It moves us still! Whatever we may say
When taking pride in what we think we think,
When rationalising things or pushing ink,
It welcomes us when we have gone astray
And look on all our works with blank dismay.
We press a button to pursue a link
Which merely tells us our horizons shrink:
Our wild aim kills us with its ricochet.

A field is like a room without a ceiling,
Hedges for walls and gates for doors. It's hateful
To think we can't go in. But it's okay,
Since nature is a host of sorts. So feeling
Like guests we tell ourselves that we are grateful
That it accepts us. Though it will not stay.

7.

That it accepts us, though it will not stay
For long enough to nurse us as it did,
May just about content us. God forbid
That we rebuke it for our sins. Today
A virus breeds and there's a price to pay.
Our Government is like an invalid
Running a nursing home. The rich, amid
Their funds and islands, try to run away.

No one can hide. We make our sacrifices
As though we can appease the gods we've cursed
While reasoning away each old taboo.

But they have left us to our own devices,
Left us with prejudices that we've nursed
For long enough to be a settled view.

8.

For long enough to be a settled view
The meadows (rooms we enter through a wall)
Need to be visited so we can learn to call
Them by their names, or give them names anew:
Like Music Meadow, where muntjac pursue
Each other; Great Mill Pond Mead where grass grows tall
Enough to hide a single deer; and all
Of Napper's Arable where moles review
The sky in punctuation marks of earth;
The buttercups in South Mead; ganders in
Bat Willow Meadow refining their fashion show;
The field near Park Farm where a doe gave birth.
They all define the routes where we have been.
Onwards has always been the way to go.

9.

Onwards has always been the way to go.
We can't relive the future or the past,
Only create the present, which moves fast
Upon itself, the way a river's flow
Defeats the expectant eye when to-and-fro
The birds behave in it. They have this vast
Assumption that the river's made to last.
Their liquid landscape is a status quo.

Another lesson from the birds, who pair
And sing about it. What is the blackbird at?
We know he has no language for goodbye.
His song-sheet says the Spring's eternal. Dare
We share with him the frail illusion that
Together we might make time stop or fly?

10.

Together we might make time stop. Or fly
Like a pair of sailing swans quite unconfined
By their mortality, rising entwined
And abstract as a page of heraldry,
Where to make meaning is to simplify
All the dire contraries of humankind.
In such a flight we could become all mind,
The once-and-for-all of every by-and-by.

But human minds are weak and fully-freighted
With all the noise of living. Nothing's clear-cut,
No revelation but a lexicon
Of possibilities. The time's awaited
When our joint mind must be divided, but
When we are parted we shall think as one.

11.

When we are parted we shall think as one
Who lost a fortune, though a billionaire.
Our years, profuse in quantity, though rare

Enough, amount to sixty. They have run
Like water through our hands, though. Not yet done,
Solid as earth, mercurial as air
Or fire. There is no reason to despair,
But let us gamble still on sixty-one.

The earth bears diamond as the air does birds,
(Tears of the gods, the Romans thought) congealed
From molten carbon billions of years ago.
Diamond is hard, but not so hard as words
We speak or write that say that we must yield
Without complaint, if matter tells us so.

12.

Without complaint, if matter tells us—so
We must believe it, without a tear or frown.
The die is cast, and we can always drown
Our sorrows in Scrabble or an old Bordeaux.
This day is precious to us both, although
I have no diamonds for you, only this crown
Of sonnets, a rococo hand-me-down
You'll say, and just another jeu de mots.

Remember Evelyn's terrace, trying to quiz
His motto: TO KALON KATEXETE? Two years
Ago, your birthday? Some Greek that took our eye.
It said the Beautiful is all there is
And we must seize it, though it disappears.
And that's just why we can't agree to die.

13.

And that's just why we can't agree. To die
First is the cruellest choice. Die second? Hard
Enough, and anyway such choice is barred
However we might think to justify
The preference. And even should you try,
You cannot cut the pack and choose a card.
Death has a way of catching you off-guard.
It comes at last out of a clear blue sky.

And that is what we have this Summer, when
The leaves are lofting in a kind of praise,
A choir of chlorophyll in unison,
Making a shade by growing thick, and then
Dappling the paths and filtering the rays,
So we may wander here beneath the sun.

14.

So, we may wander here. Beneath the sun
We circle and return from whence we came.
The place that we come back to is the same,
Though hours nearer to our oblivion.
A walk is like a knot that gets undone,
And yet it keeps us closer. We can claim
Each minute was invested in our name,
A dividend from all that we've begun,
A time to spend that may not come again.
When the dry August turns to dank September
We may be seeking answers to the clue

That time proposes, that we've looked in vain
For all these years. Perhaps we won't remember.
Come then. We'll walk. What else is there to do?

15.

Come then, we'll walk. What else is there to do
In the uncertainties of dangerous May
And Summer coming into disarray?
We see before us underneath the blue
The ancient green world that we thought we knew.
It moves us still, whatever we may say,
And it accepts us. Though it will not stay
For long enough to be a settled view.

Onwards has always been the way to go.
Together we might make time stop or fly.
When we are parted we shall think as one
Without complaint, if matter tells us so.
And that's just why we can't agree to die—
So we can wander here beneath the sun.

Traces

Tired of our talk, the summer departed.
Nothing had moved us but a favoured face
    (The yawn at the party,
    The cork on the lawn).

No need to tell that time is passing,
And frequent winters leave their trace
    (The swell of the tide,
    The weed on the shell).

The perfect shape is broken at the edges.
Something is nearly always out of place
    (The fly in the butter,
    The blood on the flannel).

Whatever begins is likely to finish,
But no-one is bound to win the race
    (The mask in the gutter,
    The face in the Channel).

The relics of the happy hour,
The might-have-been, the just-in-case,
All we have spoiled, all we have kept,
They go from us, we go from them.

And though we laughed, and though we wept,
The crimson's fading from the flower,
The leaf is falling from the stem,
And all that's left behind is space.

Unravellings

Beautifully there, but hard to unravel,
Like the famous lie of that secretive Cretan,
With its weird and multiplying venular
Branching, its twists and turns, just as nectar
Forever lures the teased bee who clambers
Over and over to suck its precious gel,
Not realising in the eager scramble
The stowaway powder adhering to its leg.

So it was also with that Theban ox-head
Hidden like the serpent in the garden
Who wove his mazy folds round Eve and hoaxed
Her and her kind into eternal danger.
Life is a labyrinth. Have you not felt
It so? Felt it however much you hated
The hero's role? Turn always to the left.
And hope without reason to evade your death.

The Bees

for Emily

Will you remember this walk when we're not here,
The flags charged with the June day's heat
Between the bristling books of the Apostles
And the high dry wall with its clumps of red daisies?
Almost a hundred years ago the border
With its yellows and greens and blueish purples lay
Beneath the same sky and its creator's careful
Fingers, and continues to lead the eye.

At the lip of each sweet salvia, as if there were time,
Time enough, or perhaps only just enough time
For their immense project, barely understood,
The bees are visiting and busying themselves.
Of all kinds and sizes, they work alone
And yet in company, humming in descant,
Broad-shouldered and with yellow mufflers,
Or small and brown. One is as big as a thumb.

Circling and clambering, they share each spray
Without hindrance, challenge or deference.
They have the air of going on for ever,
Giving a nudge to every flower in turn.
The quiet of this walk is an absolute
Defined only by the dizziness of the bees
Or the distant nest-squabble of the ravens,
The loudest topic of the afternoon.

A garden begins with gestures on an urn.
The walk leads forward, though you may walk back,
Knowing its length is finite. Will you remember
How the blossoms are pleased with their colours and shapes
In that still moment which surely comes to us all,
When in their being they are what they intended to be,
Under their sun and the hand of the garden Buddha
In his grey and ochre stone, dispelling fear?

Flowers for Bees

1. Geranium

In a green shade of the garden
These untroubled flowers
Demonstrate their five petals,
Violet shading to pink
And with white at the centre.

Are they like hands reaching out
In a kind of greeting?
Are they like faces containing a joy
Transmitted in reflection?
Bees make them nod as if they are.

Although I look at them closely enough,
Glancing up frequently from my book,
I can't catch them in the act of attention
To anything beyond their own being.
These words I write are a nod of a kind.

2. Japanese Anemone

It never understood the prohibition
Of pink with yellow. It marches from its bed
On to the lawn as if it is beautiful.

But it is! Splayed stalks like a candelabra,
Large dark-veined leaves, tough and coarse.
The bees alight on it like any other.

3. Marjoram

I might have cut the marjoram for salad,
And did so, until the rainy days drove
Me indoors, and it was all forgotten.

Their little spears of green, with over-notes
Of rust or leather, are now emerald pillars
Supporting tiny clusters of pink flowers.

I counted seventeen bees upon them, delicately
Rampaging (seventeen until I could reliably
Count no more, as they circled and changed places).

I shall, I think, straddle the back of one of them,
Gripping its tigery fur, and fly away
To see where they make their honey, and to taste it.

Lord of the Arboretum

for Louisa

In his lofty museum of trees
There was a leaf for every mood

From the fine distinctions of the acer
To the gloom of the elephant's ear.

In its winding descent the coupling
And uncoupling of water and stone

Led to a surprising lacquered bridge
Created from a few strokes of red

Where he could enact the pausing
That is philosophy's credential,

Led to pool after circled pool
Where the trees reflected themselves

Moving and yet unmoved, their reach
Completed in their fullness of leaf

And consequent downward flutter of seeds,
That sly conquest of territory

Which must however be fairly shared
In the equal judgement of chance and time.

Led to a smug tóngshi, toying
With the entire globe in bronze.

Led in fact to the edge of things
Where all the truth of the tilted woodscape

Looked out upon a blankness of field
That had nothing to think of but the sky.

And so of course he would return
Up again through the varied paths

Learning to know what the trees know,
Happy to know as much as the woods.

Woods that remembered the wise East
But cast their shadows to the West.

Horizons

East Coast traces the sun in its rising; West Coast follows it to rest.
East Coast is mindful of origins; West Coast looks to the future.

Between, there is a natural movement to find the best,
The centre of cities moving to the west.

Keels in the shingle; launch of resolve.
Waiting for invasion; postponement of migration.

Estuaries of industry; granite of poverty.
The derelict pill-box; the timely tide.

Gas-flares at night; worm-flats at morning.
Wind in the wires; driftwood and heartache.

Lending the money of guilt; spending the money of shame.
The one word whispered; the speech at the pier.

The hard apprenticeship; the villa with the view.
The barely shod; the beautifully dressed.

What do they share but an ending and beginning,
A beginning and ending, never at rest?

And a compulsive scanning from left to right
To parse the history that we must read. Or write.

Gardens

for Sophie and Elaine

Two gardens. The first is where we meet up
After too long a time, triangulation
For a dispersed family, the shortest distance
Between three points, a house in the Surrey hills
Where the old botanist promoted reflection and
An openness of mind: 'OMNIA EXPLORATE . . .'

The afternoon is mellow as its russet brickwork.
Across the terrace, tea is brought and shared.
Just beyond it is a mass of Russian Sage
Busily married by bees. A coloured pheasant
Scuttles without fear or purpose across close grass
That sweeps away from us like a raked stage.

This lavish green expanse leads from both sides
To a columned gazebo with a presiding nymph,
The marble grubby above the dispersed mosaics,
Clipped trees with inky shadows, hiding
Steep steps to further heights and the stone candle
Of mysterious Mossy Moses and his blessing.

Your own upland garden was once Victorian,
With corners of paved shade where the daughters
    of gentlemen
Turned the pages of the latest Trollope
Or perhaps sewed examples of the same motto,
'. . . MELIORA RETINETE', as they had been taught,
Or sang some Maude in a small voice of hope.

You rescued the throttled blooms, exhumed paths
And restored a walkable shape of ascent and completion
Where flowers could breathe again and share with fruits
The seasons' appropriate encouragements.
You introduced your garden to the kitchen
And now take heart from that relationship.

You may have no fountain, or Italian cave,
But you can be your own prophets or hermits,
And commanders-in-chiefs as well, sowing
The seeds of content for their yearly march to the border,
Tents of netting, trenches and ramparts for roots,
Wooden frames in the war on slug and fox.

And some necessary truce, perhaps, with that
Most ancient of inhabitants, the badger,
Who charms you in his soothing baritone:
'We are an enduring lot, and we may move out
For a time, but we wait, and we are patient, and back
We come.' For what we all want is to come back.

To philosophise in a garden is a fine thing,
In a world where nymphs are nature's sole authority,
Better still to eat it: the cut lettuce,
The sweet angelica, the peppery radish.
Never, never is there time to wait.
See, you are holding out the gathered handfuls.

Cuckoo

Why is the cuckoo
Always in a further tree
   Along the valley
Than the one she seems to be
Calling from? Who knows, who knows?

Hotel

The birds, have they been singing here
For these five years? And we not here
    To listen?
That one scuffling there, her eyes
Quick among the leaves? Her eyes
    Glisten.

She'll swoop about and scoop the pool
As she does now. She'll drink the pool
    Once more
When we are gone. And throat the air
With joy until she throats the air
    No more.

The palms have grown a span or two
And they will grow another two
    Apart.
The owners, whom we knew before,
Pretend to know us now, before
    We part.

Think of them as angels who
Greet all the travellers, and who
    Will tell
Them what it means to gather there
After so long, and late, in their
    Hotel.

These lodgings of my pilgrimage
Are staging-posts that youth and age
    Deserve.

If I look carefully, I'll spot
Some corners of a favourite spot
    That serve.

And there reflect on all I've done
Or haven't, when my days are done
    And time
Takes time to judge unjust or just
My every little action, just
    In time.

When the heart questions, there will come
A consequent resolve that, come
    What may,
Regret can never cancel my
Remembering it all, nor my
    Dismay.

It will not need another five.
There cannot be another five,
    Since now
The days, the weeks, the years fly
Like birds. And yes, I watch them fly
    For now.

'Meditation'

Sunlight in a sitting-room, memento
Of an afternoon's longueur, when Mme. Monet,
Positioned on a canapé, is pleased
To become paint, till so much time's elapsed
While he adjusts the details and design
That, No, she will not wait to see it signed!
Her finger taps impatiently. She's tried
And tried, but her book calls her. She is tired
Of sitting all these hours as a statement
Of Claude's love, art's selfish testament.
Perhaps he tells her all models have aspired
To be their painters' muses, and be praised.
But she has much to do—there are the precise
Amounts required for the day's recipes,
Seeing a consommé clear or a sauce thicken
(Those strange metamorphoses of the kitchen)
And all the children's emotions superintended.
Life is a labour. It is unpredestined.
She asks herself what living will deliver,
Extemporised and not to be relived.
She's not a piece of flesh to be appraised.
She is a person, and can disappear.

. . .

The French for 'Lent' is a famous chef—Carême!
How strange. I order a chocolat à la crème
At a little pavement table by St-Germain
Where once philosophers, now emigrants
Debate if justice can exist on earth

And reason be acknowledged by the heart,
If love itself is more than coincidental
And common understanding non-dialectic.
This is Paris, where almost every doorbell
Leads to an atelier or bordello,
And ghosts of the 1950s in this café
(De Beauvoir's chevelure, the haunted face
Of Greco expecting immediate arrest,
The pensive hangdog jowls of J.-P. Sartre)
Remind me of the pathos of all exits,
Although I know that entrances exist
And those we remember have surely had their moment.
As at the Luxembourg has M. Monet
And his tender 'Meditation'. There are no
Setbacks that will keep us from pressing on.
The painter's wife turns to her novel. Night
Comes, as it will. And art is still the thing.

The Painter in his Valley

for Syed Jamal

1.

The purpose of these pages is to write
The lines and colours that embody light.

A spirit steps, miraculously, out
From her blinding nothing into light.

And graciously she licences the fingers
To trace the shapes that will reflect that light.

Reflect it, and control it, faithful to
The energising presence in the light.

2.

Paper loves light, and like an unknown land
Opens in mystery beneath the hand.

The four quarters of a travelled kingdom,
The five edicts of the intending hand.

The page is filled with instantaneous objects
By the slowly moving and creating hand.

This is the world before the world began,
The only sound the quiet human hand.

3.

The world burst into light when he surveyed
The corners of that world, in sun and shade.

And framed the spaces that those corners made
In grace and habitude, in sun and shade.

The golden frogs announce a serenade.
The granite echoes them, in sun and shade.

The trees pretend to be a colonnade
That strayed here long ago, in sun and shade.

4.

The little deities of furniture
Stand imperturbably upon their feet.

All speak the common language of their use,
Nothing extravagant, nothing effete.

And passing ghosts of previous presences
Declare their mistrust of the counterfeit.

All the possessions of the house reply:
Simply to be here is our singular feat.

5.

She is in earth and in the streams, the queen
Of gardens, of their pebbles and their green.

She is in stone, that's happy to be seen
As blue or pink among the grey and green.

The branches bend towards her as they lean,
Naked like her, since they have cast their green.

Or reach up to the sky where she has been,
And celebrate her and resume their green.

6.

Heroic voyages are metaphorical.
Our only compass is our watchful eye.

A home is where we start from, where the oracle
Speaks riddles to us of our destiny.

We fuel our stride, we climb, we patch our coracle.
The jet describes its plume across the sky.

And in the end we know that we're historical.
The only shore we reach is when we die.

7.

The wall has shadows where there might be gates.
The wood has depths that only the waters find.

The sun makes colours in the drying wood.
The sea has the horizon on its mind.

The bay proposes a red sail to the west.
The bwlch defines its granite peaks behind.

The picture places bowls and skulls and lights
Which then become the rooms they have defined.

8.

Whatever else there may be in the room,
There's always room enough for the painter's eye.

The shapes of things dismantle, then resume
Their quiddity in his constructing eye.

His mind withdraws. It is itself a room
That owes its richness to his restless eye.

And the whole world is swallowed in the bloom
That feeds the furnace in his greedy eye.

9.

Scarcely the brush can choose what it settles on,
But like the wings of summer is soon gone.

The lane has the air of knowing where it's going,
But nothing tells the eye where it has gone.

A page is turned, and what was still to come
Is yesterday, and yet is still not gone.

The day, the year, the centuries are one,
But we in these rooms are here, and not yet gone.

Nymph

She might be dancing
But for the stillness.
She might be speaking
But for the silence.
The arm unbending
And the bidding hand,
The turn of the wrist
And the one forefinger
Across its neighbour,
Neither pointing nor reaching
Nor grasping at air.

It's the easiest of poses
To please a patron
Strolling the studio,
Twirling his cane,
Whose practised eye
Will caress the breast
And the body's twist
Down to the right leg
Across the left knee
And a garment melting
Muslin to bronze.

The eyes uplifted,
Lips parted in wonder,
The other hand's clutching
The tale she is telling,
The tears of her goddess
For bleeding Adonis,

A tale of lamenting
And metamorphosis,
Amused in the telling
Of the flower and the wounding,
The book and the roses.

Bricolage

Driftwood lady, you've a sky-blue skirt but not much else to wear,
Fraying string about your waist, a floozy's feather in your hair,
Round your neck a little golden bell that's sadly silent there.

Upwards, where the painted driftwood branches, stumpy arms
    are thrown.
Bottle-plastic makes a mouthy shout, half-chorus-girl, half-crone
(Where your heart would be, a split allowed us to insert a stone).

Felix helped me make you at I Costi in the evening sun,
Fussing over bits of flotsam endlessly and having fun.
Pleased as paint, we packed you up for England when our weeks
    were done.

What we made of hours unspooling silently at our behest
Seems so idle to me now, and yet we knew that art was best,
Leaving trails of our creations as our star bowed to the west.

Orange theatre, molten globe, declining in the restless bay,
Lighting tiny seaweed cities in its low and level ray,
Burnishing our salty faces, eager at the end of day.

We were busy gods that summer. It will never be the same.
Now you dance here in my study, looking much less like a game,
Rather, a reminder of important truths that have no name.

Not the shell of Venus. Not the many-dipping oars of Greece,
Steering for the prizes of the Pillars or the Golden Fleece.
Not the sarsens of the shore-line where invaders never cease.

Not the hopeless longings of the psychopath Pygmalion.
Not the work of thinkers that some tousled dons still lecture on.
Not the famous victories (for all the warriors have gone).

What you tell us now is vastly simpler and more commonplace.
Your frozen dance is something of it, something in your startled face
That catches moments lost, unrecognised, that wished us grace.

What you speak of now is time's elusive opportunity,
Though your bell's still silent, silent as the complicated sea
Which in better days we loved to be beside. And simply be.

Touchdown

The butterfly upon your wrist
Is an eternal solipsist:
It seems to think it's all alone.
It didn't land there on its own,
But lifted by the wind and blown
On to the skin it might have missed.

Its wings display a winning brace
Of cards—an ace, another ace!—
A blur in flight that once again
Is still, with its proboscis strain-
ing, a long-distance aeroplane,
Preparing a refuel in space.

Its docking here was chance, unplanned.
It didn't know where it would land
Nor drift to next, and therefore you'll
Not move until (it would be cruel)
It's sucked that grateful molecule
Of perspiration from your hand.

There: off it goes! The wind makes free
With it. That luminosity,
Azure and orange, all those rare
Infolded textures going spare
And thrown into the careless air,
A scrap against the indifferent sea.

Light, Flame and Air

Fluttering at the window-sill,
Midnight marauder, death's-head, goth,
The candle-seeking summer moth
Crawls on the blind, becoming still
Till morning pales, as mornings will.

Night after night these insects fly
Into our lit, seductive room
Where flame is like a rare perfume
That seems somehow to qualify
The certain outcome that they'll die.

Hand over hand I pull the string
Letting the day come flooding in
That shapes the world and warms the skin
And does the work of wakening
Each night-ghost into some new thing.

The powdery moths, rolled in the blind,
Brief blots of grey against the gold,
Become their shape again, unrolled,
Still as a photograph, defined
By sun that shadows it, behind.

Leaves of the myrtle, too, are cast
Upon this theatre of light,
Stirring like wings prepared for flight.
But, like the foolish moths caught fast,
This bush, this blind,—nothing will last.

Not even that slow-burning star,
Rich with its greatest gift, our sight,
Making our existence bright
With knowledge. Still, that time is far
Ahead. And this is where we are.

Pictures in light are what we see.
We gather round the flame of our
Desires: the scent, the touch, the flower.
And, like the moths, are never free
To settle where we want to be.

The air that lifted wing and leaf
Is drawn into our bodies, then
Is slowly given back again.
Breathing, the motor of belief:
Unconscious, crucial, mothlike, brief.

II

The Repair Shop

In a few days I shall ask to take my body to the Repair Shop.
I shall walk in cheerfully through the tall barn doors
Out of the rustic sunlight and into the laboratory of redemption
Where they will be waiting for me with welcoming smiles.
They will say 'What a history!' and 'Thank you for bringing it in',
And, as a tender afterthought, 'What would you like us to do with it?'
All the long afternoons they will work at their benches,
One with pairs of spectacles pushed back over his head,
One with a lathe, one with goggles and spray.
I know their generous ways, and I know they will do their best,
Trying to see how things work, and why some things don't work.
Much will be familiar to them, but they will joke with each other
About what is unfamiliar, and they will congratulate each other
About the progress they make in the different corners of the Repair Shop.

When I return, not daring to believe in the impossible,
Some will gather together with their hands splayed on the counter
Unable to conceal a glowing pride in their skills.
There will be a blanket concealing their long handiwork,
And others, still sewing or chiselling in the background,
Will look up, smiling in the sentiment of fellowship.
Have they been successful? Will my grandsons be surprised?
Their hands are lifted as though in sudden prayer,
Lifted as if to hide the truthful mouth and the urge to weep,
Lifted in a kind of namaste that is all love and powerlessness,
For in truth they will have to say that there was little to be done.

Cardiology Music

1.

Come now to the very place
Neither familiar nor unexpected
Where Le Bon Dieu has agreed
To be your devoted audience.

The vital muscle has become a grand soloist
Though feeling much like an understudy,
Not riven like an oak
But trapped like a moth.

2.

Petrushka has stopped dancing
Though the music goes on without him.
He lolls back with a glazed stare
And a mouth of glum expectation.

Perhaps Le Bon Dieu will pardon him.
There are extra blue nipples on his chest
And a trail of wires from his shins and shoulders
Leading to a machine that says: 'Nearly, nearly, nearly'.

3.

The prisoner is the centre of attention.
There are screens and interpreters
Since he is both a hero and an oracle
With eagerly expected answers.

The band on his left arm suggests
That he might also be the conductor,
Though in the end it sighs as if simply
Delivering a verdict that no one wants to hear.

4.

The big aria is always a defiance,
But you never heard it before like this:
A slobbery devouring in unvisited deeps
Or the gulping of the washing machine.

Perhaps if it were wholly audible
It would feel like a rinsing of teeth,
Quite a comical sound, but then
If you couldn't hear it you'd be dead.

5.

Said Le Bon Dieu to Charles Trenet
From his armchair of clouds:
'What did I tell you? That "Boum!"
Is an illusion. It will not last.'

Trenet said nothing. He is long dead.
Which is another of His illusions,
For here is Trenet still singing
His heart out: 'Boum, boum, boum!'

Bodies

Who is the I who says I might
Have been a two-toed sloth?
Reaching my fingers to the ceiling,
I count them, unbelieving.

They might look hideous if
You'd never seen a hand before.
And when was it decided (right
And left) we needed both?

Bodies are something like a source
And not a gift, not moment-perfect.
It's a delusion we are under
That we can manage them.

What else I've counted on in life
Is hardly worth recounting.
Things that we share, of course,
Are something like a wonder.

Misprint

Stealth is its policy. It lies in wait.
It is no respecter of age. It turns up late
Or far too early, without an invitation.
You may not notice this miscalculation
By your compositor, this turned letter
Or metathesis in the river of text
That flows, page after page after page, for better
Or worse, unproofed, through your perfect book of health.
It is what happens next.

Storm

The weather takes back what it gave
And we must yield. But still we crave

That calm that came before the storm,
And there is nothing left to save.

For air is changing places now,
Since air delights to misbehave.

Wildly it blusters on and on,
Eager to spin and thud and rave.

Light flickers as the sea is lashed
Up to the height of a church nave.

The tide draws back and blocks the sky,
Making a kind of seething cave

That mounts, and curves, and breaks, and falls,
Till every boat becomes a grave.

To ride it is absurd, of course,
But necessary, to be brave.

And this is me, the storm my heart,
Wave after wave after wave after wave.

Questions

How can we ever second-guess
The neverwhere of the unborn?
The unbodied, the hoped-for
Or, far into the future,
The simply never to be known?

I perched on the edge of the running bath,
An insufferable little shrimp,
Asking my mother about her intentions:
Would she produce a brother for me
Or even, dared I hope, a sister?

Such wish-siblings, not serious,
Can haunt me even now at times,
Though age brings still-possible ghosts:
Great-grandchildren I'll not meet—
And theirs, too, coming after them.

By then, the no-where will be now-here.
It will be like their being called up
After long waiting for an appointment,
Blinking into the light, and maybe
Now and then thinking about me.

But where are they now? A mystery!
In time, embodiment will enable
Them to ask such questions themselves
If only in awareness of whimsy,
Writing their little lives in empty rooms.

Purposes

That snail in the corner of the ceiling
Turning a blind eye, bruised in its socket:
How did it get so high? So far? So still?

What purpose in its concentric spirals
Of palest lemon, charcoal, cream?
No one has looked at it till now.

Crisp and light as a crust, yet somehow able
To sail on its slow jelly of a foot?
My own purposes seem no less futile.

Rescued with a chair, it squirms
And shrinks again into its shell
Until I've settled it beneath a leaf.

Survival at all is a chancy thing.
We, the prime species, will go on boasting
And playing our extraordinary games

Duped by our invention of the future
And its reasonable projects until
That coming day when death learns all our names.

Transplants

This stencil on my latte:
Is it a heart or is it a turnip?

Disturbed at each sip,
Forgotten as the level sinks.

The heart lives in the dark
With all its secrets.

The turnip, white and violet,
With its wispy beard

And its delicate reek,
Is only half in hiding.

At the field's margin
A hecatomb of swedes

Knobbled and rusty, piled
For fodder like bodies.

Wurzels throbbing underground,
Tugged into the frosty air

To wrinkle and wither,
Snuffled and guzzled by pigs

Whose hearts can beat in a man
For eight hopeful weeks.

The heart is disciplined
And measured like music.

Replaced when it fails,
Planted in the willing blood

And warmed to its use,
Assuming the beat da capo.

But what of the old heart,
Of no use to anyone?

It is clearly a remnant,
And it will not keep.

Wine

1.

That ghoul in the Qu'ran, who lent his name
To alcohol: must we avoid him too?
When we exchange our reason for vain dreams

We know that blood and wine are not the same
So why should we behave as if it's true?
Brain stuff: we've learned that nothing is what it seems.

Conviviality is quite another thing:
Between a pint at the Perch and a malt at the Mitre
Whole afternoons have been entirely mislaid.

There's something in wine that isn't merely drinking.
When the glass gets heavier and the bottle lighter
It's as if a kind of pact is being made.

It's a reviving gift from our tilled earth,
The sense of a ritual of death and birth.

2.

Between the first glass that is good for you
And the last that isn't, a whole seventy years
Of eager indulgence, never diagnosed.

A glass can be poured without thinking, it is true,
And it will be tilted between the ignorant ears
Which hear nothing, and the eyes which are closed.

But what does the tongue say, which is concerned
With assessing its own pleasure? Content to be tied
Like an accomplice in a robbery? Content

To let the body speak of what it has earned
Of pleasure? The wine will give you nowhere to hide.
The wine will tell you that this is what it meant.

Seventy years of delight that have come to pass,
One for each of the seventy grapes in a glass.

Relief

To draw conclusions from the precise force
Exerted by a handshake or a kiss
Is to confuse a delta's civilities
With the ambiguous thunder of its source,
And what the fingers or the lips endorse
Could be misleading. It comes down to this:
Emotions are such things as you might miss.
The river is the mystery of its course.

And so it may not seem to matter much
If you react with unexpected fright
To what was thought to be a welcome pressure,
Or quite inconsequentially delight
In disappointment, taking a guilty pleasure
In the dismaying lightness of a touch.

Talk or Walk

The good Doctor couldn't put
His left foot (or was it his right
Foot?) forward to walk into a room.
He simply couldn't choose.
Was it diffidence?
Was it inhibition?

He couldn't walk from a room either.
Once he had started to talk,
Out-talking the competition,
Laying down the law,
Holding the floor,
All was well. But then?

He would hover at the threshold,
Jerking and twitching,
While everyone waited.
The bookseller's son translated
From provincial Lichfield
To the drawing rooms of the literati.

When we are put at our unease
And have no idea how to behave,
We either stay, anxious to please
(Which cheek? Which knife?),
Maintaining our position,
Or we walk.

Yes, we would like to leave.
We tread the priceless Turkey carpet,
Noticing the labour of its weave.
What can we possibly say?
We are not all like the good Doctor.
Easy for him to talk.

Sometimes I feel like getting permission
To avoid this altogether and simply
Click on the walkthrough of my life.

No Plot

The letters will be found in the spidery tomb.
The madman laughs aloud. There'll come a time
When the characters are together in a room
To hear about a codicil or crime.

The swindler knows at last he'll be arrested,
The drunken baronet falls up the stairs,
The patient women, being sorely tested,
Rebel at last and leave the page in pairs.

Our histories are yet to be arranged.
We like this freedom, though it's all we've got.
There are no drafts, and nothing to be changed.
There are no chapters, and there is no plot.

Epitaph for a Star

A chance in a million! He was perfectly cast
In the role of his own life, though he almost flipped
When told it was all in the future, and not in the past,
And someone (who?) had forgotten to give him the script.
He tried his darnedest, but there were other factors
That made the going tough. The director allowed
No rehearsals and gave the supporting actors
All the best lines. His face was lost in the crowd.

The shooting proceeded in too much of a rush
For him to be shown the rushes. All those heartaches!
That foiled ambition! He demanded re-edits,
But the final cut revealed his busted flush.
There was never an occasion to save the out-takes,
And in the end his name was removed from the credits.

A Life

Always unlikely I would interpose
   My momentary shape
   Between the entropies,
(In matter's history a trivial phase).

I didn't wish myself earth's resident,
   Nor have I aspired
   To have myself inserted
Into its tale of ultimate despair.

And time is a cruel memorialist,
   Quick to resent,
   Loath to immortalise.
A man is shown the exit as he enters.

The Last Hero

1.

The latest hero
In the shade of his armour
　The steel of his gaze,
The deep glare from the barbute
In the summer of his days:

　What will he do first?
What exploit has he in mind?
　Will it surprise them?
Though it has been done before,
There must be greater acclaim.

　The raw confidence,
The sly smile from the sallet
　Astounding the field,
The charm behind the mailed fist.
He knows they have to yield.

2.

In the still hours, the moon flooding the coverlet,
The world is trotting home with bloodied teeth.

If we could recollect our dreams, then something
Might be saved, a stirring of purposes.

Saving is a restoring, not a hoarding,
Since you must spend your life before it can be spent.

After the night declares its temporary truce,
The image of the hero stares back in disbelief.

A tap trickles steadily like unwritten chronicle,
A passage of water which is as invisible as sleep.

A grimace spares him the mockery of what is to come,
Spares him the connivance, the evasions.

. . .

And here he is at last, found assembled
In every greave and gusset, laced for the day.

In every corselet and coulter, just as the years
Required: duty's the man, to the last ditch!

Despite the twinge in the culet, despite
The ache in the flange, despite it all.

He sits sullenly by a bubbling kettle,
His head in the gorget like an upturned turnip.

The profile that was noble is simply owlish,
A sprue of thinning hair, and clown mouth.

And all he keeps is kitchen counsel,
Licking the butter from his blue fingers.

. . .

The waste is the worst of it, waiting for oblivion,
Living for living's sake, the fear of awakening.

As if the skin could leak inside its silver
And the pins drop to the floor.

As if with a clatter and a rattle he might appear
Alive in the doorway to howls of derision.

As if nothing would happen at all, ever again,
Despite his occasional tug at a buckle.

Hola, Señor! The chalk-marks are against you!
Can you stir yourself to some adventures?

A fist slams into the table, an explosion
Of cheese: no more nonsense!

.   .   .

Saved or solved? Perhaps that is the answer,
That memory is simply knowing there is no problem.

No problem, as they say, indicating obedience,
Bowing before you as before nobility.

I will go and get it for you now, sir, whatever you say.
No problem, after all. It was all in your mind.

Death will fetch you its little red-hot pincers
With something like the same obedience.

Where shall it be first, ventail or poleyn?
It must start somewhere, however ridiculous.

Now, as the morning advances, he settles into thought.
A quiet time, enduring all the voices.

.   .   .

He is like the heron, who you may see from time to time
If you are lucky, with an eye for legend.

He is like the heron, attuned to the gods,
Patient and one-legged as a pirate.

He is like the heron, determined and self-reliant
In the face of utter hopelessness.

He is like the last heron, hunched in its dirty shawl
In that state between abjection and watchfulness.

His whole life is like the river where the heron stands
Still as a star while the water swells and flows.

III

Hip

1.

When she fell, he was playing chess, half out of hearing.
But in Summer the doors are always open
For the air to pass through freely.
And for sounds, too, whether of cheerfulness or alarm.

Had his only rook somehow reached the seventh rank?
Had his weak bishop finally found a place of retreat?
His tea grows cold in its grey-and-blue striped mug.
Whose move was it? He will never know.

2.

It was near the beginning of the eighth month
That she set the ladder against the plum tree.
It is near the beginning of the ninth month
That she takes her new hip into the garden.

She grasps the twin bars of her crutches like the rungs
Of a ladder that has been sundered by the gods
As a punishment for failing to support her.
Now there will be no plums until next year.

She reads beneath the late roses, turning
And turning a still swollen ankle.
Her novel might be a story about herself,
Turning and turning, page after page.

3.

What became of the plums? He slit their throats
In the thrill of vengeance, and sweetened the deed
With slugs of honey in a slow pan on the stove.
Already a few leaves are beginning to fall.

The plums have now been imprisoned in an icy future,
Which, like all our futures, is always out of reach.
Well, they may like it there, just as they liked their tree
Which dies more slowly than they do.

Pheasants at Bredon

Along the dips and turns of a mossy garden
That once was half a field, there are two pheasants
Finding things to eat. One wears his colours
As something like a continual invitation.
The other seems to be affecting little interest.
They have no idea of a future, but they have
Each other. In this they are much like us, who are
As P. G. Wodehouse wrote of the futureless,
Simply 'among those present', specimens
Of bodied time and perpetuated matter.

Those thicknesses of growth, high in the trees:
A heronry perhaps? Or that parasite
Famous as the pretext for a season's kissing?
Kissing was invented four thousand years ago
And has ever since been pretty much in season.
It gave us the idea that our chances to be happy
Are unrationed, and somehow provides an edge over
The soundless rabbit or the screaming birds.
One thing we understand: we are the only
Animal that knows that it is lonely.

We are here in a wooded county, with villages
And spires, symbols of connectedness
And strange desires. Within the utter quiet
What sounds we hear are friendly or absurd:
The short chalk scrape of that coloured bird
Bred to be peppered, or the dawn horse's
Clop and gargle as it greets the visiting children
Of the nearby stable. Enough of horses, though.
Our observation only goes to show
Two pheasants roosting in the mistletoe.

Two from East Sussex

1. Battle

Here on a misty Sussex hillside we ponder history's thread,
How it unspools steadily between unusual moments of hatred
And thus is largely an accumulation of interims
When the quite conventional government of abbot or minister
With the patient ink of monks or dull reports still to be filed
Allows the pacifist sheep back on to the bloodied field.

This town is named not by topography but an event—'Battle'
And all the signposts lead at last to an English Heritage tablet
Proclaiming the deaths of more than its present population; no hero's
Triumph, then, but pure waste, and the skill of the Norman horse
(Two thousand of them ferried across the Channel in hand-made boats
To fulfil with methodical violence an outlandish dynastic boast).
It makes us think, between the chalky downs and the flinty shingle,
Of what it can possibly mean to feel impregnably, smugly English.

2. Birling Gap

At this point of nervous descent between the Seven Sisters
And Beachy Head we find that the land uncertainly resists
The silvery sea, which looks harmless enough down there, though recent
Falls bring the cliff edge ever nearer to the Visitor Centre,
A metre lost each month! Yet in the formation of this limestone
A hundred million years is nothing, merely a single milestone.

It's the flints we come for, that trick of silica from the death of sponges, kin
To the plankton and coccolithophores. Glassy and black as ink,
They lie in nodular or tabular seams like mineral ghosts, each
One a migraine thudding in the headland, a stone ache.
Or down on the beach, the tides rolling them slowly, even the roundest
Still with bumps and knuckles, smaller, beginning to gleam, unsorted.

Yes, the world is both solid and liquid. The waves go on streaming
Through the clattering pebbles, ever patient, ever mastering.

The Swifts at the Maison Louverie

Have the swifts returned?
The house and its crevices
   Are waiting for them.

The hammock's empty,
Longing to feel the motion
   And weight of reading.

The pears and walnuts
Are starting to appear, like
   Models of themselves.

A cloud like a hare
Drifts and dissolves across
   A meadow of sky.

The black butterfly
Refuses to pose for us.
   It is called away.

A heron crosses
The flight-path of the tourists
   At ninety degrees.

The salvia blooms
And time stops to admire it.
   Then the mower comes.

Traversing the lawn
Are the mole's breathing-places,
   Little gasps of earth.

One swift plays Neptune,
Anther plays Jupiter:
    All the planets turn.

Feeding, as light fades
Round their astrolabe of air,
    As if for all time.

Danger

Lappety-lappety, the hare careers
Across the flinty fields, its ears
   The tied ends of a sack.

Two ears triangulate the sound
Of danger, when danger is all around,
   To keep it well away.

This way, that way, the hare veers
Sideways, as if it somehow fears
   To go forward or back.

To zig-zag is to give no ground.
There is a point to every bound
   And dangers every day.

What is it, then, when nothing appears?
What is it that the creature hears
   That makes him change his tack?

No pop of gun or bay of hound,
But danger's echo, that has found
   Its thrilling space to play.

The Feel of It

I happen to be here, like waking
From a dream of being nowhere.
Who could believe that now could be a somewhere,
Like a return from what I was before I was?

The year is in its stride.
The weight of cherries starts to drag the branches
Down. A cherry fills a pressured space between
The finger and the thumb.

Who could believe it?
Just a cherry, firm before it's ripe.
And yes, it has a future still,
The feel of it, like waking from a dream.

Ear Worm

I'm on the way out, but don't turn off the lights.
Just a few more bars of this song:
The notes go on as if they'd never end.
I'll be here for a while yet. I won't be long.

I took breath on the day of my birth.
I took breath to the grave.
I took breath as if my life depended on it.
I didn't think much about it. I wasn't brave.

Was I breathing before I woke?
Did I last the night?
Does it matter if it's morning?
Give me a couple of jugs. I'll be all right.

I came out of a byway of my life
Wandering in the sun
And I was somewhere else entirely,
Where I never thought I'd be. But it's all one.

It's a place to be for a little while
And any place to be
With this familiar nagging music in my head
Is good enough for me.

Across

Take me across the water, who knows where,
Take me across the water.
The swelling surface, floated silk,
Falls back to swell again, with me upon it
At the fullness of the tide.
No need to pay the boatman, save the fare,
No need to pay a boat.

The rolling surface, floating me
At the fullness of the tide
Will do it well enough,
And all above the water, drifting there
All above the water,
The passage of the clouds in their brief life
Drifting with the tide and the slow wind.

Leaning back in the water, carried there,
Leaning back in the water,
Turned by the current every way,
Which moves just as it will, with me upon it
At the fullness of the tide.
No need to stir a limb,
No need to do a thing.

Winter Cadae

1.

In winter
We
Are near freezing

Both

In body and mind,
But the thought of cycles consoles us.
A verse
Like this tries to rehearse

The formula, thus:

Unconfined
Ratio of growth
In the yearly return of Spring;
Periphery of Persephone/
Diameter, Demeter.

2.

Pale moon, our
Friend,
How you coldly

Stare

From your battlements
At our blood and tides, without concern,
And throw
Light wherever you go

That's not yours to burn!

There's no sense
In that haughty air
Of self-possession, don't you see?
It reflects badly on you to send
Back such light hour after hour.

3.

How I wish
That
We were walking

By

The retreating tide,
Stumbling over clumped laver on to
Clear sand,
Finding round sea-shells and

Look! some shapes quite new,

That have died
Not wishing to die
In the moon's cruel marooning:

Rings of glittering crushed goblets that
Turn out to be jellyfish.

4.

As the gulls
Stir
The lifting air

And

Howl down the black seas
As though the night tide made them less free
And as
Sky and ocean compass

Their circles, so the

Moon-jellies
On the endless sand
Look round as well, and everywhere
Turned yet unturned pebbles. No wonder:
Nature abhors right angles.

5.

Favoured ground:
I
Stand at a loss

Here

In the wintry light,
With the loaf-loving ducks in full voice,
The pond
Something to get beyond

That offers a choice:

Left or right?
The answer is clear.
No water can be walked across.
How much longer does it take? Ask *pi*,
I think, as I walk around.

6.

As you were:
Thumb
Between your lips

In

Babyish pleasure
Or scratch-scratch in pursuit of something
So true
That there's nothing to do

But go on waiting.

On cue, your
Doubts start flooding in,
Regular as the moon's eclipse.

Fullness of knowledge can never come.
It's an infinite number.

7.

Admire the
Blood's
Circulation:

Hour

By hour, minute by
Minute, second by second, it moves
Toward
The heart and is restored.

Its vigour improves:

By-and-by
The lungs give it power
And it is rich with oxygen,
Flows along the arteries and floods
The body with energy.

8.

Can you tell
Me
Something of love?

It

Is that notional
And elusive centre of our sphere
Which brings
Us from our wanderings

Back to what is dear

To us all,
Since its opposite
Kills us, when clouds gather above
The horizons of exploit and the
Challenging circles of hell.

9.

As a boy
I
Was always struck

By

The strange constancy
Of ratios, when a divides b,
Each time
Just the same, like a rhyme.

Now in age I see

What would be
Close enough to *pi*:
My days by occasions of luck,

My nights by indicative dreams, my
Whole life divided by joy.

10.

We prefer
The
Bright sense of eyes.

Why

Do diameters
Always relate to circumference?
The robe
Of light drenches the globe

In magnificence.

Our sight stirs
Within radii
Which, paired and opposed, define size,
An inwardness of scope, but singly
Will radiate for ever.

11.

Time is in
Name
And in nature

A

Sharpster who likes to
Play with moons and tides and ice and suns
And seeks
To mark the pack of weeks

Whose suits are seasons

And cheat you,
However you play,
Of all your hope and composure.
Time holds all the cards. It's a long game
You know you can never win.

12.

All too soon
Wide
Arcs of distress

Split

Our world apart, take
Us off balance; whereas all we need
Is that
Sense of proceeding at

A suitable speed

Where we make
What we make of it,
Calmly channelling, more or less

Like a conduit, inside and outside,
Tides of the heart and the moon.

13.

Our failing
Star
Draws all round it

In

Endless curvature
And (at a terrifying distance)
What we
Hope is consistency,

And though all is chance

We endure,
As they turn and spin,
These hands of the hour and minute,
That empty page in the calendar,
The painful return of Spring.

14.

Finally
We
Know what we want,

Though

It's impossible.
We want to say 'Not Yet' for ever.
We say
It as a kind of play

With our shared pulse, a

Tidal pull
Where moon-jellies go,
Their circumferences still cont-
racting and expanding beneath the
Moonlit waters, silently.

The Report of the Angels

We had to count them all, not say why some
Might be considered better than the rest.
Variety and equilibrium
Were, we supposed, twin features of the best.

The task, we knew, would take almost for ever,
But not for ever quite, since finitude
Was necessary to the whole endeavour,
And those already dead were not renewed.

So we completed our enumeration
Of the extensive spheres, eventually
Reporting back, expecting approbation
Of our meticulous and useless tally.

Surely not one of these insentient globes
Knew what they were? Or could begin to know?
Mere marbles spinning in their ignorant robes
Of gas, aching and ponderously slow.

But then we found, amongst the ninetieth
Decillion, one that had started such a process,
Like a ripe fruit whose bloom in the end is death,
Crawling with genius, knowledge, and necrosis.

How did elaborated matter prove
So curious about itself that it
Once found by chance a path of infinite love
And recklessly pursued the opposite?

Solstice

Earth tilts on its spindle, winding the day
To its very tightest. At three o'clock
The air is bruised. Our footsteps hasten towards
The contrived pleasures and endless interrogations
Of our fifteen hours of resented darkness.
The spirit is subdued among its shadows.

Already it is felt on the darkening streets
In the anxious aimless shapes of shoppers,
In the queue for buses, and in the lit windows
Where waiters offer to place their coloured dishes
Like conjurors in front of the beautiful
Who gather early to talk the night away.

And so the year tumbles into its slumber.
We are greedy for light. It is never too early
To pour a discreet half-glass. Never too late
To repel the advances of insinuating night
And relight the pale candle of the spirit
With the shaking flame of a newly discovered resolve.

Acknowledgements and Notes

Acknowledgements are made to the following, in which some of these poems first appeared: *Agenda*, the *Oxford Magazine*, *Poetry London*, *Poetry Nation Review*, the *Spectator*, and the *Times Literary Supplement*.

The flower border in 'The Bees' was created by Dorothy Elmhirst at Dartington Hall, Devonshire. 'Lord of the Arboretum' describes the Batsford Arboretum, Gloucestershire. The first garden in 'Gardens' is Wotton House in Surrey, the former home of John Evelyn. The Latin motto means: 'Explore everything . . . and keep the best.' Maude is the composer Maude Valérie White. The words of the badger are from *The Wind in the Willows*. The syllabic structure of 'Winter Cadae' is based on the first fourteen digits of *pi*. I am grateful to Camille Ralphs for alerting me to the form. 'The Report of the Angels' appeared in *How Many Children?* (Rack Press Broadside No. 3). I am very grateful to Sarah Howe for her meticulous editorial work on this collection.

This book is dedicated to n
for their unconditional love
This book would not have l
them. Thank you also to m
Harley, my beautiful dog and best friend, for
providing much appreciated encouragement.

Fragments from the Abyss is something I deem to be a work of 'Faction'. It is a fictionalised account of real life events and by this I mean that I have reworked my memories, feelings and experiences into a story. By drawing upon pieces, or 'fragments' of my past I have constructed a story that is largely interwoven with reality - absolute truth is sometimes kept at a safe distance - and is at times embellished with exaggeration. My fundamental aim was to create an engaging story and I aimed to show a kaleidoscope of feeling with the hope of evoking a variety of corresponding emotions in the reader. I wanted to intersperse the camaraderie experienced and a sense of humour, however dark that might be at times, as well as focus on the fraught reality of being held captive in my 'abyss'. I hope the light-hearted aspects shine through the dire straits of the narrative when necessary in order to make this novel as well-rounded as I intended.

Also written by Natalie Browne

Mad Cow: The Diary of a Fractured Personality
(written under the pseudonym Leanne Bitrowa)

*From the Inside: Short Stories That Voice the
Misrepresented*

It was with a sense of mettlesome foreboding that we embarked upon the year. The Millennium hadn't sparked the end of the world like we had all been told and nothing was actually any different to the year before. Flourishing hopes gave way to contrived efforts at improvement, forward thinking zealots trying to effect change and innovation, although none of it bothered me. I shut myself off from the world like a clam. Nothing could crush through the smooth exterior of my lack of caring to crack into my messy, maladjusted mind. I switched off, busying myself with drawings of stick women, pouring over books on Auschwitz and Belsen and watching my favourite cartoons from the 1980's. My brain would impinge upon something – one thing at a time – and that was it then, I was off, tranquilised by a solitary fixation for weeks at a time. The Holocaust held a peculiar fascination for me and I would watch many documentaries on concentration camps and their victims. I was horrified and driven to tears, but I was riveted like a moth to a flame. The life of Van Gogh became another point of interest and a plethora of other tortured geniuses and wounded souls. I became insular, introverted and increasingly insecure. I'd read novels like *1984* and *The Handmaid's Tale* and stay up late watching *Schindler's List.* All the while I became skilled in the art of manipulation, hiding stuff, covering my tracks, lying through my teeth. Things like getting up at the same exact time every morning became paramount so I could read my dad's copy of yesterday's newspaper from cover to cover

4

and slurp down a foul cup of black coffee before anyone else had batted an eyelid. I crawled from one obsession to another, all the while becoming a devious, deceitful creature. My metamorphosis was such that I couldn't recognise myself in the mirror or identify my own personality traits. The descent was vast and vigorous.

The truth was, I was trapped, though little did I know at the time that I was ensnared in a prison of my own making. Whilst everyone around me seemed to be growing up and having fun, I was burrowing myself to the point of no return, a vanishing point from which there was minimal hope of escape. The death of Lena Zavaroni the previous October was when I realised – when they all, much to my disdain, sprung up and took acute notice. In a hospital bed, aggravated by the drip in my arm, I knew that my head was only just above water, yet, it didn't take long to start sinking fast, plummeting as if a rock was chained to my ankle. I guess it was a kind of drowning, the struggle, being at the in-between place, a civil war taking place inside me. It had caught me unawares, snuck up on me like a monster hiding under the bed.

The old maxim, 'be careful what you wish for' was pertinent; the second wish on my wish list at the age of nine was *to be skinny.*

With the power of hindsight, I should have heeded that advice.

Chapter 1

I'd already made up my mind that I couldn't sleep. The enveloping gloom swarmed around me like a gigantic shroud, yet I refused to surrender. I stretched my eyelids wide, saucer-like, till my forehead ached under its furrowed wrinkling. My first night and clearly I was intent on defying this place. I tried to fidget just enough to keep my senses alert, but not too much as to attract attention from the pair of eyes boring into me from across the room. Fortunately, this set-up was so uncomfortable that sleep could not come easily and I would remain ready as a panther, poised and attentive. Listening to the rhythmical breathing that surrounded me, I was struck that it sounded almost melodic in a way, the gentle, lilting, inhaling and exhaling. It filled me with melancholy, each surge of air usurped by a wilting cadence; life ebbing and flowing out and away from the lungs. That seemingly simple task of breathing – the vital exchange of oxygen and carbon dioxide – is so excruciatingly fundamental to our survival, yet offered a poetic poignancy as I lay, entrenched in my solitude. I was not alone, but I was suffocated by my loneliness, and right now I was not prepared to invite anyone in.

Flanking both sides of the classroom, mattresses were lined up neatly on the wooden floor with minimal space in between each one. A large window gaped on the far side of the room, the pale blue patterned curtains open to expose the starless night sky. Tables and chairs had been pushed up against the wall to

create this pseudo-sleeping arrangement and an armchair stood beside the doorway like a sentinel, overlooked by a reading lamp on a small pine table.

I snapped out of my bewilderment to see two girls hefting bed linen in my direction.

"You'll have to get used to this," one of them snapped, dumping sheets and a sleeping bag at my feet. The girl was like a beanpole, I had to crane my neck to peer up at her face. She wore a disgruntled expression, which was unfortunate as she would have been pretty minus the sneer. I looked at her dumbly. "After today, you'll be sorting your own bed." And with that, she stomped off across the room with her own sleeping bag and sheets.

"Sorry about Holly," the other girl shrugged. "She's fine once you get to know her." This girl was not much taller than me, with shaggy auburn hair that fell into her eyes. I gazed at the lump of faded linen piled at my feet and glanced back to the girl's face to see a bemused smile stretching across it. She had obviously recognised my surprise at this unconventional set-up.

"If you hadn't already realised, this is where you sleep on Supervision. My name's Clara, by the way."

I nodded, stalling the avalanche of tears that threatened to extricate themselves from behind my eyes, the word 'punishment' floating briefly on my lips.

"Chin up," Clara said, "Julie's on duty tonight."

*

"We heard you arrive."

I cast my mind back to earlier that day. The grey, overcast sky hung limp and forlorn, like a ceiling begotten by mould and ready to implode due to its saturation. I didn't want to leave the house, all of my instincts cried out against it.

I was tricked. The whole thing was a cruel trap.

I hadn't agreed to the long car journey, but had been coerced to get into the car in my own conviction that I was fine and therefore everything would be all right. I sat with my head bowed and hands in my lap as the car purred into action, crawled along roads, twisted and turned around lanes, roared along the motorway, and eventually reached its destination, all the while I remained wedged between my two younger siblings, my head electrified with empty static. Staring out of the window listening to the nonsense of white noise, I felt myself spinning into a void, into nothingness, completely severed from everything around me and, in that instance, completely careless. The car came-to with a dull thud, prodding me back to reality.

"We're here," someone said, my mum or my dad, I can't recall which, and the four of them climbed out of the vehicle in sombre silence. Statue-like, I remained pinned to the spot, my instincts still clawing

at my insides, my empty stomach turning somersaults and the blood racing like lava through my ears. The door opened beside me and I hesitantly clambered out, my leaden bones unyielding as stone. Divorced from my senses during the drive here, I was suddenly overwhelmed by the startling brightness, the awe-inspiring beauty and breadth that smacked into my vision. With my clarity of sight returned, the vastness of the grounds and the grandeur of the building stood impressively before me. It looked more like a stately home than a clinic. I tilted my chin upwards, neck tendons clicking with a spasmodic ping, to see a couple of floors stretch up before me, small windows etched into the archaic stone. Dark clouds besmirched the panorama, circling the building with ominous foreboding and I subconsciously dug my fingernails into my palms. It was with immense irresolution that I dragged one foot after the other in pursuit of my family, who had already advanced to what resembled an entrance; my dad had remained following behind, like a shepherd herding his sheep, not wanting me to go astray.

Ivy erupted around the doorway, intertwining across the nooks and crannies of the grey mosaic stone, spreading rapaciously like green wildfire along the guttering and spilling over the ground, sumptuous in its liberation. A light was on in the hallway, through the door, and I thought how odd it was for a light to be on when it can't have been later than two p.m. The light instantaneously went out and it took me a moment to realise that a figure had moved to fill the doorway, obstructing the brightness within. The

woman was large, dressed in a swathe of black silk that rippled with the roundness of her body beneath and her hair was a striking medusa of rope braids that looked like a tarantula rested on her head. She extended her right hand to my mother and I watched her pudgy fingers clasp my mum's in a vague handshake as she introduced herself as Natasha. She then clamped her stodgy hand around my father's, before trying to negotiate into a similar greeting with me. I eyed her with caution before stating matter of factly, "I'm not stopping here." Natasha smiled indulgently at me as if I were a naughty toddler then exchanged a suspicious look between my parents. My brother and sister had remained quiet up to this point, though I heard a nervous giggle escape from one of them, a trickle of unrestrained and inappropriate hilarity that hung garishly in the ether, a fart in a library or a funeral joke, and I noticed that my fingernails were still embedded in my flesh.

"If you'd like to come this way." Natasha ushered us through the door with vigour and led us up a steep flight of stairs to a large homely room. We traipsed up in single file, a row of ants marching in regimented unison, Natasha leading the way, myself hanging behind, my dad keeping up the rear, lest I should take flight from his flock.

"This is the Sky Lounge," Natasha announced, making a sweeping gesture with her arm to encompass the two gigantic three-seater sofas and the two single comfy chairs. My brother and sister deftly nestled themselves into a single armchair each, whilst

my parents and I shuffled awkwardly to the large sofa on the right-hand side of the room. Natasha explained that one of the doctors would arrive presently in order to outline the clinic's policies and the duty of care to each patient. I calmed myself by remembering my morning assertion to my mum and dad that I was perfectly fine, to which they had replied, "You'll have nothing to worry about then." I had hammered it out repeatedly to them that morning that there was nothing wrong with me and there was no need whatsoever to admit me to an eating disorder clinic, for I was fine and I could exist perfectly well at home. "Existing, but you're not living," was a typical phrase espoused by my mum, yet, this morning - if only perhaps to humour me (as I was growing to realise now) - she had simply said, "If you think you're fine, then you don't need to worry about staying. We're only going to have a look around." This morning I had wrapped this statement around myself like a woollen blanket, comforted and safe in the knowledge that reason would prevail. I was not able to placate myself so easily now, seated here between my mother and father, a reflection of the journey here in which I was clamped between Leonard and Leonie. Panic tugged its deathly cerement over my head, tightening around my neck as beads of sweat began to moisten my spine, gathering like the footprints of tiny insects running the length of it. My head felt wadded up in a fog to the extent that I could no longer hear what was being said; it was as if my ears had cotton wool stuffed in them.

I don't know how much time had elapsed but my typically ice cold body was feverish as adrenaline

overtook me and I ventured a large stride forwards. Natasha and the doctor whatever-his-name were talking to my family in an effort to convince them that this Food Farm was some kind of heaven with its fancy therapy, meal plans, specialised workers and what-not. I could not be admitted to this place – I would not be subjected to this place. I heaved my legs to the exit as if my life depended on it, only it wasn't quick enough, for Natasha had stepped in front of the doorway, blocking egress, like a spider in her web, and in that split second, my dad had managed to secure me to the spot, his arms wrapped around my shoulders as my legs threatened to buckle. I kicked, I screamed, I wriggled. As small and weak as I was, I fought with all the determination I could muster, a cornered animal striking up its inner resources in sheer desperation. I bawled and shouted and shrieked: I'm not staying here! I'm not staying here! I bellowed and spat that useless mantra until my throat dried up, my body gave in and my will to live evaded me.

*

The patterns on the walls twisted and tumbled in a conglomeration of lurid reds and greens that assaulted my eyes. Affronted, I closed my lids and rolled over. I had no idea why anybody would want to decorate their walls in such an unsettling way. I jolted wide awake then, the strange sensation creeping over me that I didn't know where I was. My head was burrowed down under the covers of whatever I was sleeping in and I pawed at my face like a rodent in a

trap, disentangling myself. The lurid colours that had been sailing across my retinas were, in fact, the patterns on the faded sleeping bag with the full blaze of the classroom light bearing down on it. I rubbed sleep out of my eyes, stunned that I had managed to nod off at all, given the hardness of the floor against my limbs. My hipbones, knees and elbows felt grazed, my spine shaved by the uncompromising ground. I sat up and rubbed my back gingerly, taking in my surroundings.

"That's why we should give you new-comers two mattresses," Julie, the lady who sat guarding the door said to me, inclining her head at my stinging backbone. Suddenly I seemed to represent all the new admissions to her. "You all find it painful, at first." She tutted, "Poor mites."

I noticed a small queue assembling behind her where a lady I remembered from the previous evening was standing. Kaye stood tall, proud and matronly with her hair cut severely in a white blonde bob. Her right foot wedged solidly in the door. A toilet chain flushed and within seconds the door opened, a flash of brown and green as Alicia emerged, and the next in line went in. I joined the end of the queue behind Jocelyn, a girl I'd spoken to briefly last night. I suppose it goes without saying that she's slim. Everyone here is thinner than average ranging from fashionably petite to the point of being almost skeletal. Jocelyn's reddish-brown hair was in a pixie cut, flecked with blonde highlights; dark eyes peered

out from an angular face in an inquisitive way as I positioned myself behind her.

"How did you sleep?" she asked rhetorically. "Now for the other joys of Total Supervision." Jocelyn nodded towards the toilet. I'd refused the proffered shower or bath last night and avoided visiting the bathroom at all, but this morning, my bladder was unmistakably full. I knew I couldn't avoid it any longer. Jocelyn misread the discomfort on my face and added, "don't worry, you soon get used to it. The being watched, I mean. It's not like they're actually *watching* you do your business, most of the time they're just checking your reflection in the tiles opposite. Making sure you're not doing anything you shouldn't."

"Right….that makes it loads easier," I rolled my eyes and Jocelyn started laughing an infectious chuckle that almost had me laughing. It was quite astounding how bowel movements were soon to become a treasured component of daily humour and an antidote to the many downsides of this environment.

"How long have you been here?" I asked.

"Since October. Six months."

I looked at her, curiosity building, my eyes drawn to her striking jaw line and her protruding collarbone.

"How long have you got left?"

"Long enough," she moaned. "I'm hardly ever above my line, hence why I'm kept on Total. I'm on a ridiculous amount of calories as well, yet still going through this rigmarole." She had a plumb voice, well-spoken, as if her tongue polished each and every word before it left her mouth. "I should have reached target by now but every single weigh-in I'm below my line. It's been ages since I just had a post-meal." I stared at her as if she had just spoken a foreign language.

"It's ok," Jocelyn soothed and she explained everything to me. Well, not right there and then in the queue for the toilet but, over the course of that morning, she delineated all that I needed to know about the mechanics of this place and its regime. The basics were that each patient was given a specific target weight upon their admission, or thereabouts, and this would be arrived at with a weight gain of at least 1kg per week. Patients would be weighed twice every week on the mornings of Mondays and Thursdays. Obviously the patient's food consumption was engineered in order for this size increase to be achieved. Calories were counted meticulously by the 'powers that be' to ensure everyone got larger, and they sure did! Anybody failing a weigh-in and falling below their prescribed 'Line' of weight ascension would be evaluated and consequently denied privileges and activities, have more food thrust upon them or be given additional hours of supervision, leading inevitably up to the dreaded Total Supervision. Clearly, eluding weight gain was considered a cardinal crime here. Whatever

the reason for losing weight - or being unable to put any on - it was believed to be the result of breaking the rules: puking meals up, discarding food, over vigorous exercise or just being too damn clever.

"So what's your secret?" I asked.

"What do you mean?"

"Well how come you're on 3,400 calories a day *and* on Total Supervision, yet you're losing weight?"

"I'm not actually losing weight," Jocelyn purred innocently, "I'm just not consistently gaining enough."

One revelation surpassed another in this obscure place. I was still smarting from having been dumped here by my beloved parents, an abuse of trust that would take a while to forgive and more than time to heal. It didn't feel entirely real and, like a dream, I considered myself immune to consequences. Last night for instance, in a moment of madness, I lunged for the entrance at a chance opportunity to escape and was seized immediately, not by a nurse but by another inmate! Gobsmacked at this lack of solidarity, I was escorted up to the Sky Lounge by two members of staff who proceeded to monitor me on a two-to-one basis for the next three hours, every movement on my part scrutinised to within an inch of my life.

Hope dwindled as I sat in that lounge, the others in the room transfixed by the television. I stared out at

the impenetrable blanket of sky that stretched beyond the window; a suffocating expanse of air that also could not free me. In a flight of fancy, I envisioned the window, open and inviting; offering me salvation, my ragged legs clambering over the white ledge, my frame contained within, holding steady for just a fragment of a second and then all would be gone. I'd plummet, the whorl of air rushing in a vortex that swallowed me into nothingness. I snapped back to reality. It was hopeless - hopeless fantasy. At tea-time I hadn't even managed to discard my cheese sandwich successfully. That had been another moment of madness; a hasty instant of insanity where I had acted with no regard for potential reprimands. Rosie, the small lady (nurse, carer, or support worker I wasn't sure which yet) with the Irish accent (not of the delicate lilting variety, but with the scary invoking the fear of God type harshness) had instantly collared me. She must have eyes in the back of her head or something, for she snapped round the instant I'd disposed of the sandwich under the dinner table.

"Leanne, where's your sandwich? You can't have eaten it that quick," her words shot out staccato-like as she jerked her head under the table in an effort to discover the offending item. "Leanne. Why did you throw your sandwich on the floor?" Her hand clutched the limp white bread, a slab of cheese dropping from between it to land with a discernible thunk on the tiled floor.

"I didn't," I muttered.

"What was that?"

"I didn't," I repeated, a little louder this time.

"Well, what's this doing under the table then?"

I met her with stony silence.

"Hmm?" She looked me directly in the eye. Rosie may be small but I could tell this was a woman not to be messed with. Her impossibly pale blue eyes seemed to pierce right through me, I had to look away. I don't even know why I'd chucked the cheese sandwich now; it was such a silly impulsive thing to do. All eyes in the room rested on me, I could feel the weight of them.

"Joan, make Leanne another cheese sandwich please!" Rosie was still staring right through me as she issued this command. A collective gasp shot up around the kitchen. "Shush! Anyone else want another sandwich?!" she challenged.

Joan was an elderly woman, dressed in an apron bearing the words 'stay out of my kitchen'; she was most probably overjoyed at the prospect of busying herself over another chore in her vicinity. She brought the plate over within seconds and placed the two slices of bread, filled to bursting with cheese, before me with a flourish.

"Eat," commanded Rosie.

"I'm not eating all that! I'd already had two bites out of the sandwich!"

"What, the sandwich you'd thrown on the floor? Well, you should have thought about that before you chucked it then." I took an instant dislike to this ruthless woman. I mentally noted the fact that I'd need to exercise caution around Rosie in future. I couldn't hold it against Joan, she was merely following orders; it was Rosie who was cold-hearted and cruel for the sake of being cruel.

"I'm not eating it." I pushed the plate two inches away from me. Rosie nudged it back, almost immediately.

"Yes you are," she countered.

"I'm not," I insisted, "I'd already eaten some of the other one. It's not fair!"

"Who said anything about fairness coming into it?"

I knitted my brow and summoned my most morose expression. I needed to set a precedent here. I had to demonstrate that I wouldn't comply by their rules, especially when they operated unjustly. Rosie continued staring right at me, a woman possessed, her eyes burned like sapphire orbs, too bright, too intense, and too callous.

"You can eat it, unless you'd like it tube feeding through your nostrils." Rosie delivered this stark

warning with the malicious cool calm of a serial killer. I glanced opposite me at a younger girl giving me the sweetest and most encouraging smile possible. Elle's eyes gleamed like warm emerald pools, the complete antithesis of Rosie's icy stare, and she mouthed the words, "go on" in such a reassuring way that I took a bite out of the dreadful sandwich, if only to remove all the emphasis from me. I may have lost this battle but I hadn't given up just yet.

*

There are two kitchens at Rose Farm, the Blue Kitchen and the Brown Kitchen, aptly named because the Blue Kitchen is fitted with pristine white cupboards and deep blue marble worktops and the Brown Kitchen is the colour of mud. The Blue Kitchen has a breakfast bar with modern metallic beams and fancy stools, all of its appliances in matching blue. It resembles a holiday apartment, you could almost imagine coming in from the seaside and padding barefoot across the tiled floor, everything light and airy and fresh. The Brown Kitchen is cramped and dark and, worse of all; it is the kitchen I'm relegated to because I can't be trusted. That's the fundamental purpose of the Brown Kitchen. It's the dining area supervised by staff. Why? Because they seem to garner some perverse enjoyment from watching sick people eat. They derive immense pleasure from seeing the torment in our panic-stricken faces each time a mountainous bowl of cereal or a plate swimming in grease is thrust before us. You hear of all the Bramble Lodges, Oakley Manors,

Anstey Houses and Briar Orchards in the world, yet I had ended up in a Farm and, like livestock, we were being fed up, pumped full of fat and protein to make us docile and compliant. And as time went on I'd sleep through most of the day, awaking only at mealtimes and for snacks, so my very existence was like that of a cow: I was alive merely to eat and sleep.

That first morning at breakfast I was incredibly nervous, unsure of what to expect and, because of that, I followed Jocelyn into the Brown Kitchen and sat next to her. There were eight of us altogether that morning all congregated around one of the two large teak tables that virtually filled the room. The cooking area was at the far end where two members of staff were already standing in wait, one of them was weighing out cereal whilst Joan was turning muffins over on a baking tray. Kaye was pouring water into pint glasses and positioning them at each place.

"Come on in, hurry up and sit down," Kaye urged. "We're running late as it is."

Rachel, the nurse weighing the cereal, began asking what type of cereal we would like. She turned to Alicia who was sitting closest to the food preparation area.

"I'd like a whole normal please," Alicia said confidently, taking a huge swig of her water and making a grab for her spoon. Rachel took a bowl that was half filled with muesli and then weighed out a

portion of cornflakes to pour over the top so that it all balanced precariously in the one bowl. Rachel passed the Mount Everest in a cereal bowl to Alicia who dug her spoon in and began devouring her breakfast with relish. I felt a light jab in my ribs.

"Don't look so scared," Jocelyn whispered. "A whole normal is the muesli with the crunchy nut on top – if you have the larger portion of cereal, you can opt for the smaller dessert at lunchtime. It depends how many calories you're on, of course, but that's usually the way it works."

"And what is it she's having?" I pointed at Clara who was being handed a bowl of flakes.

"She's got a half flake," Jocelyn said. "You can't have a whole flake because they don't have enough calories in them – they wouldn't all fit in the bowl." I glanced back over at Alicia's towering monstrosity. "You can have a whole muesli though. The whole normal is the mixture of the two."

"I can't see what's normal about that!"

Jocelyn laughed, "I know. And they think we're the weird ones."

I had a whole muesli as it looked the least intimidating of the options. We had to drink the entire pint of water and a small glass of orange juice and then the muffins were dished out. My stomach

was retaliating already against this onslaught; I didn't think it would accommodate anything else.

"Be careful with your muffin," Jocelyn advised quietly.

"What do you mean?"

"The butter." She squeezed the muffin subtly, yet roughly, thick golden butter oozing out over her hands to be conveniently mopped up by the sleeves of Jocelyn's jumper. I stored the information in my memory that I must wear long sleeves to breakfast every morning. "Just don't let them catch you. You'll be given another one if they see you."

All eight of us were marched up to the Sky Lounge once the morning feast was over. Alicia, Holly, Clara, Elle, Casey, Andrea, Jocelyn and me. I'd been informed that as it was Saturday there were less of us at the clinic; quite a few patients were on home leave and some would be out with families in the daytime during their visits too. Jocelyn had said that it was easier to 'get away with things' in the week when there were more patients for the staff to keep their eyes on. A couple of the patients from the Blue Kitchen were still moping about the place too but they mainly kept their distance from the Brown Kitchen lot, deeming themselves superior in their right to eat unobserved.

Rachel appeared at the door to the lounge. "Jocelyn, your dad's here."

"Wish me luck", said Jocelyn, getting to her feet.

"What for?" I asked.

"I'm hoping my dad's going to get me out of here this time."

The rest of that first day was painful. Not only was I so terribly lonely now that most of the others had left for visits, but my stomach felt like it was on the verge of rupturing. I had never felt this bloated in my entire life. I don't think I had ever consumed this much food. I peered down at my previously sunken stomach to see the white flesh stretched tautly over a distended belly. There was a morning snack at 10:30am comprising a Double Decker chocolate bar and a chocolate chip cookie, plus the obligatory pint of water. Lunch soon came round at 1pm: fish pie and sweet corn, followed by apple crumble and ice-cream. Fortunately I didn't need an afternoon snack, but tea time arrived at 5pm and I was forced to gorge on a huge cheese and onion pasty with an enormous portion of baked beans. It was all about the supersize portions here, not to mention the insistence on cheese and chocolate. I was fit to burst and stranded on Total Supervision. All I longed for was a surreptitious trip to the bathroom so I could purge my load and deflate down to emptiness. Hollow is what I could tolerate; it's what I felt comfortable with.

When bed time came I couldn't have been gladder. Sleep represented escape and following a traumatic first day in this unmitigated hell hole, I was about to

indulge in some much needed nothing. The confusion, sense of abandonment and the isolation I felt got swallowed by the night as the zzzzzzzz came to my rescue and I was dead to the world.

Chapter 2

As if in some horrendous nightmare, I had gained a stone. I stepped off the scales – huge industrial ones that measured weight with absolute precision – and retrieved my t-shirt from the floor. I stood alone in the small weighing room (for lack of a better name) shivering in my bra and knickers, the pimpled goose flesh making my body look hairier, the downy fur standing erect from each bump covering my pasty skin. My stomach looked enormous, unusually filled with food, like a melon perched on two cocktail sticks. The scales read in kilograms but even my rudimentary mathematics could manage the conversion to pounds – it was quite extraordinary how I'd picked up the numeracy element that was a prerequisite for anorexia. I'd arrived less than a week ago at 25kg exactly and today weighed 31.52kg. I pulled on my jeans, noticeably tighter around the middle than they had been just days ago.

"Water retention," Kaye said, making a note of my weight in the black folder that was assigned to me. "It will ease off after a while of eating and drinking regularly."

Things had to get worse before they could get better though as later that day I was waddling about like the Michelin man. My face bloated up like a balloon and my ankles swelled up so much that I could actually feel the fluid sloshing about in them as I walked.

"Jeeesus Lea!" Clara exclaimed, rearranging the cushion that my right ankle was resting on, "at this rate, you'll be at target in no time!"

"Look at the state of me!" I kneaded my doughy face between my fingertips, "surely it's not possible for me to get much bigger than this!"

"Trust me; you can get bigger than *that*. You're *tiny*, and at least it's just water," said Joce, aiming to reassure me.

I sighed unhappily, my latent distrust of the nurses overcoming me. "What if it's all a calculated plot? Maybe they planned this. I don't get how I could have gained so much in less than a week, surely that's gotta be dangerous!"

"That's paranoia Lea. Honestly, it will go down and they wouldn't just let you keep putting weight on and on until you burst! Keep your legs raised and the water should, in theory, flow back and re-circulate through your body."

"Given the amount of crying I've done this past week, I'm surprised I've got so much water left to retain!"

Jocelyn laughed gently as if to excuse my maudlin introduction to Food Farm. The water works had been playing up all right; I'd spent that first week snivelling like a lachrymose infant. It was unforgiveable really, my behaviour. On the threshold of becoming an adult, yet I was still a sappy little cry-

baby, unable to hold it together one iota. Maybe this water retention was my punishment for being such a nuisance.

"You're not the first to blow up like a balloon. Holding onto water is quite common when patients first come here, it's the body's way of storing nutrients after deprivation." Jocelyn was on course to study triple science at university. "There was one other girl who apparently put on *more* than a stone in her first week."

"What happened to her?"

"She evened out and gained weight normally. She's still here – Lauren - I don't think you've met her yet, she's in the Blue Kitchen and is allowed home on leave a lot of the time. She'll probably be discharged soon."

"I think I've seen Lauren actually, she's the girl with the long dark plait, looks very young." I almost added, *she's the one with a round face too,* but thought better of it.

"Yep, that's her! See? She's reached her target and she doesn't look gigantic, does she?"

My only response sounded spiteful and I resented myself the instant I'd validated my thoughts. I bit my tongue, holding my words in check. I noticed Holly and Alicia in my periphery, sniggering away carelessly.

"And you swear that I won't just keep on expanding?" I recognised how ridiculous I sounded the instant I'd said it.

"Honest, Lea. Nobody here actually gets *F-A-T.*" She spelt it out as if it was an elicit word, something dirty or illegal.

"Really? Is that so? Well, look at Matt," Alicia snickered.

"Alicia!" Clara shrieked in horror.

"What?" Alicia asked, mock-surprised. "It's not like you haven't thought it as well."

Holly inflated her cheeks to imitate a puffer fish, whilst Alicia crumpled into a fit of giggles. Clara looked at me apologetically.

It was an unfortunate fact that male anorexics at Food Farm had to achieve 100% of their 'normal weight', whereas females had to get to 95% for their prescribed target. I'd only seen Matt once since I'd arrived and he seemed friendly, a couple of years younger than me and due to leave in a fortnight. I didn't take too kindly to Alicia's snide remark; she was certainly someone to keep on my radar. I think this place was at a disadvantage being overpopulated by girls and I anticipated that cattiness could, at times, run off the scale. Matt was the only boy here and even he was being discharged soon, leaving

behind the likes of Alicia and Holly and their
oestrogen-fuelled bitchiness.

It had been raining all day, and with my retaining
fluid and the torrential storms outside, I was sick and
tired of water. It had been miserable. My ankles had
been consistently throbbing all afternoon and I kept
having to alternate which leg I had elevated on the
chair opposite. I hadn't had anything to keep me
occupied in the classroom so I had covered the piece
of paper in biro sketches and the ink had stained my
hand. My sleeves still carried the sickly sweet stench
of butter from breakfast and I had half a potato rostie
concealed in the pocket of my combat trousers from
lunchtime.

I urgently wanted some schoolwork to do but after the
previous place I'd stayed at – before I escaped and
my parents tricked me into coming here – had banned
all educational pursuits. I was behind in my studies
and Food Farm had to make contact with my school
in order to have work sent here. It could take a few
weeks and in the meantime, I was stranded in the
classroom, a beached whale watching everyone else
excel. It was infuriating. Boredom was dangerous.
The place I'd been in before was a child psychiatric
unit (admittedly it sounded scary but at least it wasn't
a feeding farm) and I'd only been there two and a half
months. It was solely me who was not allowed
schoolwork, the other patients all attended the little
schoolroom there on a daily basis, yet I was confined
to bed rest. The nurses hid my papers and
assignments so I had to get really sneaky and have my

teacher send them to my home address. Needless to say, the unit didn't find out that I was busying myself with essay questions and exam papers whilst I was home on weekend leave, and I ran away anyway so it's irrelevant. With schoolwork prohibited, all I was good for was idling about in the living room, whilst the other patients were in school complaining how unfair it was that I got to lounge around doing nothing all day. Either that or the insufferable bed-rest; again, the word 'punishment' enters my mind.

The point is that I needed to be doing something worthwhile with my time and sitting here twiddling my thumbs as I expanded like an inflatable ball was far from thrilling. At least Food Farm was allowing me to do schoolwork and I hoped to sit my exams too, in spite of the schooling I'd missed. I just needed to exercise patience and wait for my work to be sent. I rapped my knuckles against the standard issue classroom table, willing time to press on, wishing my life away.

The evening passed in a daze. I could register nothing except how full I was. My stomach – containing mammoth portions supplemented by water retention – bulged over the waistband of my trousers, and it was not only disheartening, it was uncomfortable. I was repeatedly being cautioned by the nurses for fidgeting, particularly by Helen, who would always make everything into a question.

"Leanne would you like to sit still please?" or "Leanne would you like to stop exercising?" This

wasn't exercising; it was simply a futile attempt to manoeuvre myself into a position where my stomach didn't threaten to explode its contents over the room.

I had finally wrestled myself into a spot on the floor on my knees, my back rigid, my stomach not allowing too much overhang. Behind me on the sofa Jocelyn sat waiting out her three hour post-meal with Emily who was now on Total. Across the room, Holly and Alicia were counting down their two hours with Clara who was still on Total. Between the two armchairs nestled little Anne – also on Total – and over in the other corner of the Sky Lounge sat Andrea and Casey, an inseparable pair, on a four hour post-meal. Helen's beady black eyes were somehow on everyone all at once. She stood over by the doorway, a troll guarding its bridge, arms folded across her ample chest, dark brown hair scraped over her scalp in a tight ponytail. I observed her over the top of the book I was pretending to read. Suddenly, like a whirlwind, Bethan breezed into the room and in her melodic Welsh voice, purred "Come on Alicia, you're off now! And you Holly!" Helen looked as if she was about to say something, but, in an instant, the three of them had linked arms like schoolgirls and had danced out of the Sky Lounge, their retreating footsteps pattering like raindrops down the stairs. Clara sighed, clearly wishing she could have left with them. I glanced at the clock and it was a minute before 7:30pm. In another hour, Jocelyn would be scampering off too (more than likely to the nearest vacant bathroom) and I would still be sat here stuffed

to the brim with stodge, envying Joce's opportunity for release.

At 8pm two of the evening staff arrived, Julie, who had kept watch that first night and hadn't been in since, and a lady I'd not met before, Larissa.

"So, who wants their shower first?" Larissa asked and immediately Clara shot up almost at the same time as Andrea, (which I couldn't understand as Andrea was only on a post-meal, so she could shower after her supervision ended). "Ok then Clara, off we go." Larissa had a laid back Jamaican accent and wore large purple hoop earrings and a necklace in the same colour, her skin as smooth and rich as dark chocolate, emphasised all the more by her long white dress. Andrea slumped back in a sulk and I wished that Jocelyn had still been here so I could have asked her what all the fuss was about.

"Leanne, would you like a shower?" Julie asked and, again, Andrea was visibly itching to get up and go with her.

"Andrea sit back down," Helen barked, "you can shower when your post-meal ends." Andrea scowled, first at Helen and then at me, before plonking herself back down next to Casey.

It was the Green Bathroom that I chose. It was the most private and secluded, for it only had one small window and possessed a quiet, relaxing ambience. Not that it mattered really as, from experience, the

nurse or carer would stand and blatantly watch as I showered. In the six days that I had been here, I had showered twice; the first time I was pinioned by Rosie's piercing eyes for the duration so that I was in and out quicker than lightning. The second time, I'd been supervised by Mother Teresa and her ubiquitous Bible; she had psalms rolling off her pious tongue like bitter honey as she stood with her back to me, glancing at my reflection in the mirror to ensure I was behaving appropriately. I had little doubt that this evening I would face the same humiliation.

I had my pyjamas, shampoo, shower gel and two towels wadded up in my arms and as I reached the bathroom door, I noticed Julie lean back against the wall and remove a magazine from her bag. I continued through the mint green door, expecting Julie to follow me, however, she pushed the door-to behind me and said, "Call me if you need anything hon, I'll be right here." I was in shock. Now I understood Andrea's eagerness, for here was my very own 'get out of jail free card'. I had the bathroom to myself. There would be no one watching me, no indignity and nothing to stop me from ridding my body of this excess of stodge. I had no time to waste surveying my surroundings; freedom was mine for the taking. I didn't care about getting the water temperature right or using enough shampoo. I didn't even bother to run conditioner through my hair. The minute I stepped around the shower curtain, I turned the water on full –so as not to elicit suspicion - and I violently poured the contents of my over-filled stomach down the plughole, using my finger to swill

the excess away. Purged and liberated, I was able to exit the bathroom that evening feeling wholly cleansed, my insides purified. I decided that I liked Julie and on the walk back to the lounge, I talked animatedly with her, enjoying this feeling of newness. I felt like a completely different person.

Chapter 3

The day I was told my target weight was not a joyful one.

I had woken five times in the last hour. I'd always wondered if it was possible for your brain to physically hurt. I felt as if shock waves were being triggered throughout my whole nervous system.

It was 6:30am and the dawn swam in the distance like a pale yellow and lilac watercolour painting, mild and non-threatening. However, my mind was doing somersaults. My body felt like it was being gnawed at by insects. I missed sleep, but at least I was snuggled under a duvet in a bedroom, and no longer sprawled on a questionable-looking mattress on the classroom floor. I had been in this bedroom for a couple of days now, sharing with an Asian girl called Jasmine who was my age, at her own target weight and due to be discharged in a matter of weeks. In fact, Jazz had managed to have her target weight reduced by seven pounds as a result of resuming her menstrual cycle. She was over the moon: stunning and slim and smiling, to boot. At 5ft10 she towered over me, her long supple limbs, catlike and elegant, her sleek black hair tumbled over her shoulders in a cascade of silk. Willowy was the word. How lucky, Jazz's period offering unexpected salvation! The renowned curse becoming a blessing in this instance….

I lay supine on my crumpled sheets, pondering what my meeting with the Tarantula, who was now assigned as my key nurse, would bring. I would receive the vital number that my body was geared towards. It was like the Holy Grail, especially as I'd been waiting around getting fatter and fatter for two weeks, my fate suspended in the balance. I was sitting in the middle waiting. Gone was my old self, old body, my former identity, so it seemed, and I was yet to see what I would be forced to 'grow into'. My once concave stomach had heaved itself outwards like a tumescent mound of rising bread dough and flesh was beginning to seep in between my ribs. I didn't need to look in the mirror because I could *feel* the overall puffiness of my face. However, curiosity got the better of me at times. My mousey-blonde hair hung straw-like around my shoulders; months of re-growth showing at the roots and a pair of sad blue eyes looked imploringly from the round pale moon face. I'd inadvertently traded cheekbones for a second chin.

I dressed slowly, in a daze almost, lamenting the tightening of my favourite jeans around my middle. I couldn't wear them; I'd be forever tugging at them and pulling them loose. I threw them in the corner angrily and walked to the wardrobe to find another pair. Biting back sobs whilst rummaging through one of the drawers, I found only t-shirts and tops, all of my trousers had gotten too un-wearable. In the end, I found a long skirt with an elasticated waist and although the weather wasn't mild enough to wear it, I pulled it on bitterly, scrunched the elastic into a small

loop and clipped a safety pin through to hold the elastic waistband tighter. My rustling and pacing had woken Jasmine. As she stirred, her pink flowered duvet moved gently, roses and chrysanthemums shaking their heads.

"What's going on?" Jazz slurred.

"Nothing fits me anymore!" I slumped to the floor, my head in my knees. "I hate it!"

"Calm down", soothed Jazz. "What's this all about?"

"I just can't bear it here anymore."

"It's ok." Jasmine sat up.

"All the food, the weight gain. Being here. I can't stand it! I never asked for it! I just hate it here so much Jazz!" I loathed how melodramatic I sounded, but I felt as if I had reached another breaking point. My emotions bubbled in a conglomeration of chaos and despair, like a volcano within, needing this outburst. I hadn't been welcomed into this place, but reprimanded for merely being 'me', punished using the one thing I was battling against and was inexplicably afraid of. The staff here brandished food as a weapon of attrition, all the while berating and belittling us because we were sick. The only people who held their arms open in comfort, who offered empathy, were some of the other patients, locked up together with me in this prison. We had a mutual understanding and a shared affliction.

"Ahhh! It's your nurse session today, isn't it?"

I nodded, wiping my eyes with the back of my hand.

"Now I understand. Try not to worry Lea."

My body trembled as I tried to gather myself together. I was sure that everyone was tired of seeing me reduced to tears and I hated the thought of being such a burden on everyone around me, especially those few who had given me such warmth.

"Try not to worry." Jazz reiterated, "We all have to reach target. Nobody here wants to but it's inevitable sweetie and just look at you – you're so little, at least your target weight will be small. It'll be a diddy little number. You'll be fine". I thought back to how Holly and Alicia were laughing at Matt's expense the other day.

"But what if my target weight is monstrous – I mean, I feel enormous now! I can't imagine getting any bigger than this."

"You've only been here, what – two weeks? You'll adjust, honestly, and even when you reach your target weight you'll have time after that for your weight to distribute and even out." Jazz locked her huge chestnut eyes on mine as she knelt down beside me, "Come on, cheer up….if you're so 'enormous' as you put it, why are you still having to secure your clothes with safety pins?!" Jasmine started laughing as she pointed to my dip-dyed lilac skirt, held snugly around

my waist with its trusted safety pin. I shrugged; I suppose I couldn't argue with her there. It didn't make it any easier though.

At breakfast, I offered to pour the orange juice into the glasses, up to the second rim on each glass. Some mornings we were given an orange to eat instead of juice and I hadn't yet made up my mind which I preferred. The only people in the Brown Kitchen were Kaye and Rachel, diligently sorting out the morning's feast, and now that I was off Total Supervision, I could move around the Farm more freely. I was still sanctioned by a three-hour post-meal, though that was nothing in comparison to the toils of Total. As I came to fill what would be my own glass, I hesitated, checked that neither Kaye or Rachel were looking, before drizzling the tiniest drop of juice and smearing it around the inside of the glass. I pressed my lips roughly around the rim to make an imprint. Job done. Nobody suspected a thing and the meal ended with me leaving the room with a full croissant secreted up my sleeve. The day was off to a flying start!

Lunch time that day saw another success for me. As it was Wednesday, it was fish and chips, nobody's particular favourite, least of all mine, as the staff had thrown my vegetarianism out of the window with complete and utter disregard. Believe me, I'd argued till I was blue in the face, however, any riposte on my part in defence of my ethics were met with threats to tube-feed me lard or, even worse, to tube feed me the animals that I held so dear. It was a no-win situation.

"Most of you lot claim to be vegetarians when you get here," sneered Kaye on one occasion. "But, for the majority of you, it's just another food to cut out". It angered me deeply that my beliefs were considered to be just a whimsical elimination of a food group. However, it had reached the point at which arguing was achieving nothing but exhaustion. Similarly, I had met a stalemate whilst creating my 'Dislikes List'. I'd listed meat as number one and fish as number two, deeming myself to be quite sneaky at the time, but these were dismissed immediately.

"You need the protein from meat and fish," was the explanation Kaye offered for why I had to boycott my morals. "When you're better and healthy and you're out of here, you can eat or not eat whatever you want."

The obligatory three 'C's were banned from the list too: Cheese, Chocolate and Cream, much to the disdain of every patient here. In the end, I'd settled for beetroot and corned beef (two foodstuffs that I truly couldn't stomach) and added chocolate cake as a third dislike, just for the hell of it. That felt like a minor triumph.

Helen was dishing up the fish and chips that day and the Brown Kitchen was rammed full of not-so-hungry residents. I was sitting beside Jazz, with Elle on the other side of me. Joce sat across the far end in between Clara and Andrea. The other spaces around the table were filled by Holly, Alicia, Casey, Bethan, Anne, Emily, Layla, Fliss, Laura, and Robyn. Tanya,

41

Maisie and little Piper - who was the youngest at six years old - were seated on the other brown table. Maisie was a former patient who had returned for a fortnight following an illness which had caused her to lose a significant amount of weight. Her parents, fearing the return of her anorexia, had hastily got her referred back to the clinic and here Maisie was on a two week holiday of excessive calories and Total Supervision. Tanya was a relatively new admission from Greece and although her command of the English language was good, the nurses thought it was important to segregate her on the other table with little Piper. Piper, who for all her cherubic innocence was a pain in the back-side; Sick-Bag is what she was secretly referred to by some of the others. However, Piper proved to be my blessing that lunchtime, for her 'incident' allowed me the opportunity to smuggle my whole portion of fish and a handful of chips into my spacious combat trouser pockets.

The smell of disinfectant already marked Piper's presence in the Brown Kitchen that afternoon, so we were well aware that projectile vomiting was on the cards. When it happened, Helen, Kaye and Joan threw themselves into a panic as gastro-eruptus took place in the form of clods of mushy peas and undigested battered fish. Puke-phobic Laura fled the room in tears, causing Kaye to run in pursuit and the scenario provided some welcome entertainment for me as well as some respite for my aggrieved stomach.

*

42

Prior to my key nurse session, I'd had a fantastic vision of being hauled away by the Tarantula and her envisioned eight legs into a dark and dismal lair, my tiny fly-like body paling in comparison to this predatory beast's. I'd be thrashing about frantically, batting my meagre wings in a futile effort to escape, wholly at the mercy of the gigantic Natasha and her food-filled web. Grated cheese melted around the entrance in dripping crusts, chocolate oozed from the walls and mayonnaise sloshed thickly on the ground. The stench of sweet unsalted butter assaulted my nostrils and the smell of baking permeated the air in waves and bouts. A sofa of assorted cream cakes beckoned me over to be consumed in the very act of being seated. Absolutely nauseating….This was, of course, nothing like how the meeting panned out. Once again, I'd allowed my imagination to run riot. Natasha merely appeared, filling the doorway to the Sky Lounge, and called my name. Her teeth gleamed white and perfect. I envied her that stunning smile. Her hair still sprung from her head like thick black ropes, and she was dressed casually in a navy blue poncho and white baggy cargo pants. I still hadn't forgiven her for preventing my getaway that first evening, not that I stood much chance of running very far. I cringed from the memory of the struggle, my matchstick arms fumbling abysmally for freedom.

Natasha led me down the hallway to a room I hadn't had the opportunity to enter before, and she beamed at me from ear to ear as she unlocked the door. The room had a certain freshness about it, the scent of furniture polish lingered in the air and the window

over the far side was vented open half-way. Lime
green curtains flapped merrily in front of the glass.
The walls were adorned with several seaside pictures,
one of a rowing boat, another of a beach. It was all
too quaint and nice for the likes of me. Me and my
stupid life, my silly insignificant life.

"So Lea," she chirped, interrupting my reverie, "How
are you finding it here?"

"I hate it."

"I'm sure you do." Natasha's tone dropped as if I'd
insulted her. "Everyone hates it at first."

I hesitated, expecting her to continue, but she just
reached for the black folder with my name printed on
the front. The individual pieces of paper sounded
delicate as she pugnaciously flicked the pages away,
one by one, to get at one with a set of charts on it.
My name was printed indelibly on that page too, as
were my date of birth and the date of my admission. I
squinted awkwardly to see if I could glean much
more from the document, before it was snapped shut
in a loud clomp.

"Well, I'm sure you know why you're here," Natasha
stated.

"I'm here to put on weight," I said flatly.

"No, I mean here – sitting in this room with me."

"I'm here to get my target weight".

"It's more than that. You're here so that – together - we can go through what is to be expected of you and what will happen here. We're going to work through this together, you as patient and me as your key nurse. We can trust each other and if there's ever anything you want to ask or anything you're worried about, just feel free to ask me."

In my head, the image of a tarantula backing me into a cream and custard-filled corner, a dozen chocolate bars falling on my head, made me want to laugh. I tried to focus on Jasmine's conversation earlier that day, about how fortunate I was to be five foot zero and how that would gain me access to a miniscule target weight. Jocelyn had goaded me into a similar sense of security by telling me that I was small-boned and therefore it would be not only unfair but *unhealthy* to make me gain too much weight. Joce was studying science after all so she knew what she was talking about. I felt my confidence bolstered by the support of my friends.

"But I am getting my target weight today, right?" Panic ascended within me like bile, my nerves reacting in abject fear that this precious number would not be revealed today, my fate stalled even more.

"You girls are all the same, so fixated by scales and weights. It's such a shame you can't just *be.* " The

Tarantula caught my aggrieved expression and added, "Yes, we will discuss your target weight."

The tension oozed out of me like poison from a wound, my ability to think restored, my nerves granted a degree of respite.

"First things first", Natasha said in her upbeat voice, "I need to check your blood pressure and your reflexes, as these weren't done on the day you were brought in". A flash of recognition passed between us as we both automatically remembered that fateful evening of my admission. I almost made a joke then about how below-par my reflexes must have been as I hadn't been quick enough to escape, but I thought better of it, judging Natasha's earnest expression.

"Have you spoken to your parents?" she asked, catching me by surprise.

"No," I replied sullenly.

"They were only doing what they thought was best. Don't be too harsh on them," she said softly. "Are you speaking to your brother and sister? What were their names again?"

"Leonard and Leonie, and yes I am talking to them. They didn't put me here".

Leonie is like a best friend as well as my sister, for the bond we share is watertight and time has soldered us together like charms on a bracelet. We've always

wrote little notes to each other, usually with stickers of rainbows or stars decorating them, and she still sends me letters and cards through the post at the clinic. I've always been pretty close to Leonard too, though he has detached himself from me in recent months, stymied by my inability to eat. Illness – particularly, mental illness – is something that Leonard fails to comprehend.

"I'm pleased you're still speaking to them but go easy on your poor mum and dad. It wasn't an easy decision to make. Most parents say that when they drop their daughters – or sons – off. You'll understand when you're older and have children of your own."

"I'm never having children! I don't want the burden and knowing my luck they'd probably turn out like me!" I don't know if it was intended as a self-deprecating joke or as a statement of fact, but I felt suddenly foolish and wished I could stuff the words back into my mouth.

"You may change your mind," Natasha mused, "Now, pull up your sleeve for me."

Natasha gasped in alarm at my forearm, its network of red and white cross hatchings; a map with no discernible directions, just indicating a senseless maelstrom of anguish.

"What have the nurses said about these scars at weigh-in?"

"Nothing. They're too busy staring at how fat I'm getting."

"Don't be ridiculous. What have they said?"

"Nothing really," I shrugged, making light of it. "Just to keep an eye on me, maybe."

"They look healed, at least. How long ago did you do this?" The Tarantula rotated my arm, inspecting the grooves left over from assorted burns and slashes.

"About a year ago," I muttered evasively.

Her eyes glazed over with tenderness and concern. "How old are you Lea?"

I liked that she called me Lea, the monosyllabic abbreviation of Leanne, informal and intimate. I relaxed under her maternal gaze then and replied with a voice that didn't sound like my own, it came as if from somewhere deep within my very soul. Natasha shook her head gently.

"Seventeen and you should be out living your life. You should be *experiencing* it. You ought to be having fun, exploring the world, breaking hearts, getting drunk. You should be enjoying yourself, and yet, here you are." She nodded her head towards my limp mutilated arm. I was beginning to warm to her now, her cool, calm unadulterated caring, and I felt guilty for having made her recoil in horror whilst

merely doing her job. I was behaving like an obstinate brat.

She took my blood pressure gently and I was amazed that the blood pressure band not only fitted, but gripped my bicep firmly. She read my mind, "It's a child's band. You've not suddenly gained how ever many tonnes you were thinking of just then, in case you were wondering." Natasha smiled and I couldn't resist smiling back.

It would be a long time before I smiled at the Tarantula again.

Chapter 4

"Soooooo?" cooed Jocelyn as I joined her at the classroom table, her brown eyes illuminated like a child's on Christmas morning.

"It's worse than I expected!"

"Come on, what is it?" she urged.

"I'm going to demand a change of my key nurse. I think Natasha made my target weight higher on purpose."

"Why do you think that?"

"I dunno. But, just look at her!"

"Just because she's overweight, you think she's trying to make you big too!" Joce sniggered, more amused at my plight than I felt she should be.

"It's more than I've ever weighed in my whole life!"

"*Come on* Lea, just tell me what the weight is!"

"It's absurd, it's utterly beyond belief, it's...."

"Just tell me what it is!" Joce's impatience boiled over.

"47.5 kilograms". I spat the number out with vitriol. "I can't believe it!"

Jocelyn rolled her eyes, "It could be worse. Just keep your fingers crossed you get your period back early. That's what I'm pinning my hopes on."

"How likely *is* that though?"

"Well, it happened for Jazz. She avoided a whole half a stone! Just imagine how lucky she must have felt!"

"Does it happen often then?"

"I think so. I've heard a few stories of girls having their target weights lowered, never any more than seven or eight pounds, but hey, it could make all the difference!"

Apparently, menstruation was the female body's health barometer.

"I guess," I bit my lip, deep in thought for a moment.

"What else did Natasha talk to you about?"

"Nothing much, she mainly repeated stuff I'd already heard. My therapy sessions start on Tuesday at 6pm. Great." I added with sarcasm.

"Which doctor have you got?" Joce asked, her lips quivering as she tried to suppress a smile.

It had become a bit of a joke about the unfortunate names of the two leading doctors at Food Farm –

Doctor Dicken and Doctor Beaver. I won't go into detail about the particulars, needless to say the jokes were crass and at their expense. In fact, I hadn't heard anything positive about the doctors, nothing that afforded me much hope anyway.

"Doctor Beaver", I said and Joce burst out laughing. "What's wrong with that?" I asked, genuinely concerned now.

"Nothing!" Joce could hardly get her words out for giggling. "Actually, I really wouldn't know as I have Dicken. They're both lousy doctors! What has Dicken got to do with Beaver? What is a Beaver and where is a Dicken?" She exploded into a fit of unmanageable laughter then, which hadn't reached me as I was still raw from the revelation of my target weight.

"I'm still going to see about changing my key nurse," I announced stubbornly. "The Tarantula almost had me liking her, as well."

"Just because she's overweight, come on Lea, that's hardly fair." She stuttered her words in between giggling.

"It's not that…"

"Who's that over there?"

I whipped round dizzyingly fast to stare not very inconspicuously at the girl standing across the room.

Her shy gaze met mine in an embarrassed collision and she instantly turned away as if we were two magnets of the same poles. I was awestruck by her swathe of crimped blonde mermaid-hair, stretching down the entire length of her back, thick, glossy and nourished.

We were meant to be taking part in Art Therapy, which was basically a glorified Craft Club. The session would inevitably end with glitter carpeting the floor, two or three pairs of scissors having gone 'missing', and a patient making an impromptu disappearance which would result in us all being told off. It was a shame really as I loved art. I could whittle away many an hour painting or sketching, completely abandoning myself to the elements of creativity, experimenting with myriad tones and textures, splashing an array of colour with artistic abandon. This passion of mine was certainly not shared with this bunch of anorexics. Elle and Ruby enjoyed gluing things to the table and Holly liked leaving a big mess for us all to clean up. Even Joce, who would usually be attempting something inspired, was cradling a blank piece of paper this evening. The girl with the golden waterfall of hair was standing with a blonde lady, presumably her mother, and one of the doctors and Rosie. She was clearly being shown around, led into a similar trap as I had been. Her face was sullen, devoid of any emotion whatsoever and I shivered, pondering the abominable fuss I had kicked up on my arrival. Dignity and decorum were certainly not my forte.

With an abrupt, officious handshake, the doctor and the mother parted ways, leaving the young girl at the mercy of Rosie. They were facing in our direction and naturally I smiled at the newcomer, although this was not returned.

"There's Holly and Clara over there, and here are Jocelyn and another fairly new resident called Leanne," enthused Rosie. "This is Millicent."

"Millie," the girl interjected with the tiniest voice I had ever heard. The sound that issued from her throat was like that of a startled mouse or a gurgle from a brook or a stream. Rosie completely ignored her – or perhaps hadn't heard her squeak - and just continued making introductions in her pompous way. "Over there is so-and-so and that's where they do such-and-such." I wondered if they had shown her to the gigantic food cupboard yet. That's the reason we were here, after all.

"Right girls, it's up to you to make Millicent feel welcome," Rosie dictated, making me flinch at how she had completely ignored Millie's abbreviated name preference. "I'm off to start the meds rounds". She quite literally wiped her hands alternately across each other – swipe, swipe - as if washing her hands of the new girl and the situation, before sauntering off to ruin someone else's day.

"Do you know how long you're staying for Millie?" Jocelyn asked, making polite conversation. Millie shook her head. "Where have you come from?"

Millie shrugged. She was clearly not much of a conversationalist.

"I love your hair!" I enthused, "It's absolutely gorgeous!"

"Thanks," came her taciturn reply.

"How did you get it so long?" I envied her length and volume, my hair had been falling out in small clumps prior to my arrival. I wondered if she had some trick up her sleeve for keeping it so healthy.

Millie shrugged, "It's always been like this."

"Well, I'm going to have to love you and leave you." Jocelyn sighed, her supervision time over. With a blasé message warning me not to fret about my target weight, "it would all distribute out in the end," she was gone.

I was left swirling black chalk about on a large sheet of paper. Millie took the seat that Joce had vacated and hoisted one leg underneath her as she began rhythmically swinging the other leg that was dangling. Silence smothered us like a blanket. I felt unsure of what was the appropriate thing to say to this enigmatic patient that had become my responsibility somehow.   I glanced around the classroom and noticed that I had inadvertently slipped into a void, alone with the new girl in absolute quiet whilst the world carried on calamitously around me: Holly was chasing Clara with a contraband scalpel blade

completely unnoticed by the nurse on guard and Ruby was pouring bits of scrap – felt, wool, pipe cleaners, tooth picks, lolly sticks, multicoloured fabrics – into an abandoned rucksack, an impish smirk engraved on her face. Alicia and Bethan were hunched around the art cupboard, blatantly doing something that they shouldn't and getting away with it. I snapped round to look at my neighbour who, with a raised eyebrow, uttered in a teeny-tiny sugary sweet voice, "I see it's all fun and games here then." The irony wasn't lost on me and I was, at last, delighted to find someone who was perhaps even more acerbic than me.

*

The simplest way to describe how I got here is this, that anorexia is a stone rolling down a hill, gathering momentum. It got me alone and it singled me out as its prey. Like a cancer sufferer, an Alzheimer's victim or an alcoholic, I did not choose my disease. Anorexia crept up on me when I was at my most vulnerable, at my lowest ebb, during my darkest moments when I was blinded by my own inadequacies and wracked with debilitating self-loathing. It pulled a searing cloak tight around my head and wrenched me asunder, binding me to it irrevocably. Together, anorexia and I, we tumbled down that hill, picking up speed, gaining velocity as we hurtled to the point of no return. That is how I got here. Here, I am in Hell.

Mother Teresa says we will go to Hell – us girls - because we don't pray. Well, I won't be going to

Hell, because I'm already there. I'm back on Total Supervision. Millie is on Total also and we drag our faded mattresses out from the cupboards, me hauling Millie's out for her first whilst she holds the door so that I can grab the second one for me. Our arms are like the pale, fragile branches of trees as we drag the cursed things along the floor. Mother Teresa comes and snatches the rope ties from us the minute we have unfolded the mattresses and I wonder how she has the audacity to be so self-righteous. Millie has started to refer to her as 'Mother Teresa' as well and I smile to myself at our small defiant act of solidarity. Millie has only been here a few days but we get along superbly. We instantly clicked that evening in the classroom and I realised that she is the most cynical, yet bleakly exuberant person I've ever encountered. I know that's hard to comprehend, but she is like the embers of a fading bonfire. Tiny and quiet, Millie gives the impression of being timid and unassuming yet she's actually a firecracker, bursting with brutal effervescence and scathing scepticism. I smoothed out my sleeping bag on top of the mattress, which I'd inspected for the usual curly dark hairs and bits of filth from being spread over the floor repeatedly. I caught Millie carrying out the same inspection.

Millie made a face, her features contorting in disgust.

"Vile, isn't it?" I stated.

"I don't know how they get away with it," Millie remarked. "I thought this was the NHS."

"Apparently it's around £500 a day to stay here, and most of us are funded through the National Health. However," I cocked my head, gesturing towards Mother Teresa. "The likes of us lot sure need punishing."

Millie affected a haughty tone and added, "you're all going to Hell, girls, you don't pray, you're going to Hell, to Hell, girls, you're doomed, doomed!!" She began wailing "you're dooooomed! Dooooomed!" repeatedly in an eerie ghost-call echo that had my shoulders shaking with hilarity.

"What's that racket?!" Mother Teresa's stout neck twisted round in an effort to detect where the sound was coming from, but Millie had promptly quietened, leaving me and my bowing shoulders the only indication that anything untoward was going on.

"You, there," her bony finger singled me out. "Move your bed. You can sleep over here, next to me."

"But, I …"

"No buts, come and put your things over here where I can keep my eye on you."

"I wasn't…"

"Shush." Mother Teresa spat the word out abruptly and I thought better of trying to fight her when her weapon of admonition was food. I skulked over to the armchair that was still standing sentinel at the

door, dragging my made-up mattress bed along the dusty ground. Millie gave me a look of abject apology when I turned around, although, in all honesty, I was grateful to her for having had the opportunity to laugh unrestrainedly again.

It wasn't my fault I was back on Total. It was the medication they had put me on and its odious side-effects. Following my consultation with the Tarantula in which I received the news that I was to be transformed into an elephant, my key nurse had decided that antidepressants would be conducive to improving my state of mind. I'd retaliated, sensing that whatever they plied me with would essentially be an endeavour to make me more compliant. However, it was signed off with Doctor Beaver and I was put on a daily dose of a medicine that has since been banned for children and adolescents due to its proven association with suicide, among other things. My consent was not warranted. The second day of being on the medication, I slept through virtually the whole day, being poked and prodded awake to be fed, watered and toileted, my existence resembling that of a new-born baby. That evening my dishevelled appearance and general apathy had been noted, thus prompting the decision to put me back on 24/7 supervision. I was livid, though in my drowsy state, this irritation translated as mediocre moroseness. I was too lethargic to put up much of an argument and consequently, here I was again experiencing the delights of having a mattress on the filth-infested floor and being scrutinised in my slumber by a religious nut. Millie had been on Total since her

arrival and considered it serendipitous that I had joined her in this castigation. If we must suffer in silence at least we mustn't bear it alone.

I'd never taken drugs before but this is how I imagined it would be. Hazy, woozy, disorientating. I had lost my footing and fallen into a trance. It would have been terrifying, if I'd had the wits about me to have recognised fear. My heartbeat was not my own but the frenzied sputtering of a rabbit's in the headlights, eyes wide beacons of shock, an aura of alarm infiltrating the air. My body felt so removed from me, it was like death. I'd mellowed, that was for sure, because I really couldn't fathom the motivation for anything. Time drifted in the way that clouds traverse the sky, steadily and with magnificent heaviness, conveying a sense of impending doom that I was somehow blinkered to. I couldn't care less. I was looking out at the world with grey-tinted spectacles, everything subdued and slightly off-focus, colours dimmed or removed completely; all sounds seemed to be pushed to the outside walls of my mind, like background noise. The thoughts and feelings that had been so overriding, filling me with venom and anguish, melancholy and desolation had deserted me, leaving my mind lighter than a feather. I was floating in a foggy unreality. I was weightless and inconsequential, drowning in a milky nothingness. I could cope like this, an empty shell, an unhindered vessel. Sleep came warm and delicious and I luxuriated in it like a cat lapping up cream. Instead of speaking, I slept. Instead of thinking, I slept. I didn't bother to shower or brush my hair, or read my books,

or worry about school and exams, or question why I was here or how I could escape. I caved in, I submitted and I slept.

Although I hadn't been in a room of my own for long, I missed it; the privacy had seemed a luxury and the novelty of being able to see my own belongings, priceless. I doubt if Jasmine really minded that I wasn't sharing with her as she was readying herself for her great departure. Jocelyn was still on her post-meal supervision so I could see her whilst she was counting down the minutes to her release, although I was growing exceptionally close to my new friend Millie. Once the inertia of the medication faded, I emerged from my cavern of fog, reborn and revitalised, bolstered by a strengthened resolve to combat the injustice of this place. I wanted either restitution or revenge, and a means of liberation. In Millie I found a willing accomplice. I was quietly enraged by the drug-induced stupor I'd been plunged into and combined with the regularly inflicted cheese sandwich punishment, the indignity of bathroom supervision and the mattress putrefaction on Total, Millie and I vowed to rally together and we spoke of revolt. Some of our conversations were laden with humour – our defence against Food Farm and its attempt to suppress the spark in us – although, at times we spoke with deathly seriousness about how we intended to flee.

Until that night when Mother Teresa separated us, Millie and I had slept side by side, plotting our escape (with or without apocalyptic pyrotechnics) and

imagining a life beyond Food Farm. Most of it was make-believe but it was refreshing to make jokes about the clinic and the world outside, to ponder how things could be different and how we would change the world if we could. In the Sky Lounge we sat in what jocularly became known as 'the naughty corner' for one of the carers had noted that "it's always the quiet ones you have to watch out for". Such comments constituted nothing more than water off a duck's back, and as my weight increased, so did my fire.

Chapter 5

If I thought the week couldn't get any worse, I had another thing coming. Weigh day and Helen on duty. If she was pouring the cereal at breakfast, we'd all get extra milk and that was a fact. Kaye had made quite a habit of guarding the toilet door in the mornings, listening for the tinkle of urine splashing against porcelain, making certain our bladders had completed their mandatory pre-weigh-in emptying. I always strained to hold it back, just allowing the initial trickle as evidence that I had 'been', storing the remaining fluid as stock weight to fool the scales. I must admit that I was usually pretty good at this, it hurt like mad - a burning sensation spread across my abdomen - but it was worthwhile. I exited the toilet swiftly and stood in anticipation of the number on the dial.

"Leanne," Helen's throaty voice summoned.

A colossal sigh was emitted from my very soul and I thought *here we go again.* I sloped into the room and reluctantly stripped to my underwear.

"What's this?" Helen's hand grabbed my wrist which was adorned with three individual bead bracelets. "Off."

"You've gotta be kidding?" I said.

"Take them off, now," demanded Helen.

"They're only little beads, they're practically weightless."

"No jewellery allowed."

I huffed, irked, and flung the three bracelets over to where my pyjamas lay crumpled in a heap. The turquoise bracelet rattled as it hit the wall on its descent. Karma beads, they were called.

"Am I going to have to call someone?" Helen said it with an exaggerated air, rolling her eyes, trying to make me think that I was making a nuisance of myself. I felt like answering back, but I halted, remembering that Helen would be in charge of breakfast. I didn't want more in my bowl before I'd even made it to the table!

"No Helen," I replied submissively, taking a slow and deliberate step towards the scales.

I was below my line.

Helen was busy noting this in my black folder and I felt the colour drain from my face. I was in for it now.

"What have you been up to then, Leanne?" Helen was tapping the end of her pen against the table.

"What do you mean?"

"This," Helen struck the chart in front of her with the pen. "You're on Total Supervision and you've fallen below your line. Are we not feeding you enough? What have you been doing?"

"Nothing."

"Hmmm we'll have to see about that, won't we…"

"I've not actually lost any weight though", I interrupted, "Look!" I grabbed the folder and spun it round so that I could get a better view of the graph. My line ascended like an elevator and I could see that I had dipped slightly below – I hadn't gained a kilogram this week, but I hadn't actually lost any weight either.

"Give that back here," Helen barked.

"I was just looking," I said defensively.

"You have no right to just grab things off my desk!"

I apologised, sensing that it would help my case; however, Helen flung her next epithet at me with malice. "From now on you're on 3,500". She raised her voice so that she could be heard beyond the weighing room. "Kaye, Nicola, from now on Leanne's on 3 thousand and five hundred each day." She flashed me a self-satisfied smirk.

"Ok, we'd best let Natasha know, so she can amend her care plans", squawked Kaye. Nicola was helping

the other patients tidy away the mattresses, whether she heard this information or not, I couldn't say.

I was incensed. A rise from 3,000 to 3,500 just for a minor slip? It was barbaric. Most people's calorific intakes where increased by a hundred or two, to aid them to get back on track. I felt that I was being penalised - maybe I shouldn't have thrown those karma beads. Indignation rose at the back of my throat but it would do me greater harm than good for me to vocalise my rage. It was another notch of injustice to bear – to remember and report back to Millie. My desire to abscond had been galvanised.

*

Breakfast was a joke. Helen may as well been spoon-feeding me the cereal, she was up so close in my face.

"Would you like to eat it properly, Leanne?

"Would you like to put more on your spoon, Leanne?"

"Would you like to stop separating the flake and the muesli, Leanne?"

No, no and no, I would not! It seemed to be 'Victimise Leanne' day, especially where that ogre Helen was concerned. The other girls sat squirming quietly in their wooden seats, sympathy exuding from them just enough, as they also relished the relief that it wasn't them.

"Joan, I think we'll be needing another bowl of flakes for Leanne, as she's so expertly picked them all out of her muesli."

"What!" I spat, furious.

"I warned you, Leanne, and yet you persisted in separating your cereal."

"That's how I like it. Lots of people separate parts of their food. It's called *having a preference*".

"Not when *you* do it, it isn't. It's a form of obsessive compulsion and that's not allowed in Rose Farm. You know that. In fact, you all know that. Anyone caught separating their food will be given more."

"What? That's ludicrous!" My typically quiet nature was easily riled where threats of extra food was concerned. Additionally, I hated Helen and made no secret of that.

"I think you'd better keep your voice down Leanne, else you'll be getting more than just another portion of flakes".

I felt utterly deflated. I was so consumed with anger that the wind had been knocked from my sails and I closed my recalcitrant mouth, unwilling to invite any more trouble my way. Joan brought the dreaded bowl of flakes over and Helen proceeded to mix them in with the muesli that remained in my bowl. It was triple chocolate muesli today so the milk had formed

a muddy slush at the bottom, rendering it a most un-enticing sight.

"Maybe you'd like to think of what you do, before you do it Leanne?" A self-satisfied smirk stretched across her large white face, bringing to mind the Cheshire Cat, only uglier and, more importantly, chubbier.

I refused to look at Helen. I wouldn't give her the satisfaction of seeing me this enraged and this close to tears. Instead, I ate the cereal like a trained monkey, shovelling it into my mouth in the exact same way she had instructed. She kept her eyes on me the entire time, awaiting the moment I deviated, but I didn't. I just kept plodding through until the bowl was empty and I even brought it up to my lips to drink the remnants of milk from it, much to Helen's alarm.

"There's no need to behave like an animal…" But it was too late, I was already wiping my mouth with my huge sleeve, mopping up any dribbles. A chortle or two could be heard around the kitchen.

"Don't encourage her!" Helen warned, "Else it will be extras for you too."

Nicola and Kaye were patrolling the rest of the kitchen, keeping their eyes peeled for renegades. There was no chance of squeezing the butter out of my muffin this morning and no light at the end of the tunnel for the day. When we were all finished, those

of us on supervision were marched up to the Sky Lounge by Helen who, to my bitter realisation, would be monitoring us for the majority of the day. I curled myself into a tiny ball, making myself disappear, seeking refuge in sleep.

*

"Leanne, it's time."

A large man stood in the doorway to the Sky Lounge and I stared up through the dissolving wall of sleep. It took several seconds for him to come into focus and I saw that it was Doctor Beaver. It's time? Another couple of seconds elapsed before it came to me. It was time for my therapy session. I'd been weaving in and out of sleep again all day so felt rather perplexed at the advent of this overweight, balding middle aged, middle-class man in the entrance to the lounge. I sat up cautiously, feeling rather light-headed, and stared at him, nonplussed.

"Would you like to come with me?" he asked.

A number of answers punctuated with expletives came to mind, but I smiled like a meek little mouse and scampered along behind as Doctor Beaver led me out of the building.

We came into the back garden, which was beautiful, an opulence of colour, a variety of flowers laid neatly in rows, their hues bleeding into each other, like a sea of wonder amidst the prevalence of green. There

were trees, big and small, hedges, and ferns and also potted plants were littered closer to the exterior walls. Everywhere saw a captivating abundance of Nature, making me at once feel remarkably blessed. We walked down the pathway that snaked all the way to the end of the garden, passing the pond and its surrounding shrubs, a flicker of gold visible beneath the iridescent surface; past the little outdoor swimming pool and the wooden benches that reclined beside it; past this idyllic wonderland that I wished was my own back garden. It was an outdoor Utopia, but was somewhat taken for granted, overlooked by the other girls - adolescents equally selfish and self-obsessed as me – yet I looked upon this haven with affection and yearning. It brought back memories of playing in my parent's garden when I was younger and unhindered by anorexia. Back before food became the enemy and my mind was uninhibited; no obsession of numbers and scales, I was unshackled by a tape measure. I was a child and I was happy.

As I strolled down the garden path, I was struck with such an overwhelming longing for how things used to be; only I saw no way out from the life that had caved in for me now. I'd been such an ebullient girl, content and gregarious, devoted to my family, and anorexia had been the stake that had savagely severed us apart. All I wanted was to be happy, but I had scratched the surface of a self-perpetuating itch. This illness had taken me under its wing, taken me over and the wedge between my family and I had expanded in the process. As the weight dropped off me like melting icicles, so my relationship with those

I loved fell away into anorexia's cold, dark chasm. I felt so awful for my parents who had brought me into the world, imbibing me with life, and loving me unconditionally. My mother nurtured me in her womb for nine months to deliver me, my father anxious to see me born. It was unforgiveable really, that I was the fruits of their labour, their so-called 'gift'. Defunct, I was like an order that has gone awry. There was something wrong with me, only my parents couldn't return me for a refund or replacement. I was not what they had ordered, not anymore.

We arrived at two log cabins at the very bottom of the idyllic garden, one either side of the snaking path. Doctor Beaver introduced the cabin on the left-hand side as his, the one on the right belonging to Dr Dicken. He reached into the pocket of his bottle green tweed jacket for his key.

"Shall we go inside?" He led the way.

I was struck by the homely scent of sandalwood as I stepped inside the rustic log cabin. The wooden walls were red – not bright red like a post box, but a luscious timber tone, illuminated by the shaft of afternoon sunlight that came spilling through the window. There were two windows, one on the same side as the door and a smaller window facing back towards the clinic, which resembled a tiny spec of grey from here. A painting of a meadow was on the bare wall opposite the door and combined greens, yellows and reds, to create a very ambient image. I

remembered that everything in here was orchestrated to 'relax' me. I was subconsciously being put at ease. It was a far cry from the previous outpatient therapy I'd had with my shrewish psychiatrist who I couldn't resist lying to. The Evil Man, I'd called him and the sessions were uneventful and uninspiring, a complete waste of my time. Good luck Doctor Beaver, I thought sardonically, seating myself on the plush beige sofa. I could not fathom how this 50-something year old man could even entertain the notion of looking into my mangled mind. Ten minutes of complete quiet wafted through the room, Doctor Beaver sitting there like a grinning fool, his hands positioned as if in prayer.

"So…." The doctor clearly couldn't bear the silence any longer.

"So, what?" I countered.

His face collapsed like ice-cream melting into sand. What was the point of him sitting here waiting for me to speak to him? What was he expecting me to say? It was up to him to do the work, that's what he was paid so handsomely for, wasn't it? As if reading my mind, he said, in his haughty voice, "Why are you here?"

"What do you mean, why am I here? I'm here because my parents brought me here *against my will*. I don't want to be here and if I could leave now, I would." It was the most I had spoken for a long time

and my mouth felt dry, my tongue expanded within it like a toad stuck in a pothole.

"What is it that's troubling you, Leanne?"

"Lea," I corrected. "Nothing in particular is 'troubling' me, I just hate this place and I think it's ridiculous that I'm here."

"So, it was perfectly normal for you – a 17 year old girl, bright and happy with a caring family - to be starving yourself almost to the brink of death? To be weighing just four stone, your parents at their wits' end, does that sound normal to you?"
I gulped. "Define normal".

Doctor Beaver breathed the weighty sigh of a self-satisfied but mildly exasperated old man who had most probably consumed a hearty evening meal, his large torso rising and falling from the effort of breathing. His black-rimmed glasses rested on the end of a protuberant nose, which had grey hairs springing out of it. I thought it a shame that his ears and nostrils were besieged by sprigs of grey hair, yet his comb-over was a poor attempt to conceal being follically challenged on his cranium.

"What do you hope to get out of this clinic?" He continued.

"I just want to go home."

"You are nowhere near a healthy enough weight to go home, I'm afraid."

"Well, can I have my target weight lowered then?" It was worth a try.

"Your target weight has been properly calculated based upon your age, height and recommended body mass. This is the very minimum that you must be, we are not expecting you to put on an excess amount of weight. You will still weigh less than the average person does."

So this was his justification for my mammoth target weight. I couldn't believe it. Even I was beginning to tire of the discussions centred on my target weight. I was fed up of hearing about and talking about the damned 47.5kg.

"I've never weighed this in my life though! I've never weighed any more than seven stone." My voice squeaked embarrassingly at the end, sounding less stoical than I was aiming for.

"That's because you haven't been at a healthy weight for such a long time. Now that you are older, you will naturally be expected to weigh more than you did, say, two years ago."

I was fighting a losing battle with this issue. All I could do was hope, wish and pray for the premature red flourish, the sooner the better, to stall my arrival at seven stone, eight pounds. The therapy session

was up quicker than anticipated and it was even more pointless than my deceitful discussions with the Evil Man. Nothing had been achieved here, as far as I could tell. Doctor Beaver merely repeated, "It's time," indicating that my allotted hour was over and he led me back through the luscious paradise of the garden and back up to the Sky Lounge.

"How did it go?" Millie asked, drawing herself up closer to me so that we could whisper between ourselves.

"The walk down through the garden was lovely. I think that's as far as my thoughts go regarding this afternoon".

"Evening", Millie corrected. "It's twenty past seven now".

"Not long till evening snack then", I groaned.

"How many calories have you got left?"

"Three-hundred. It'll probably be a Double Decker and a cookie. Or a Boost. Please don't let it be a Mars Bar."

"This soon before bed time as well!"

"Don't remind me!" My stomach turned at the thought of more food.

Snack time wasn't a complete nightmare. In spite of the sickeningly sweet confectionary I was forced to eat by Nicola this time, not – thank God! – Helen, I was also informed that my supervision had changed. Rachel arrived to give me the good news.

"Right Lea!" she exclaimed. I had grown to quite like Rachel, even though she was a nurse and a distributer of meals. She had a liveliness and a *joie de vivre* that couldn't help but rub off on me. Her attitude was optimistic, without being unrealistic, and she handled matters in a firm but fair manner, which I admired. I looked up as I was finishing drinking my water. Rachel was wearing khaki trousers and a navy vest top, her mousey hair was pulled in a loose ponytail. She flashed me an enthusiastic smile and said, "Guess what? You're off Total Supervision. Every day at 9pm you're released from Supervision until after breakfast in the morning."

Jazz and Matt had left earlier that day amidst a flurry of congratulation and fond farewells. The only thing that could have made it more celebratory was if they had dished out sweets and chocolate on their way out, glasses of champagne spilling lavishly out of tall thin glasses. Unsurprisingly, the celebration was more for the actual avoidance of foodstuffs that the two Food Farm graduates would anticipate. Jazz had tears in her eyes – whether these were tears of sadness or of joy, no one would ever know – and she hugged me close, candidly wishing me all the best. I congratulated her on her departure and vowed I would miss her lots too, though I struggled to contain my glee at having Millie

replacing her as my cell mate. That was if she ever got off Total, of course!

Thirteen hours of supervision wasn't perfect, but being free at 9pm each evening was better than nothing. I was freed from that vile classroom – I found glitter in my underwear the other morning after a night with a mattress on the floor. I had a bedroom to call mine again at least. Hooray for small victories!

I wriggled down under the duvet, enveloped in darkness; my face concealed, body foetal, simulating warmth, allowing just the top of my head to be visible for the sake of checks. Oblivious to everything, maybe there's truth in the cliché (or is it a proverb?) that 'ignorance is bliss', for as I lay curled up in my self-contained sanctuary, serenaded by Silverchair, my eardrums being tickled by melodies and my soul soothed, I felt truly at peace. Alone, nestled in the alcove of this wooden beamed attic room, I could forget where I was. I could pretend that I was on a holiday, somewhere else, and that none of my life was real. I could return to a time when I was happy, a time when I was 11 years old, and enjoyment came free and easy. It was jarring, the realisation that I hadn't felt unadulterated happiness since I was 11. It saddened me yet filled me with guilt at the same time. I should have pushed the memories away then, but they came in a surge of reminiscence, both painful and sweet, of holidays at the seaside, the five of us, snapshot smiles, squinting in the dazzling glare of the sun. The carefree days spent abroad, surrounded by a

healthy mixture of family love and sibling bickering. Lazy hours lounging around the pool, Leonard and I fighting over the inflatable Lillo, our skins toasting golden brown, and Leonie's hair bleached nearly white. The simplicity of an ice-cream and thinking nothing of slurping through copious cans of fizzy pop. Hot tears glided down my cheeks as the aptly timed 'Ana's Song' filled my ears. Lamenting the transience of childhood and the lost freedoms of the past, I turned the volume up and, smothered in the gloom, I cried myself to sleep.

Chapter 6

I feel like I'm plummeting from a cliff and nothing is available for me to grab onto. There's nothing to assail my fall. I will be spattered against the ground and mixed in with the rubble, nothing but hopeless debris.

I wake up, my head racing. There is a massive knot that pulls itself tight in my stomach, and it thrusts every essence of me together until I am suffocating. Hibernation is such an inviting prospect. I long to crawl into a place of respite, like a hand into a glove. It has descended upon me again, this jet black cloud of despair. My face is soiled by last night's tears, and I feel lost and helpless in my self-imposed pit. I'm not just lonely. I'm all alone in my own abyss.

I extricated my leaden arm from under my head and shook it like a useless lettuce leaf. Darkness enveloped the room, the only light apparent was a sluice of moonlight slithering through the gap in the curtains. It was still night. My cassette had stopped playing. I clicked the 'open' button and flipped it onto the other side, hitting 'play'. I retracted like a tortoise back into my shell.

*

Tentatively, I opened the curtains to be greeted by a milky blue sky. There was no sign of sun, but promise hung pendulum-like in the air. I felt

unhinged but well-rested. I needed to be ready to face whatever the new day would bring.

The days fluttered between Day Supervision and three hour post meals. As my weight fluctuated, the amount of monitoring I required oscillated between almost always and almost always *after meals*. Sometimes, being on a three-hour post meal was tantamount to having a full sanction, for if breakfast finished at 8:30am and the next snack was due at 10:30am, the supervision parameters smacked right into each other. Most of the nurses and carers keep a tight reign on us during supervision, others were more lax and naturally we gravitated towards those who were less observant and more careless. I once managed to achieve a two hour post meal, albeit a short-lived privilege, and on one occasion I was erroneously let loose completely for two days of near-paradise – no supervision whatsoever - abruptly halted by the revelatory weigh day where I had lost 3kg. I think my eyes pinged out of my face when I was informed that I was off supervision and I made the most it with complete abandon and no reverence for the repercussions.

Millie and I, although we shared a bedroom in Food Farm, had never actually spent the same night in the room yet because one of us would be subjected to Total. At this point, it was Millie who was still on the dubious classroom floor and with no free time of her own. She sometimes vocalised her jealousy, watching my ability to trot away liberally when my time was up, particularly for the long afternoon

between lunch post-meal and tea. I understood and I empathised as there was nothing worse than being cooped up and isolated for hours without respite. The minute I confided in Millie about Damascus Hill, I regretted it, fearing it would increase her envy. However, my fears were allayed by the mischievous twinkle in her blue eyes.

"I'll come with you when I'm off too!" Millie beamed, excitement rippling across her typically solemn face.

The thing about Damascus Hill was that it was but a stone's throw from the clinic, a mere amble around the corner and through a little jitty to a marvellous retreat. To me it represented escape; a means to an end. In retrospect, I'd overlooked the fact that it was stunning; a rural haven with verdant hills that rolled endlessly into the distance, neatly clipped trees framing the spectacle. I'd follow the jitty a short way, with its flowering weeds and tiny stones, then take the turning to the right, which led directly out to Damascus Hill. It wasn't actually a *hill* but an immense area, private grounds in fact, which were rumoured to be owned by a convent – every time I trespassed on that land I kept my eyes pinned wide, in expectation of seeing an old woman roaming in a black and white gown. I'd prepared excuses in my head, just in case, for instance, I'd lost my way, I was searching for my little sister, or *Silly me, I hadn't realised this part was out of bounds!*

There was a little copse a couple of metres from that discreet entry. My pace would quicken, adrenaline building, my heart pumping furiously, as I literally scrambled to the seclusion of that small thicket. Hastily looking both ways and all around, I would bend over and with a large intake of breath I would retch until my lunch was ejected into the bushes. I'm not proud of myself - looking back - as, like I said, I was simply and selfishly satisfying a means to an end. I don't know if that land was owned or frequented by nuns but all I can say is that I was very fortunate that I wasn't apprehended. It felt wrong at the time. Not that I cared, for my anorexia stole any kind of moral compass when an opportunity to break the rules was presented. When Millie and I would end our post-meals simultaneously, we would flee from the building, stifling laughter like naughty children, and both pick diagonal spots apart on the copse, each allowing the other privacy as we vomited over this somewhat hallowed ground. It seemed so sacrilegious that afterwards, with an empty belly and rebellion coursing through my veins, I would feel empowered and ultimately alive.

The limited number of available toilets in Food Farm was what necessitated this al fresco endeavour. As soon as patients' post-meals were over, there would be an exodus from the Sky Lounge (or wherever we were being held) and a stampede down the stairs in a race to acquire a bathroom with a functional-flushing toilet. The White Bathroom was a no-go as it was exactly that: a room with just a bath in it. The quest was rendered all the more difficult as upstairs was

classified out-of-bounds to patients before 6pm. There were the Green Bathroom and the Blue Bathroom that you could stealthily manoeuvre your way to if you were luckily. If those options were out of the question though you wouldn't be afforded the luxury of a bathroom, but would have to quietly do the deed in one of the two individual toilets, which were along frequently patrolled corridors. As if it wasn't bad enough that the evidence could be sniffed out – chicken tikka infusing the air like a stupendous neon sign – it wasn't just the staff we had to be heedful of, for fellow residents were just as likely to spy us out. There were the calculating and bitchy likes of Alicia and Holly who would grass you up just for their pleasure of watching you have to consume another meal and have supervision extended. Then there were the jealous girls unable to puke on self-will or the wannabe good girls who found it so heartbreaking to observe your plight that it increased their own struggle. The solution to all this was to slip out for an innocent meander around the grounds, and then take the surreptitious road to Damascus.

*

The afternoon crept in like a thief in the darkness, stealing away minutes and stashing hours out of sight. Sitting at the classroom table, my head resting on my forearms, I was jolted to a start by an abrupt tap on my shoulder. It was Marcella, the science teacher, peering down at me with her thin-rimmed glasses perched precariously on the tip of her nose. My eyes instantly transfixed by her shock of red hair

that shot out of her scalp in all directions, I realised that I was rudely staring at the poor woman.

"Leanne, your work has arrived," Marcella said in clipped, precise Queen's English, rather contrasting with the unorthodoxy of her hair. She thrusted a thick wad of papers at me, resting on an A4 brown envelope that had been roughly torn open. "I think that should keep you out of trouble for a while". She winked, surprising me again, before turning on her heel, leaving me gaping at this piece of luck.

"You can close your mouth now Lea," said Joce, noting my elation.

"Wow! I can't believe it! I finally have some work to do!"

"I don't know why you're so over the moon about it", said Millie in her characteristic whisper as she absent-mindedly defaced her exercise book. "I'd love to have nothing to do."

"No, this is amazing! I may actually have a chance of sitting my exams now." I saw a future open up before me like ethereal lilies unfolding in an idealised sepia nostalgia. I had almost been blessed with a second chance.

"Do you really think you'll be able to cram enough studying in?" asked Joce critically. "I mean, there isn't that long left until the exams start, is there? And you know what the nurses will be like, they'll strike

you down in flames if you try to over exert your frail little body."

I could imagine the staff fiercely adjudicating our revision. Jocelyn arched her eyebrows at me. She'd been trying to dissuade me from studying for my GCSE's in her belief that I should get away with not studying or working whilst I could. She'd hopped on the 'gap year' bandwagon, stating that there would be plenty of opportunities for me further down the line. I secretly felt that she just wanted someone to languish about with, rather than being the only one who had nothing to focus on.

"It'll be fine. They can't keep an eye on me all the time as I'll have the evenings to myself. I'm determined to try and do well."

I detected a glimmer of jealousy in Jocelyn's eyes. "Well, I'm off to university as soon as I'm out of here and I don't need GCSE's where I'm going." Her father owned a villa in Portugal and apparently she had persuaded him to let her live there when she was discharged. Her dad was well-renowned for something or other in the realm of physics. He also had a snotty girlfriend called Clarissa who was young enough to be Jocelyn's sister.

"You've got the motivation," said Millie. "Go for it, if that's what you want." She pushed her exercise book across the table towards me. "Here, you can do mine as well, if you like!" I opened the pages at the middle and grimaced.

"What on earth are you studying Millie?"

On one page there was a printed diagram of a human heart, the parts neatly labelled in Millie's microscopic writing. On the opposite side was a collage of emaciated women and internal organs with ransom-note cut-out style captions littering the page.

Millie half-heartedly lifted and dropped her bony shoulders in a shrug, "I was bored."

I glanced at Jocelyn who was busy eyeing up the skinnies on Millie's page.

"*She's* not that thin, Millie, what's she doing in there? You can't even see her dinosaur! But that one, she's definitely anorexic. And as for *her*, oh my God, she's got cheekbones to die for!"

"What the hell is a dinosaur?" Millie asked, her curiosity piqued.

"It's your spine, you know, when it juts out with all the individual notches showing through the skin." Joce slouched, jutting her backbone out to demonstrate, poking her fingers into the ridges. "Mine lacks definition now, of course", she added regretfully. Millie and I copied her, both smoothing our fingers over our own spines when Layla appeared in front of us.

"What are you guys doing?" Layla called everyone 'guys', she had some strange idiosyncrasies, mainly

borne out of the fact that she was from Australia. I took an immediate liking to her when we met as she was warm and friendly and, foolishly I questioned her about koalas and kangaroos and how many poisonous snakes she'd encountered. I thought she was mysterious, coming half the world away and I bombarded her with questions about what it was like growing up where she had lived. Whereas anybody else would have been irritated by my incessant questions, Layla bore it all in good stead and was happy to talk at length about her life and old home.

"We're comparing our dinosaurs," Millie laughed.

"Ah, right," said Layla, knowing straight away what we meant. "Lea's dinosaur is the most prominent. How long have you been here now Lea?"

"Coming up to three weeks, I think."

"Yep, you'll have that protruding for a while yet. What were you when you got here?"

"25kg".

"Nah, not your weight. What percentage were you?"

"Oh, 52. I think. Yeah, it had been 52 percent." It hadn't entered my mind since my admission. I'd been informed that I only weighed 52% of what I should, prompting me to try to imagine what half a person would look like.

"You've got a long way to go yet", said Layla.

"Don't tell her that," Joce rebuked. "You'll scare her to death!"

"Well, just look at her. Of course she's got a long way to go. She's so skinny, I bet she still looks like her photo."

I remembered having the photograph taken on my first day. I caught a glimpse of the picture as it shot out of the instant camera. It was horrendous. I was grinning like an idiot, my teeth too big for my face, and my lank hair hung like an afghan hound's over my eyes. There was no denying the fact that I was sick. The bones across my chest and shoulders penetrated the t-shirt I was wearing, resembling fossils strewn under black sand.

"I've seen Lea's photo and yes, she does look practically the same, except…" Millie stopped talking suddenly.

"Except what?" I exclaimed, taken aback.

"Nothing, it's nothing," Millie mumbled evasively.

"No, what did you mean by 'except'."

"Really Lea, it's nothing."

"It's your face," Layla said, brash and straight to the point.

"It's nothing bad, Lea, but it's just the swelling from the water retention. It's made your face, erm…rounder, since that photo." Millie's effort to rescue the situation hadn't been entirely successful.

*

Following our evening meal of oily salmon fishcakes in a sea of baked beans, sloshed down with blackberry yoghurt and three chocolate chip cookies, we were led into the other lounge – a downstairs living room directly below the Sky Lounge. It was a darker and more dingy-looking room, mostly due to the absence of the abundant natural light permitted upstairs. This lounge was ordinarily inhabited by patients of the Blue Kitchen, self-righteous and arrogant individuals who chided the likes of us for our defects. A mutual dislike extended between us, an innate mistrust and suspicion, particularly circulating about those of us on supervision because we were naturally at the bottom of the hierarchy. We were considered uncontrollable and unpredictable; whimsical animals at the mercy of our prosaic instincts. We envied the freedoms of those in the Blue Kitchen. Plus, they had been getting away with removing the pecan nuts from their muesli, and sneaking it into ours, making our breakfasts laden with more fat and calories. Their hypocrisy infuriated me, that they could revere themselves as superior, yet take liberties at our expense.

Millie and I had installed ourselves in the same corner as the room above and Jocelyn lounged across the

arm of the adjacent chair doing a crossword puzzle. Nicola was supervising us this evening, which was a welcome surprise as she didn't berate us like Helen and Rosie would. Sat on the opposite side of the room beside the TV, Holly and Alicia were giggling away with Bethan and Clara and on second observation, I realised this lounge was somehow smaller than the Sky Lounge, as we all seemed more intimately packed together. The clock said 6:49pm; just over two hours until I could retreat to my room. Time slowed down when I was under observation and irritation prickled my skin like nettles. In addition to the one window in the room, there was a patio door – locked obviously – but it granted full view of the garden. There was, in fact, something akin to a patio just beyond, grey slabs laid on the ground and a small stone bench just a little distance in front of the door. A potted shrub stood either side of it. I'd never seen anyone sit on this bench so I imagined it was just for show. I veered my focus round to the left to see six large industrial rubbish bins – all black, this was before the implementation of mandatory recycling - two of which had their contents spilling over the top. I noticed a twitch of movement, as if one of the bin liners was flapping in a non-existent breeze. Fascinated, I continued to watch as three enormous black rats emerged from the bin and proceeded to scuttle along the fence behind. One of them the size of a small dog had something questionable hanging from its jaw as it disappeared behind the large oak tree at the other side. I turned to see Millie also watching this bizarre parade and, with a wry smile,

she said, "At least we're not the only ones being fattened up around here."

"Is it really a new patient?" asked Bethan, "is someone new coming to stay?" Excitement fizzed through the room the instant Nicola had said an introduction was taking place upstairs, hence why we were ensconced in this lounge.

"It's gotta be a girl, it's always a girl, why are anorexics always female in this place?" Holly moaned.

"You never know, it could be a gorgeous hunk, an amazing swarthy man ready to take me in his arms and sweep me of my feet! Ooooh just imagine!" Alicia licked her lips suggestively and Bethan's eyes widened.

"Don't be stupid," moaned Holly, tugging at knotted strands of her hair.

"Is it a boy? Really, is it a boy?" Bethan was jumping about all over the place now. At 15 years old, she exuded enthusiasm and youthful charm.

"Oh Nicola, if it is a boy and you've just made us eat those stinky fish cakes – my breath will smell rank!" Alicia's face crinkled in horror, as if having been instructed to eat a dog turd.

"Forget about that!" shrieked Bethan, "Look at the state of me! I'm almost at target now, no boy'll ever fancy me! I'm absolutely huge!"

"It'll be a girl, I'm telling you. It's always a girl," Holly said resignedly.

"Well what about Matt then?" Bethan asked.

"Yeah, what about him?" countered Holly.

"He was hardly what you'd call 'boyfriend material'." Alicia turned her forefingers into quotation marks above her head.

"And he ended up leaving here fat", said Holly and all three of them collapsed into disorderly laughter.

Nicola observed this exchange, not wanting to get involved, but as the voices hurtled off the Richter scale, she was obliged to step in to quieten the melee.

"Girls, girls! Quiet please." Her voice was drowned out by the throaty chuckle of Holly and the high pitched squeaks of Bethan and Alicia.

"What is all this noise about?" Helen demanded, her white face appearing like an apparition at the door. "Calm it down right now, or else there'll be extras for the whole lot of you". Her arms were folded across her body and her eyes fixed in a challenging glare that focused on no one and everybody at once. Holly's mouth snapped shut and Bethan crept back to her

hidden haven behind the sofa. Alicia plonked her bum on the ground, head raised with a defiant pout. I felt my head swim, the sudden silence – the calm after the storm – like a blow to the head and I was grateful I was sitting down. Helen dismissed Alicia's pleas for information about the apparent new recruit, merely stating that a very important meeting was underway upstairs and we were all to remain quiet, unless we wanted our stomachs lining with a cheese sandwich or two. Helen gave a nod of assent to Nicola, her face the consistency of watery scrambled egg, her chins wobbling, priding herself on having diffused the situation. Nicola politely thanked her and Helen vanished from sight with as much tenacity as she had arrived. Alicia, Holly and Bethan paused a moment, ensuring her complete departure, before resuming their former conversation.

"If I breathe in really hard, look, I might just get away with looking a size slimmer, what do you think?" Bethan was standing up, the patio-door her pseudo-mirror as she strutted this way and that, sucking in her stomach, twirling around and examining her physique.

"There's no need to breathe anything in, you're thin as you are", said Alicia appraisingly. She got to her feet beside Bethan. "Look at the size of my butt! No amount of squeezing in will get rid of that!"

"Oh pur-leazze", moaned Holly. "We probably haven't got a new patient and even if we have, I'm telling you, it won't be a bloke!"

To be honest, my interest was still arrested by the gigantic rats carrying out their reconnaissance raid. There were two of them out there now, huge black lumbering rodents, their fur glistening in the waning light, their claws ferreting industriously through the rubbish. It was practically criminal how much food was wasted here and I speculated the media frenzy should it ever come to light that this place had a vermin problem.

*

It took a month before I spoke to my mum and dad. I would later remark how it was the longest silence I've ever completed, knowing full well it was a cruel, ill-begotten grudge. I cringe thinking of how needlessly hurtful and brazenly self-absorbed I was. A different time and another me. The day I found my voice for them was during a visit. I was sat on the edge of my bed, stubborn and sullen, when the four of them arrived, dad adopting his best smile as if trying to detract attention from my mum's red-rimmed eyes. My brother was busy investigating the individual trinkets and objects that rested on my shelf whilst my sister was standing loyally at my mum's side. I was still below the required 70% that would enable me to do the more normal activities that people took for granted: walking to town, leaving the unit, even the banal aerobics class that took place on Thursday after tea. In other words, we were confined to the clinic, much to the displeasure of Leonard, who had been forced to abandon his trip to the cinema with his best mate to come and visit me. Leonie shifted

awkwardly, catching my attention, and for a fleeting moment I saw my mother give her a gentle nudge in my direction. Leonie stepped forward timidly holding a carrier bag that she held towards me, the features on her face suspended in trepidation.

"It's just a little something for you Lea."

My anticipation soared tangibly inside me and, with an irrepressible smile broadening across my face, I took the bag from her, opening it with the zeal of a greedy child. An audible gasp escaped my throat as I stared in awe at the contents. Inside, were a mini compact disc player – brand new – and a selection of my own CDs from home. Incredibly, the CDs chosen were my favourite album by each of the bands picked: 'In Utero,' 'The Holy Bible,' 'Live Through This,' 'The Colour and the Shape,' 'Freakshow,' 'Antichrist Superstar,' 'Ixnay on the Hombre,' 'Is This Desire?' I made a cursory count and there must have been 20 albums here, carefully conscripted from the towering compilation of music from my room.

"It was your mum's idea," said dad, observing my dumbstruck countenance. "Leonard and Leonie chose which CDs they thought you liked best."

"There's something else in there too," said Leonie, prompting me to move the CDs aside and look beneath them. In the bag was a photograph album that I immediately recognised as my own. I'd had it since I was seven years old: bottle green faux leather cover, slightly worn on the corners so the brown of

the cardboard showed through. Leonie misread my alarm. "Don't worry, we didn't go rummaging about in your room. I knew exactly where it was, in the same place the day you left. I thought it might help you if you got lonely or if you missed us."

I was overwhelmed by emotion then and forgetting my self-imposed silence I looked up at the four of them in unison and said, "Thank you."

Their thoughtful gifts had been the bridge I needed in order to restore our connection and I had crossed it that day. After a month of stubbornly digging in my heels in resistance, I had ceased fighting and the liberation I found was a welcome surprise. For the duration of my visit, we talked like a normal family and I – for the most part – behaved like a normal person. I'd renounced my bitterness and antipathy, and calmness wafted like a soft fragrance on the breeze. When the time came for them to head back home, I felt bereft but my resentment was appeased. I was lighter on my feet, in spite of my increasing weight, and my frown had recalibrated into a smile.

That evening I wallowed in some cherished nostalgia. Lying on my stomach on the bed, I turned the pages of the photo album to watch myself be born again. One headphone wedged in soliciting my eardrum, the other dangling from my neck so as to remain on the offensive if anybody was to encroach on my seclusion, I listened to one of the CDs my family had rescued for me. I cradled the photo album in my arms lovingly. The first pictures featured me as a baby, so

tiny and helpless; eyes filled with promise, glistening like deep blue pools, ruddy cheeks aglow, illuminating a face with innocent radiance. It was hard connecting this baby with me; knowing what I knew, I saw that this child didn't stand a chance. There was no choice for the baby in the pictures that was me, it was almost tragic.

There was a soft tap-tap at my door and Larissa's head appeared in the small gap. I appreciated her respect of our privacy; she wouldn't dream of just barging in on one of us unannounced. Her courtesy went against the grain of this place and I liked to think of her being rebellious in her own little way.

"Hey, Kurt Co-bain, it's lights out." Larissa pronounced it distinctly 'Co-bain' in her captivating Jamaican intonation. Surprisingly, she called me that not on account of my dark rooted dirty blonde hair constituting an assumed homage to Kurt, but because of my omnipresent t-shirt with his face emblazoned on the front. I had just so happened to be wearing that exact same t-shirt on every shift she worked for the first few weeks I'd been here.

"Ok, night night," I said, closing the photo album and sitting up.

"You have a visit today?" She asked, nodding towards the photo album.

"Yep," I smiled.

"You talking to your family now then, hey?" Larissa looked at me smugly, though not in a bad way. She seemed genuinely thrilled that I had reconciled our relationship. "Good for you honey."

"Thanks."

"It's still just you in here then?" Larissa gestured at the other bed, close to the door, made up, immaculate and empty.

"Yeah, Millie's still on Total."

"If it's not one of you it's the other." Larissa chuckled and rolled her eyes at the same time. "Good night sweetheart and see you in the morning."

With that, the room was flung into darkness and I let my head wade down into sleep.

Chapter 7

My alarm clock whirred gently against my temple,
though, as usual, I was already awake. Thursday
morning had reared its formidable head again. I
flicked the switch to stop it vibrating and gave it a pat
of thanks for its reliability. I threw the covers off and
felt my way in the darkness to where my wardrobe
stood. Bending down, arms outstretched, my palms
against the wardrobe door, I sloped onto my knees
and located the first of several two litre lemonade
bottles. I'd started the necessary 'tanking' last night
before getting into bed, drinking one of the bottles to
start me off. I felt the pressure on the walls of my
bladder now, hours later. I lunged for another of the
full bottles, unscrewed the lid with as little noise as
possible, and took a huge glug from it. Careful so as
not to make the plastic deflate and cause a
disturbance, I gulped the water in as perfunctory a
manner as possible. When I'd finished, I unscrewed
the cap of the next and drank that one dry as well.
There was a third bottle, but my stomach lurched as I
contemplated imbibing any more. Sickness rose to
the back of my throat and I stood up quickly. I would
not throw up. I refused to undo the good work I had
done. Clamping my right hand over my mouth I
glanced at the alarm clock, lights edged the face
informing me that it was 7:45am. Only fifteen
minutes until we faced the scales.

To my absolute delight, the water loading had
worked. I was still above my line, and remained on a
three hour post meal supervision. I would just have to

99

keep up the rigmarole of tanking before weigh-ins. The prospect of aching nausea and excessive bloating wasn't something I looked forward to, but it was a necessity if I were to survive in this place. At 65%, I didn't have far left to go until I would be granted the oh-so sought after privileges. The only 'privilege' I really desired was to get beyond the exterior walls of the clinic. The imposed incarceration resembled a prison sentence; I was being held against my will and punished for my crime of self-inflicted hunger. There were rumours of an up-coming trip to an undisclosed location, which would have excited the 'old me', but barely struck a nerve in current circumstances. Clearly, I would seize any opportunity that arose, craving release from captivity, and it wouldn't be long until I could accompany the others on any mundane evacuation from Food Farm.

Fortunately, breakfast was exempt from what had become the customary dramatics and arbitrary calamity, as Rachel and Nicola were on duty with Joan in charge of the kitchen. The morning saw a tranquil interlude from the recent tumult overriding the Brown Kitchen under Helen and Kaye's reign. I welcomed the serenity and joviality that the calmer and less overbearing nurses brought with them. I was almost lulled into a false sense of contentment and security that morning, enjoying the laughter and relaxed conversation at the table. I actually felt less inclined to take advantage of their kind natures and decided against shoving my croissant up my large sleeves. It was unlike me to be guilt-tripped into doing anything that involved eating, so I was rather

flummoxed by my attitude today, wondering if it was something they'd put in the water. As cynical as ever, I couldn't accept change for the better wholly at face value.

The highlight of the morning remained the same. When the mail was brought in after breakfast on six of the seven days of the week, there was always a kafuffle, as we fought to get at the nurse wielding the precious post. Lack of contact with the outside world was obviously accountable for this anxiety over obtaining our letters and postcards from family and friends; we were desperate to establish communication with those out there in the 'real world'. The mail had to be opened and inspected prior to being handed to us. It was truly shocking the amount of illicit items that were popped in the post box. This morning I had three envelopes and I clutched them tightly to my chest as I steered my way through the morass of eager faces. Extricated from the throb of excitement, I slumped into the little beige sofa beside the oven of the Brown Kitchen, the soft cushions surrendering under my weight, the smell of freshly baked bread wafting delectably under my nostrils.

"What have you got today Joce?" I asked.

"Not much. Just a note from my dad." She released a disgruntled choking sound from the pit of her throat, before saying. "How about you?"

"Three."

"Oooh, get you! Who from?"

I studied the handwriting on the front of the envelopes, discerning Leonie's delicate hand right away on a lilac envelope that had pink geraniums sprouting at each corner. Another was from a friend from back home, Scary Mary, and was a small white envelope addressed to me in chunky jet black lettering, executed in marker pen. There were no clues for the third letter so I tore that one open first, ignoring the opening that had already been made by whichever member of staff had checked it. I took out the single sheet of faintly lined A5 paper and saw that it was decorated with spidery writing that nimbly pirouetted across the page. The capitalised address across the front had thrown me, but now I recognised this handwriting from the margins of my school exercise books. The succinct letter read:

Dear Leanne

I'm sorry to hear that you are having to stay at Rose Farm – I can imagine your distaste at that! I hope you have settled in and you are in positive spirits. I was surprised when a letter came to request work for you at the clinic's address and I realised that you must have been admitted. I hope you are still able to complete your studies, however, I understand that your health must take priority. If there is anything you need or anything I can do, please let me know. Best wishes,

Mrs Pringle

Touched, I re-read it several times, trying to fathom why my teacher would take the time and effort to personally write to me.

"Come on Lea, what is it?" Jocelyn urged, her pointy chin resting on my shoulder.

"It's from my teacher."

"Wow, you're clearly today's winner Lea. Congratulations – friend, sister *and* teacher. I'm the loser with nothing but a lousy scrawl from my dad." She turned the piece of paper around in both hands and thrust it up towards my eyes, too close for me to make out any of the writing.

"What did he say?"

"Oh nothing, just the usual rubbish. Apparently he and Clarissa are going to Prague next month. He says he'll hopefully get me out of here by then so I can join them. Yeah, right!" Joce scoffed loudly, ripping the piece of paper in half and in half again before scattering the remnants over the bin at her side.

"What's that you're chucking in the bin Jocelyn, something left over from breakfast?!" Holly was watching us from where she was still sitting at the table, her eyes glowing with mischief. Alicia started giggling inanely. Joce merely met Holly with a stare of disapproval, which seemed to incense her. "Oooooh, maybe you're emptying crumbs from yer

103

pocket into the bin!" Holly taunted, her voice rising
several notches to catch Nicola's attention.

"Oh shush Holly!" A voice rang out bountifully,
though it wasn't Nicola's. Our heads turned at the
sound of Bethan's little voice chiding her friend as
she swept into the room with an armful of daffodils.
Clara was scurrying after her, picking up the ones that
had come loose from the arrangement and fallen to
the floor.

"What are you doing leaving the room Bethan –
you're on supervision?!" Nicola's face adopted a
look of horror.

"I only wanted to make the kitchen look pretty,"
Bethan beamed, gliding over to the sink to fill a pint
glass – a makeshift vase – with water. "Clara, you
find some more glasses for these." She inclined her
head towards another pile of the yellow trumpets that
were sprawled across the kitchen worktop. I stifled a
laugh, noticing the veins starting to bulge in Joan's
forehead at the sight of the outdoors being dragged
into her kitchen. A trail of soil followed Bethan
through the kitchen. Clara flung open cupboard doors
with dynamism, clattering about the contents that
were neatly stacked within.

"Enough!" Rachel shouted, her call silencing the
whole kitchen. "Bethan, I appreciate you trying to
beautify the kitchen but just sit down for a moment,
will you? And Clara, please, close that cupboard

before you break something and give Joan a heart attack."

The two boisterous girls slid down over the arm of the sofa beside Jocelyn, forcing us to edge over to make room.

"Thank you." Rachel gave a slight nod, pleased that her order had not fallen on deaf ears. "Now then, we have a new patient waiting for us in the Sky Lounge, so we need to be keeping the noise down. We don't want to go frightening her off before she's even met us."

"Told you it was a girl," Holly huffed, a self-satisfied smirk opening across her narrow face.

"Quiet!" Rachel hissed at her.

"Right then girls, there should be twelve of you here to come with me." She began counting us one by one. "Beth, Clara, Joce, Lea, Millie, Anna, Andrea, Casey, Robyn, Liss, Fliss and Holl." She gave a cursory check that the number in front of her matched the fingers she had counted before rounding us together and rallying us up the stairs.

I could hardly believe my eyes when I walked through the door. She didn't look real. I found myself staring, mesmerised, and I loathed myself for doing so, but this girl surely couldn't be alive. As if witnessing a car crash, I kept politely turning away only to find that my gaze was immediately drawn

straight back, for I was alarmed and allured; I was at once awestruck and repulsed. She was the most emaciated person I had ever seen. Dressed in a lemon strappy top, her entire ribcage looked like exposed bone, her collar bone jutted and curved to meet the bones in her shoulders, and all the fissures were roughly carved out of her face. She was literally nothing but skin and bone. Two dark eyes stared out of the deep hollows on her agonised face and her legs looked non-existent in the navy jogging bottoms that hung off her fragile frame. She sat with a pained expression on the sofa next to Natasha and a woman who was certainly some kind of doctor. A tube fed into the girl's nose.

"This is Marilyn," Natasha declared to a wall of stunned silence.

You would have been able to hear the proverbial pin dropping as nobody dare speak. This girl appalled us in more ways than one. Not only was she a shock to behold, but she was the genuine end product. Her quest for perfection may have eroded any evidence of beauty, but it had been an almost successful result and there wasn't one of us who didn't envy the skeleton in front of us. I say 'almost successful' because this achievement had not brought the alleged happiness one would expect. She looked desolate and disconsolate. In fact, Marilyn looked as if there was absolutely nothing left of her both physically and mentally. She tugged half-heartedly at the tube, causing Natasha to eagerly yank her clawed hand away. The doctor – someone who I had never seen

before, but it wasn't Beaver or Dicken – delivered firm instructions to Natasha and Rachel that this new admission must not be left unsupervised for even a second under any circumstances. My reverence increased for this girl and with it so did my jealousy.

"She keeps trying to take the tube out," the doctor warned, "but it needs to be kept in until she agrees to eat something." The dreaded tube feeding looked more horrific than I'd imagined and I couldn't bear thinking what was being pumped up her nostrils. The instant the doctor left the room, the atmosphere relaxed.

"Who was that?" I asked Clara who was standing stock still at my side.

"That's the infamous Deedee." Clara said her name as if I should have known who she was. The look on my face must have given my ignorance away. "She's the founder of the clinic. It was Deedee who set up this place." That explained the quietude that overcame the room in her presence – everyone had to be on her best behaviour for the patron of Food Farm. I wondered if she was paid in pounds of lard or in the moans of obese former patients. "It's extremely rare that she makes an appearance," Clara continued.

"That new girl must be something real special then," I said, envy permeating my tone.

"Yeah," Millie squeaked in acquiescence. "Look at her wrists! They're the size of a kitten's ankle!"

"Well, don't worry, she won't stay like that for long," Clara mused. "Especially with that thing up her nose, she'll be on the increase in no time."

Bethan was trying to make conversation good-naturedly with Marilyn, as Joce and a couple of the others buzzed around in close proximity. Natasha's eyes were clamped on her like a vice. Marilyn was as quiet as Millie had been on her first day, although I learned a few facts about her via expert eavesdropping. She had been flown over from Cyprus where she had been living for the past five years and although she was nineteen, she had been sectioned under the mental health act and forced against her will to come here. Standing at 6ft2, she was another statuesque to make me feel inferior. Upon her admittance she was 48 percent. *Less than a person* I thought chillingly.

Marilyn was typically averse to treatment and she kept asking for the tube to be removed. Natasha advised her that it would be taken out if she would eat something, yet this request was met with disdain. I marvelled at the way her skin stretched tautly over her bones as if she were wrapped in cellophane. I couldn't help but stare at her gaunt face when she spoke, her hollowed cheeks revealed the teeth through her face. A network of veins pulsed visibly beneath her skin, her arms besieged by blue worms that writhed and encircled them. Like a spectre or something supernatural, she was hypnotising to behold.

"Like looking in the mirror." Joce's voice at the back of my neck made me jump.

"I wish!"

"There's no point staring, there's no going back now, you know." Joce said. "Even for her. We all get bigger eventually."

"Maybe I'm not ready to resign myself to that fate just yet."

"You should. You've got to just accept it Lea." Her eyes were sharp, her elliptical face no longer quizzical, but knowing.

"You're beginning to sound like one of the nurses." I hadn't meant to sound quite so accusing, but the words tumbled out before I had chance to monitor my tone.

"Well, maybe I just want to get better and get out of here." This was news to me. Where had her feistiness gone? Where was her resolve? I sat mulling over her words, my eyes still transfixed by the ghostly figure wasting away opposite. Perhaps Joce had experienced a change of heart. Instead of feeling jealous of this young woman, perhaps Joce felt sorry for her.

"I I um…" I stammered, not knowing what I wanted to say.

"You're wasting your time if you're hoping for an easy way out."

"I'm not."

"She's nothing to idolise either. That poor wretch has a difficult journey ahead."

It felt like I'd been slapped round the face. It hadn't occurred to me to pity Marilyn, but the realisation charged through my head now that perhaps her situation was not something to be lauded. Instead of wanting to emulate this waif, I should put my mind towards helping her and, at the same time, trying to help myself. The intentions were embryonic - there was definitely a long, long way to go – but the arrival of Marilyn, and Joce's response to her certainly provided a catalyst for an improved attitude, however short-lived it would be.

I would usually retaliate at any affront, but instead I followed Joce to where the small crowd of girls were gathered around the new recruit. It reminded me of my introduction to the patients on that first evening following my opportune cheese sandwich flinging. After being seated in the Sky Lounge, I had been confounded by a cacophonous flapping as if a gaggle of geese were taking flight around my face. Questions were hurled at me left, right and centre, all eyes enlarged upon me, making me wish I were invisible. Poor Marilyn was being inflicted with the same scenario. She was relatively calm and seemed forthcoming with responses to their questions on

where she lived, what she liked to do, pretty much the standard stuff. I was only partially listening as I remained irrevocably captivated by her. I'd accepted the fact that she wasn't pretty – attractiveness was compromised by anorexia - but there was something haunting about her which overwhelmed me. I felt on tenterhooks, unsettled and wary, as if something – anything – could happen at any moment. There was an air of unpredictability encompassing her which had me spellbound as I stared at her sunken face, her dark hair falling over one side of it like a skein of silk. Up close I could see that she had a hospital bracelet dangling off her wrist and bruising to her arms, indicating that she had recently been on a drip. I didn't pluck up the courage to ask about it though; I merely gawped at her whilst she underwent interrogation.

I was struck by an overriding poignancy then as I contemplated what had made this girl the way she was today. Nobody chooses the misery and despair that accompanies an eating disorder and certainly no one expects the eventual degradation it produces. It was difficult to imagine a life beyond the shackles of this disease, but we all had one (past tense). I *had* had a life; there had once been more to it than this. I allowed myself to drift off into the realm of memory, forgetting today, turning my thoughts away from Food Farm, in a reverie recalling afternoons at the park as a kid, chucking bread in the duck pond, mimicking my brother and getting hurt trying to climb trees. I remembered the time I broke my arm competing with Leonard to swing higher than him in

the park. It was the little park just down the road
from where we lived. The shops backed onto it and
the walls were emblazoned with language that was
equally as colourful as the graffiti. I was standing up,
perched on the thin plastic plank of the swing, white
knuckles clenched around the metal ropes. I insisted I
could go the highest, powering the swing through my
knees, revolving my hips in just a way as to generate
speed. I maintained a rhythm, my spirited volition
increasing as my body pumped the swing higher into
the air, my hair splayed over my face like a jellyfish,
scrunching my eyes shut against the piercing glare of
the sun. I was winning for a while, until the fateful
moment I lost my grip and landed with a
bloodcurdling smack on the tarmac. I should have
listened; that was my problem. I always had to be
right, I always insisted on being the best.

Lost in reminiscence, my mind was elsewhere. It was
as if I'd forgotten where I was. Nobody had seen it
coming. The lounge had become so tranquil that even
the Tarantula had relaxed her ensnaring gaze. Rachel
was across the room helping Holly and Alicia to
reprogram the TV and the plucky chatter had
dissipated to a gentle hum. In a sudden, short, sharp
motion, Marilyn had exited her seat and had
proceeded to deftly sprint towards the large window
left entreatingly ajar. A gasp echoed round the walls
as we all imagined the train of events before they had
even occurred. Rachel expelled herself like an arrow
towards Marilyn, pinning her arms behind her back in
a manoeuvre that was firm without being aggressive.
Natasha appeared at her side seconds later, shutting

the window and assisting Rachel to move this flailing vertical branch of a human being back over to the sofa.

Disaster averted, Marilyn unleashed a horrendous tirade as she swung her lanky body about under the intense grasp of the two nurses. She was cumbersome, but far from strong or weighty, yet the stream of unpleasant noises that poured from her mouth made my admission outburst appear comparatively tame.

She wasn't the first to be sedated and she most probably wouldn't be the last, although this was a rare occurrence; the terror awoken by the threat of the tube was usually enough to render most patients submissive. The hours whittled away, up and down the stairs from the lounge to the kitchen and back and repeat ad infinitum. The talk centred on this new girl – as it always did, for a 'newbie' was ostensibly the talk of the clinic for the first week, all gossip generated at their expense – and just what she would try to do next.

I was in conflict with myself again, at pains to decide which way I wanted to go and what outcome I sought. The darkness still ensnared me, the desire to starve and purge and obliterate myself overriding, yet, following my family's recent fortuitous visit and the arrival of Marilyn, I felt that I craved something more, something more wholesome and fulfilling. As usual I was being pulled in two opposing directions by diametrical factions. I wanted the best of both

worlds. Somehow, today my mind was sharpened, my eyes were searching for potential remedies, and I even contemplated if maybe recovery wasn't such a bad thing. I didn't know what I wanted and I wasn't at liberty to make the decision.

*

"Slow down Layla." The usual meal time refrain from all staff members interchangeably. Sometimes, Helen would threaten to dissect Layla's food into bite-size pieces to prohibit her from treating tea time like a binge. It was cheesy cottage pie with baked beans and even more cheese this evening, or as I called it, 'cholesterol time bomb'. Layla was quite an exception in this place; rather than despising food, she worshipped it, and was around nine pounds above her target weight. She had been known to raid the kitchen, and even the food cupboard on a couple of occasions, to gorge on the contents before diving into the nearest bathroom to excavate her insides. She was not afraid of utilising laxatives either, seeming to have a preoccupation with eating and a desire for catharsis. Needless to say, Layla remained on a three hour post meal for the entirety of my own stay. I didn't mind the rapidity with which Layla devoured her food; in fact, I found it preferable to Robyn's labour-intensive nibbles and sips. We would sometimes be seated in that wretched kitchen for up to an extra hour because of Robyn's mediocre mouthfuls. And don't even get me started on Laura who slurped her food as if performing a lewd act. I shivered with revulsion at the mental image.

"Why can't we have more fruit?" Alicia's voice piped up at the far end of the table, high-pitched and nasal. "It's so unhealthy, all the chocolate and biscuits we're forced to eat."

"You have the choice of either an apple or a chocolate chip cookie with your tea," Helen pointed out.

"I know and I always choose the apple. But I think we should be allowed more fruit."

A groan rumbled around the Brown Kitchen. "Don't try and justify them giving us *more* food, 'Liss!" Clara retorted, elbowing Alicia in the side.

"Ouch! I'm not, I'm just thinking that we ought to be fed a healthier diet."

I thought back to being taught all about healthy eating in science class at high school. The centrepiece of my title page was the emblem of a salubrious diet, a red and ripe apple, the light glinting off its smooth surface with a pearly sheen. 'Bad foods' were relegated to the bottom of the page, the edge festooned with cakes, cream and chocolate, all with big red crosses slashed through them. This infatuation with healthy eating was how it all started; I wasn't to know that a seemingly innocuous diet was the genesis of something far more insidious. I observed the benefits: my skin cleared up, rendering me more fresh-faced, and I initially had more energy and a renewed vitality. But my life, and with it my

health, started to unravel at an accelerating rate, plunging me into the cold dark chasm of despair and delusion. The notion that looking at wafer thin models in magazines precipitated my descent is a misguided myth. There was and still is something rotten at my core and for some inexplicable reason I was predisposed to this. In any case, this would be my destination. My desire to be healthier fitted with my personal quest for perfection, my aspiration to be the best at everything and to outshine everybody else. Such lofty goals can only bring about disappointment and, in this instance, a near-tragic close-call.

I couldn't blame the science teacher any more than the models in the magazines. The media wasn't to blame and nor were my family. Even my peers who mercilessly bullied me at school – labelling me a freak, spitting at me in the corridors and trying to trip me up – they were not the cause of who I had become. I was fulfilling some kind of unknown destiny, some genetic discrepancy. If it hadn't been anorexia, it would more than likely have been something else. A void inhabited my soul and there would always be something I sought after, yielding with a sense of desperation in my futile and destructive efforts to try and sate it; I was perpetually trying to fill the gulf at the heart of me. My personal healthy eating crusade at high school had only hastened the inevitable.

"Hands up, who would like an extra piece of fruit." Helen smiled, her nicotine stained teeth almost an exact match for her mustard tinted t-shirt.

Unsurprisingly, two hands shot up, one belonging to Alicia and the other was surprise-surprise, Layla's.

Chapter 8

To say that most days were the same was an understatement. Days fogged and merged into one vague stretch of food and sleep and eating and weigh-ins and food, and even more food. I could close my eyes for twelve hours, open them and nothing would change. This place threatened to suck the life clean out of me, I was falling asleep and fading; paling into a shadow of my former self, I was the negative of a photograph. At times I felt like giving up, but then my true self would come to the forefront and shake me to my senses. It was an indeterminable mission to be at once doing what I should be and avoiding it at all costs. A perpetual civil war, my instincts and my brain at loggerheads vying for control over my behaviour. It would have been far easier to have opted for the simple life, to bow down and do as I was told, however, docility runs contrary to my nature.

Almost a month in and I had reached the esteemed 70 per cent; I'd been given my golden ticket and I grasped it with both hands. Although my weight had escalated at an alarming rate, I was joyous at having some control designated back to me. Millie had already been eligible for the privileges associated with being at this weight goal; however, she blankly refused to be involved in anything. Jocelyn and the others would pick and choose what activities they would partake of, usually seeing what opportunities were presented to 'get away with something'. Most of the excursions away from the vicinity of Food

Farm offered the chance of over-exercising or ridding oneself of food whether it be from a packed lunch or from one's own belly. It all depended on the who, where, when and how of each situation.

Tuesday morning was swimming at the local leisure centre and involved a trip on the small minibus, Heart FM annoyingly blaring from the radio, all the windows opened in an effort to necessitate shivering. I'd keenly agreed to go, in spite of my anxiety over parading about in my swimming costume. I tried to persuade Millie and Joce to come along.

"Come on Millie, it'll be fun! How about it?"

Millie shook her head obstinately, "I can assure you it won't be."

I looked at Joce. "How about you?"

"Not today Lea. I've not shaved my legs for I-don't-know-how-long. There's no way I'm stripping off when I look like a gorilla."

"I've not shaved my legs either, I didn't think we were even allowed razors in here."

"Oh yes, you can shave your legs and whatever other bits you'd like to remove hair from, however, it's all under the watchful eyes of one of the staff."

"That's supervised too?" I asked, aghast.

"It sure is. I think even the Blue Kitchen's have to be supervised whilst shaving as well."

"Wow." Millie said

"I know. I've only requested a razor once and I've decided, never again, not until I'm home. That's why I've stopped going swimming. I'll do the Thursday aerobics class with you though Lea, or the self-defence on a Wednesday, if you're up for that?"

I flinched at the mention of the self-defence class. It was run by two rather attractive young men and involved too much shouting in time to the movements. My nerves balked at the thought of it. I imagined my face turning an embarrassing shade of tomato red.

"What – self defence? With all that ackkking and huhhhhing?!" Millie said ironically, twirling a strand of her hair around her finger. "And jumping about screaming hi-yaaaa!"

"Erm, yeah, I don't think that one's for me. I'll probably give the granny aerobics a try though," I said.

We all laughed, complicit in the knowledge that the intensity of the aerobics class was low enough to be practically comatose. Our laughter was interrupted by Kaye's caterwauling cry, announcing that swimmers had five minutes to ensure we were ready and lined up by the door.

"At least it's not Thursday's triple chocolate muesli," Joce prodded me, grinning, and I remembered the paragraph in 'From Stick Insect to Elephant in Six Months'. We had written about the possibility of throwing up in the swimming pool.

On Tuesday mornings at 10am patients can go to the local swimming baths so do a restricted number of lengths. Of course, you have to have reached a certain weight so as not to horrify the unsuspecting families who would be appalled at the line of skeletons slipping into the water. Two nurses accompany this enterprise in case anything should go awry, however, you can paddle fast under cover of the water to burn more calories and, with about twelve patients to monitor, it is possible to blend in with the 'normal' swimmers and do something more strenuous. The actual session in the water is only twenty minutes so not a lot of energy incineration is allowed to take place. If you're intrepid enough, however, you could secretly puke in the pool. You would have to swim swiftly away from the scene of the crime, lest the swirl of triple chocolate muesli sticks to your flesh and gives you away. What an appealing thought!

Swimming was a straight-out success. Not only did I overcome my self-consciousness to the extent that I didn't care who saw me, I swam two lengths more than the designated limit and I'd thrown up breakfast in the toilets from the get-go. I'd be up for this malarkey every week. I felt as if I was beaming on the way back, stuffed like sardines into that minibus.

Even the chirpy pop nonsense that cauterised my eardrums didn't expel my glee. The journey back to the clinic, I felt my old self congratulating me and I was allowed some peace.

I think I was high from the swimming trip for the majority of the day and the relief in the realisation that there was a means of rebellion. In spite of Food Farm's stringent rules and surveillance, there were small ways of beating the system. The rest of the day had been uneventful. Having missed morning snack time, the requisite calories would be tacked onto my afternoon extras (I insisted I'd rather have them in the afternoon than extending my supervision into the evening by having to eat at 8pm).

Lunch consisted of stinky fish pie, oily potato rosties and vegetables laden in butter. The minute my plate was placed on my mat, two rosties were in my pocket. I played with the vegetables, smearing them around my plate, sluicing the ceramic with grease, which I furtively mopped up with my sleeves. Since Marilyn had arrived I had been able to slip under the staff's radar somewhat. In the Brown Kitchen this lunchtime, Kaye patrolled matronly as ever, eyes trained on Marilyn who was now eating without the need for the tube, but was still provoking suspicion. Rachel was in the kitchen with Joan, the atmosphere relaxed and jubilant, putting me at ease. I was sat in between Millie and Joce and I had the distinct impression that they were both benefitting from this *laissez faire* ambience. Also seated around at the table were Clara, Holly, Alicia and Bethan, and

grouped together at the far end Andrea and Casey were sitting together with their heads low. Little Anne, diminished in between Marilyn and Emily, was opposite me and Fliss, Robyn, Laura and Layla were sitting nearest to the food preparation area, chatting cheerfully to Rachel. Tanya was still on the opposite table though seemingly out of choice, as she was no longer relegated to it but naturally went and selected her chair territorially as a cat. Maisie, the girl who was meant to be staying for a fortnight, had been discharged, and nobody knew what had happened to Sick Bag Piper, for she had gone home one weekend, never to return.

After lunch had finished and the supervisions were about to be led upstairs, Kaye apprehended me, her face darkened with a mix of anger and irritation. My eyes flicked around the kitchen to see vague glances in my direction. I felt my heart rate accelerate, wondering what Kaye wanted to talk to me about.

"Turn out your pockets Lea."

"What?" I was dumbstruck, I almost couldn't speak.

"Turn out your pockets," Kaye repeated, her tone even.

"Why?" I asked, stupidly.

"Don't ask 'why', just do it."

Panic rose within me and I felt light-headed. I darted my eyes frantically to find Millie, a pillar of calm in this torrential storm. She gave me a reassuring smile, but it was betrayed by the worry etched into her forehead, and I learned then that I was in trouble. Kaye was instantly standing over me, her hand rummaging in my right pocket, turning it inside out. She was muttering belligerently.

"If you're not prepared to do it yourself, I'll have to dig through your pockets for you."

I was speechless, paralysed by dread. Kaye yanked me round roughly so that she could repeat the action in my left hand pocket. My mind raced as if competing with my heart beat. I was petrified, certain she was to rifle through the other pockets in my trousers – khaki combats with large pockets next to my knees – and then my sneakiness would come to light. My mental faculties overcome by a blitzkrieg, I just stood there mute as a puppet. Kaye retrieved her hand and boldly steeped back.

"There's nothing on her, Rachel!" Kaye called out with vexation to the other nurse. "So-and-so just wasting my time again! Off you go Lea, go up with the others."

II relaxed, the guilt and fear ebbing away like flotsam on the tide. Millie crossed over to join me.

"You'd better chuck it in the bin now, before we leave the kitchen, "she instructed. My mouth must

have been hanging open in confusion. "The potatoes. Holly grassed you up, told Kaye that you'd snuck them into your pockets. If you don't chuck them now, you might still get caught out."

I did as she said. As the others were all clearing out of the kitchen, I plunged my hand into my side pocket, my fingers recoiling at the succulent texture of the greasy rosties. I scooped them up and deftly chucked them into the bin, covering them over with a discarded polythene bag that rested on top.

"Thank you, Millie. That was a close-call."

"That bloody Holly, she's always trying to get us in trouble."

"She's just jealous that she never has the guts to hide food. It would have been a cheese sandwich penalty for me as well, more than likely," I moaned.

My guard was restored at teatime as was my adherence to the rules. My dislike of Holly had turned into full-blown hatred. Ensconced in our corner of the Sky Lounge after an unsavoury meal of mayonnaise and egg sandwiches (the ratio completely skewed to favour calories instead of flavour) Millie and I deployed entertainment and triviality.

As Alicia lay sleeping on the sofa after tea, I whispered to Millie, "digest, digest, digest…." It went without saying that sleep assisted digestion and we would revel in the snoozing of fellow pukers,

particularly Alicia, who we also didn't like very much. She hadn't earned our friendship or even our tolerance, being a bully just like Holly. Millie instantly repeated the same incantation, "…digest, digest, digest," as if willing Alicia's food to be unable to be regurgitated. This became a favourite past-time and we hoped that when Alicia's post-meal ended, all she could emit from her belly was a bowl of useless froth, all food substance, fat and calories absorbed. We talked about the other patients, starting with Holly and decided it would be a fun game to imagine what breed of dog they would be. We often liked to while away the monotonous hours under observation in jocular ways.

"Holly would definitely be a Poodle," I said, thinking of her mass of unruly dark curls. "A Standard Poodle, as those are the taller breeds of Poodle."

Millie released a squeaking guffaw and said, "That's spot on Lea! What about Alicia?"

We pondered Alicia in silence, thinking of her round wholesome face, lively disposition and feminine attractiveness. She was quite a girly girl, a typical seventeen year old, with a figure that dipped in and out in all the right places. She had a nice smile, but it belied a bitchy interior.

"She'd have to be something fairly small and cute looking but with a regal-something-or-other about it. Like a King Charles Spaniel, perhaps?" I said.

"No way, she's gotta be more snappy and spiteful than that. A Jack Russell, more like."

"A Jack Russell with bows on then," I laughed, not able to control my amusement. Kaye glanced over, intrigued by our discussion, yet only encouraging me to keep my voice down. Millie's soft squeak was quiet by default.

"That sounds about right."

"Marilyn is undoubtedly a Whippet - and Fliss too, even though she's at target she's practically a gazelle. Marilyn's a Whippet and Fliss would be a Greyhound, or rather a *blonde-hound*," I mused.

"I wish I could be an elegant Whippet or Lurcher or something skinny," Millie chipped in forlornly.

"Me too," I agreed. The two of us never broached the issue of what dog breeds *we* would be; we were far too sensitive to parody ourselves and each other, although it was entertaining to imagine the other girls as the canine counterparts we had ascribed them.

"Laura would be like one of those dogs – what are they called? Like Dougal from The Magic Roundabout. Is it a Pekinese or something?"

"Oh, a Skye Terrier! Why's that?"

"She's just like a little doormat, isn't she? She's a little scuttling creature and she's always doing as

she's told. She's so desperate to impress, you'd imagine her to roll on her back for a belly rub for finishing her tea!" Millie locked eyes with mine and we broke down into a tumult of hysterics.

"The way she eats her food too…."

"Oh don't!" Millie implored.

This exercise persisted for a while as we went through each patient, and even some of the nurses, designating a dog breed for each of them, based upon their appearance and temperament. So wrapped up in our puerile game, I almost didn't notice Dr Beaver appear before me, exasperation staining his countenance. I never walked of my own volition to his therapy hut as he had instructed.

"Leanne it's time." He tried to smile but it didn't success in blotting out his antagonism. I dragged myself arduously to my feet, resentment emanating from my pores.

This was to be the last time that he bothered coming to fetch me for the therapy that was apparently meant to be so essential to our recovery.

Chapter 9

It was a rare treat for Millie and me to be simultaneously relinquished from supervision and belched forth to embrace an afternoon rife with opportunity. We left the clinic around 4:35pm to go for a walk, stopping by Damascus Hill – as was customary, to get that bit of business out of the way - chatting and laughing as we mooched along lanes to nowhere in particular. The sky was a cloudless expanse overhead with a hazy tinge as the sun blazed through, making the air look almost like liquid. We'd arrived at June, the heady summer days were upon us, and today was the first time since my arrival that I'd genuinely felt warm.

There was virtually no breeze and the stagnant trees stood over us like voluptuous effigies of green lining the edge of the street. Cars rumbled along in the far off distance, but where we walked, it was a ghost town, it was as if we were the only souls left on the earth.

"Are we going to bother going into town?" Millie asked, wiping sweat off her brow with the back of her hand.

"Do you want to?" I asked.

"Would you mind not answering a question with a question, Leanne?" she said, comically mimicking Helen's tone.

"You got that spot on. You sounded exactly like *the Beast.*"

"Or the Ogre."

"The Mars Bar Witch."

"Mars Bar *Bitch*, more like."

"Cadbury Dairy Milk Fruit and *Nut-Case.*" I thought for a moment, gazing up at the perfection of the flawless sky. "We should head into town. Look at how lovely it is today."

"Will we make it back in time for tea though?" Millie queried, nibbling the skin around her little fingernail

"Sure," I said, although I wasn't.

The sunshine had given me a burst of optimism, working in a similar way to alcohol on the brain, lowering my inhibitions and making me feel invincible. As we walked, I experienced an inexplicable sense of contentment, and I realised that I never wanted this feeling to leave. I'd inched my eye-line just above the parapet of my abyss to see something not far short of perfection. In that moment, my outlook was transformed.

We reached town faster than expected and we weren't even power-walking. It's a fact that nobody can power walk without looking like a lunatic. A mass of people bumbled about with overfilled carrier bags or

screaming toddlers hanging off their wrists, only a few individuals standing out as being livelier, the sun having provided them with salubrious refreshment. There were people moaning about this or that, complaining about the heat or the price of petrol and it struck me just how much dissatisfaction there was in the world. As I looked beyond myself and my petty problems I saw but a snapshot of a greater landscape of despondency. It was startling really.

"Everyone seems so downbeat," I said.

"Why shouldn't they be?" Millie replied.

"I don't know. I guess I just imagined people would be happy on a day like today – the sun shining, the birds singing…."

"Who are you today, Mary bloody Poppins?"

"Don't be silly, I'm just….I don't know, I'm just in a good mood, I guess."

"What, even knowing that we've got to be back at that hell-hole in less than 45 minutes *and* we're more than likely going to be late?"

The realisation immobilised me. I'd unconsciously decided it before the thought had been given flight.

"I'm not going back, Millie."

"Huh?"

I cleared my throat. "I'm not going back to the hell hole."

"Where are you gonna go?"

"I've no idea but I'd rather go anywhere than back there."

Millie looked between me and the wide open beyond.

"You can come with me if you want?" I ventured. "I mean, you don't have to, but you could. It would be great if you did come with me, but I wouldn't mind at all if you didn't."

I could see Millie's mind cogitating, weighing up the pros and cons, her head and her heart battling for dominance. She sighed deeply and I knew what was coming.

"I'm sorry Lea, but I'm gonna go back."

"That's ok".

"I would have come, say a couple of weeks ago, but now that I'm finally off Total and allowed to leave the clinic....well, I just don't wanna jeopardise that."

"It's fine Millie. Don't worry about it. You won't say anything to them about me will you?"

"No, no, of course I won't!"

"Thank you."

"Of course, I wouldn't tell them anything. I'll just say that I wanted to head back, but you wanted to have a look in one of the shops or something".

"That's great, thank you so much."

"Well, I suppose I'd best get moving. I really will be pushing it to get back on time."

"Helen's already at the door, armed with the tub of mayonnaise!"

"The Fruit and Nut-Case", Millie smiled. "Well, take care and good luck".

"Thanks, you too." We hugged tightly and then, without another word, we parted ways. I wasn't disappointed or annoyed or anything like that. It was one of those scenarios where it would have been fantastic if Millie was accompanying me on this adventure but it would be equally as exciting if I were to embark upon it on my own. The sun had started to dim and I instinctively looked at my wrist, inwardly cursing myself as I had left my watch on my bedside table. I had no idea what the time was. The blue of the sky had faded, merging into a mixture of pale yellows and oranges with a slash of cerise above the tops of the trees that streaked off into the distance. I hadn't been walking for long but already the riotous hubbub of the town had receded behind me and the shops had been replaced by empty houses and strange

derelict buildings. I reached a crossroads and stood still. I had no coin to toss to make the decision for me. I carried nothing but the clothes I was wearing. I looked up and along both of the roads, considering my next step as if weighing up a move in chess. In some juvenile way, perhaps it was just a game to me, and maybe that's why I didn't mind that Millie hadn't come with me. I didn't want to be culpable for whatever happened, especially as she was younger than me by a year and a half, having only just turned sixteen. I didn't want to be in charge by default because I was older; I avoided responsibility like the plague.

I wondered what they would be having for tea that evening and was glad of the void filling my stomach. Hunger pangs are welcomed, recognised as my 'normal' and that feeling of being full and sated that is appreciated by so many is absolutely reviled by me. I had no idea how this had come to pass, just how this obsession had so overwhelmed me, but it had. It had me, hook, line and sinker. Perhaps it was all wanton vanity gone astray? But whenever I questioned it, I understood that I didn't want to get better, I just wished I'd never gotten ill in the first place.

The road turned chalky, sprigs of drying out weeds springing out forlornly and I kicked up the dust with my battered old boots. I wondered at what point my feet would start filling out. I envisioned my ankles swelling up like tree trunks, leaving no distinction between my calves and my feet, bloated slabs of flesh stomping humongous footprints that scarred the

ground like those of an abominable creature. Stomp, stomp, stomp. I saw my thighs enlarge, their circumferences immeasurable, the skin bulging, blotchy and red, under the pressure of so much fat. Podgy, or was the word pudgy? Podgy sounded like stodgy. Dumpy, that was another word allocated affectionately to the rounder figure; perhaps I'd become a dumpy girl? Plump, there was another word for fat; *They say I'm plump* like Courtney Love sings. 'From Stick Insect to Elephant in Six Months' was what Joce and I had called our version of the Food Farm Handbook, our unique and satirical guide to the clinic. We'd enjoyed mocking the place, descrying its ridiculous rules and regulations and exposing it for the farcical feeding farm that it is. It was still a work in progress and I guess we wouldn't get the chance to complete it now. Reality sucked me back into the present with a small, sharp shock.

Footsteps quickened at my back and I turned to see a familiar face.

"I changed my mind. I do want to come with you!"

Millie's hair had blown all over the place and she stood bent double, elbows resting on her knees, as she tried to get her breath back. I resisted the urge to scoop her in a massive hug. I must have wanted her to come along with me more than I'd realised.

At first we marvelled at this newfound freedom and soared through the crimson sunset, riveted by our sense of adventure. Clouds had started forming low

on the horizon, pale wispy peaks that resembled distant mountains, the sky turning into a vast smudge of reds and oranges and pinks interspersed with pale yellow pirouettes. Our bodies cast elongated shadows, stretching us out to form eerie representations of ourselves, two lost twiglets in the oncoming twilight.

We chattered away trivially, animated by adrenaline, our arms swinging liberally through the cooling air. Millie recited from her treasured calorie-counter book (it was an omnipresent battered little book that was either wedged in her pocket or stuffed down her sock) meaning to test my inadequate knowledge but actually boasting her calorie expertise. Funnily enough, the 'Calorie Counter' was the only physical item Millie and I carried, other than Millie's wristwatch and my bangles. It seemed our lack of organisation waned in importance when compared to the fat content of a cheese and onion pie or the calorific difference between a Kit Kat Chunky and a Wispa. We discussed a variety of things as we traversed the streets and outskirts of town: music, hobbies, the opposite sex, favourite films; conversation naturally coming round to the relief at having abandoned Food Farm.

"No longer having to hear Kaye's whining voice," Millie specified as a crucial plus point in having vacated the clinic.

"That's no biggie!" I exclaimed, "I can think of loads of better reasons than that! No more cheese

sandwiches, no more supervision – no more *bathroom* supervision!"

"I thought we were just naming people we were glad to be away from, like Helen and her 'please would you like to sit down', 'please could you stop separating the milk from your cereal," Poison Ivy who's such a cow, Mother Teresa who is insane, and Denise who perves in the shower."

"Ugh, I know!" I grimaced but I was laughing inside.

"How did we even end up there?" Millie said rhetorically.

We slipped into silence and I considered how nefarious it was, my innocent diet that I'd embarked upon less than two years ago which had resulted in such chaos and despair. It wasn't will-power, it was an unfathomable force beyond my control that had propelled me on this downward trajectory.

"Have you any idea where we're going?" Millie asked light-heartedly.

"Nope, no idea at all." I kicked up a cloud of dust, watching the individual components take flight, reach a kind of inertia – almost as if in slow motion – and then disintegrate as powder in the air, reduced to nothing.

We'd slowed our pace after a short while. The excitement hadn't worn off, but in the waning light,

we were taking greater care to conserve our energy. I foresaw the two of us walking for days, unrestrained from worry. Our only concern was remaining anonymous; apart from that, our minds were weightless and we would stroll along genially, oblivious to the rest of the world.

"Do you think our parents will know by now that we're gone?" Millie asked, out of the blue, jolting me out of my imagination.

"Most probably," I shrugged, trying to make light of something that I didn't want to think about.

"Good," Millie said bitterly.

My ears pricked up like a dogs, my interest arrested. "Why good?"

"I hate them."

I waited for Millie to go on, keen to know what was wrong with her family, but she didn't say anything. With her gaze averted, she just scuffed the ground with her black plimsolls, dust smothering them, clouds of dirt forging a smokescreen in front of her. Impatience got the better of me.

"Why do you hate them?" I asked, trying to keep my voice neutral.

"It's my mum. She does whatever Roger tells her to – that's her boyfriend. He's my little brother's dad

and supposed to be my step-dad. He's nothing to me. It was his idea to send me here and the place I was before here, and my mum just went along with it. It never matters what I say or want. I hate them."

"What about your little brother?"

"Oh Lewis? He's adorable. I've got nothing against him."

"Even though he's Roger's kid?" I don't know why I asked that, but I was enthralled at this point, drawn into the drama of someone else's life.

"He's only two and he's lovely. He's the only one I can actually put up with."

I was mystified as to how Millie could despise her family, finding her situation a far cry from my own. The guilt started to pummel my insides then and I actually felt a lump forming in my throat as I contemplated my own family, worried-sick at home. They deserved much better than this.

Time swept us along in a vortex, which was both cold and unnerving. After what must have constituted hours of walking indefinitely into the enclosing darkness, we reached the Underground. There was nothing else to do besides take our chances at ticket dodging and, to be honest, we had nothing to lose. We alighted at the final stop and, utterly clueless, we headed right, in the somewhat mawkish hope that it would be a step in the right direction. Millie's watch

told us it was 8:30pm - the clinic would have called the police hours ago – so it was crucial to keep our heads down and just get as far away as possible. I hadn't given much thought to anything other than the here and now and all I felt in this instant was how painfully inclement the night was. I was freezing. The voracious wind pummelled my dip-dye skirt and a flimsy cheesecloth top was all that protected me from the elements, as well as a bra that I still didn't need. I can honestly recount this particular evening to be the most unbearable coldness I've ever experienced. My teeth were involuntarily chattering, my jaw like one of those wind-up toys, giving me a headache. It was brain-freeze without the prerequisite ice-cream. Millie was dragging her feet too and in one mutual exchange, we realised that we needed to cement some sort of plan.

"We can't just keep on walking forever," Millie said. "Maybe we should find somewhere we can try and get some sleep?"

"It would help us get through the cold too." My breath formed a distinct white fog in the air before me.

"I never thought I'd say this, but my legs are killing me."

I laughed, "You, the former power-walker and manic exerciser!"

"I know, who'd have thought it?"

"I'm so freezing." The words shuddered out of my mouth in frenzied chatters.

"Because you're still skinny. You're only just 70 percent aren't you?"

"74. Aren't you cold?"

"Yeah, but judging by your mad chattering teeth, I'm not as cold as you. You're hardly dressed for the occasion either!"

"I hadn't woken up with the intention of running away on my mind. Besides, it was warm earlier."

"There's got to be somewhere nearby that we can go in, a hut or something." Millie was hugging herself in an effort to generate heat, her blue sweatshirt and patterned cotton trousers hardly the most conducive to warmth either.

Everywhere we walked looked the same, we could have been repeating laps for all we knew. The only thing that changed was the ever decreasing temperature and our deteriorating energy supplies. By 10:30pm we were at a loss as what to do. Millie and I were exhausted. Thoughts tugged at my mind of how it was all my fault, I'd initiated this whole escapade and I was to blame. My feelings were punctuated with guilt at having drawn Millie into this predicament and leading her with me towards whatever outcome we would reach. As heavy-hearted

as I felt, no amount of guilt or anguish could alleviate the intensity of the cold. I could no longer feel my fingers and toes and the skin on my face felt like shards of ice were being driven through it. When we reached the park we merely continued to walk like numb automatons repetitively putting one foot in front of the other; it wasn't until we made a cursory sideways glance that we realised we were no longer on the path. Immersed in the gloom, it wasn't easy to decipher our surroundings, but looking intently about we realised that we were in some kind of outdoor enclosure. I toyed with the idea of staying here, for we were away from harm and very much out of sight, cut off from vehicles and people, and we wouldn't have been the first people to spend the night on a park bench. Before I had chance to transmute my thoughts into words, Millie had already verbalised them. The decision was made and we were stopping here, however, after trawling the perimeter twice and inspecting the entire vicinity, there was nothing sheltered at all. The least exposed area was by a small building, a block of toilets with the doors locked. Millie and I sat down on the side that was protected from the wind. Millie emitted a sound of relief as the weight was taken off her feet. I shivered convulsively, fearful of getting through the night in what felt like the arctic.

I must have dozed off. My eyes flared open in alarm, something pricked against my forehead. It took me a second or two to get my bearings. Millie and I were cocooned like baby monkeys desperate to maintain warmth. I felt something against my forehead again

142

and something prickled the back of my head. And again. And again and then it dawned on me. I nudged Millie awake, my mouth too dry to speak and pointed ahead. It was too late. A fusillade of water erupted directly in front of where we sat huddled. I tensed the muscles in my deadened legs to force them to wrench me from the ground. Millie and I were still clasping one another and in a joint effort we heaved ourselves up and ran as if our lives depended on it. We sprinted through the showers and round the other side of the block of toilets. I didn't know whether to laugh or cry. We'd narrowly avoided saturation, the fringe of my hair was wet, dripping in my eyes, but we'd been extremely lucky. The involuntary rush of terror had got my heart racing and for a moment I'd forgotten how freezing cold I was.

"What the hell was that?" shrieked Millie

"Sprinklers," I said, "They must be on a timer. We weren't to know they were there."

"What do we do now?"

"I don't know. I don't really wanna stay in here now though. I think we should keep looking for somewhere less exposed."

"At least we managed to get *a bit* of sleep."

"That place would have been ideal, if it hadn't been for the unplanned shower."

"What kind of idiot sets them on at night?" Millie seethed.

"What kind of idiot tries to sleep right next to them?" I raised my eyebrows and Millie collapsed in a fit of giggles. I joined in, each laugh timed to coincide with each shiver. "Come on, let's get out of here and on to somewhere else. This is a disaster."

Vacating the park wasn't that simple, for the entrance we had come in had been locked. I almost couldn't believe it. We'd have to climb over the door. I began to wonder if there was any point leaving the park but an icy gust of wind rattled my teeth and I knew that there had to be somewhere else we could go. At this point I even invited notions of knocking on strangers' doors, hoping they'd take pity on us and take us in. The banner on the door stated park opening hours were 8:00-22:30. The warden must have locked it only just after we had arrived and he wouldn't be back to unshackle it for another six hours. Millie was getting her footing on the door. It was a large archaic door made of sturdy wood and although it was tall there were makeshift footholds, in the form of wooden beams, running across. Once again, I questioned my attire for such an activity. I hoisted my skirt up to knee height and waited for Millie to near the top. She gracefully flung her legs around, shuffled down the other side and dropped daintily to her feet like a cat. I groaned internally, dreading the climb. I may have weighed less than Millie but I wasn't anywhere near as elegant as she was, especially as I tried to control my flapping skirt as my

wispy top was intent on getting caught on the stray nails embedded in the wood. My hair kept getting in my eyes as well, as if I didn't need anymore impediments in the darkness.

"Are you nearly there yet?" Millie called from the other side.

"Near enough," I called back through clenched teeth.

"What's taking you so long?"

I fiddled about with my skirt, which was also getting impaled with rusty nails, and managed to throw my legs across, as Millie had done, however, I was facing the wrong way. Whereas Millie had shifted herself round so that she was still facing the door, I was looking outwards, my arms outstretched behind me. Millie had been able to gently shimmy down and drop to her feet.

"I can't turn around!" I yelled.

"It doesn't matter, just jump. It's not far."

I had a sudden fit of vertigo and I felt as if the ground was retracting up and down – I watched it hurtling closer and receding perilously away.

"Just jump Lea!" Millie said, impatience tingeing her tone.

I counted slowly to three then took flight like a wounded bird only to land like a sack of bones on the earth.

"Ouch," Millie said, voicing my discomfort.

"Come on, let's get going."

*

"It's not the same Underground that we got off earlier, is it?" Millie asked. We hadn't been on foot long when we reached the train station. It was completely deserted, yet still illuminated throughout, giving the illusion of occupation. Relief washed over me in waves as I envisaged the warmth produced within. We scurried over and discovered that it was wide open to anyone and everybody. It looked like just a normal train station entrance – a walk in area, followed by turnstiles and ticket payment booths. We didn't care for the rest of it, all we required was somewhere moderately temperate, indoors, with no breeze and certainly no sprinklers. We made a furtive surveillance of the entry area, checking there were no people lurking in the shadows and no alarms detecting our presence. With our brief assessment carried out and everything seeming in order, we nestled down tenuously in a small anteroom to try and get some sleep.

I don't want to move. I want to be rescued, damsel in distress style. I want to be swept up off my feet and escorted over the threshold into utopia. In the deep

recesses of my mind, I realise that I can't stay huddled here forever, but right now I really don't care. I inhabit the here and now and nothing else matters. Tears throb their way from my eyes again and I feel too shattered to even care. Dignity shed, I sit sobbing like a four year old, my hands filthy, mud caked to my boots and my hair slicked to my scalp with dirt and grease. This was all a bad idea. Escaping was such a mindless thing to do, yet I couldn't have tolerated Food Farm for a moment longer. I'm fed up of walking this tight-rope of living, or trying to live. If red is anger, and green is envy, then blue must be the colour of despair.

I started awake to the sound of muted voices. The muffled conversation had filtered out from the disjointed dream I was having and it took me a few seconds to detach subconscious imagination from reality. My cheeks were still damp and I hastily wiped the evidence of my tears away, before shaking Millie roughly awake.

"Huh?" she groaned, inhabiting that sleep-to-waking purgatory, her eyelids struggling to unseal.

"Shhh!" I hissed, my forefinger jabbing at my lips.

"Wha?" Stricken, Millie whirled her head around.

"There's someone here," I whispered, continuing to smooth the dampness from my face before climbing cautiously to my knees.

"People?" Millie asked.

"I heard them. Just a moment ago", I grasped the edge of the wall with my fingertips and peered round. "I think there were two of them. I heard two male voices."

"What would they be doing here?"

"Who knows?" I carefully studied the room diagonal to where we were situated, trying to make out any shapes through the frosted glass. My eyesight wasn't perfect and in this unusual lighting, lit up too brightly in only select places, I felt like I had blinkers on. Millie pivoted round on her knees so that she was peeping over my shoulder.

"It's six minutes past three," Millie revealed in a susurration.

"We've been here all night," I whispered back.

Something flickered at the edge of my vision and my head swung to meet it. An empty spider's web draped across the corner of the wall, gossamer intricately woven and suspended from the brickwork, ensnared my face as I struck it round. My anxiety was piqued, every fibre of my being on high alert. I noticed Millie nibbling her little finger and her nervousness set my nerves even more on edge. There was a light on in the little room, but no indication of any movement within. Judging from where we were squatting on the concrete floor, the room across from

148

us was such a miniscule box that maybe people wouldn't actually utilise it as a workspace. It may just constitute storage or be a superfluous dumping ground. I started to question if I had really heard anybody speaking. Maybe I had just dreamed it. I strained to conjure the dream I'd been engaged with and, typically, I drew a blank. I couldn't recall anything and, in fact, I couldn't even remember anything associated with the voices I thought I had heard. I began to seriously doubt myself. My nerves had worked themselves into a paroxysm, that was all. I'd been fraught with anxiety and my senses were heightened to my surroundings like that of a cornered animal. I realised I was still holding my breath and instantaneously exhaled with relief. I wheeled back from my crouch onto my bum, a stab of pain as I landed unexpectedly on my tailbone.

The buzzing of electricity was the only sound and after so long it seemed to become an extension of me, for the thrumming felt like it was taking place above, around and inside me. My head was filled with a fizzing as if my brain was hotwired and the lights flickered too distinctly amidst the desolate gloom. Millie and I sat silently, our guards relaxed, listening to the encroaching hypnotic hum. I closed my eyes in an effort to shut out the rippling commotion of the train station and tried to focus on something else. I thought of my family, what would they be doing? Would they know that I was missing? How would they be feeling? It didn't bear thinking about, as I pictured my mum's red-rimmed eyes and my dad's exhausted face. Within me, ruptured the all-familiar

149

guilt and if I didn't mitigate the sensations of remorse and longing, I was in serious danger of sobbing like an infant yet again. I wrapped my arms around my knees, pulling them into my chest, and allowed my head to flop into the nest created by my forearms and the backs of my hands. I heard Millie start to purr nasally at my side. I cast my mind back to a year or so ago when my mum had taken me to see our GP about my 'weight problem', thus setting the wheels of this machine in motion. The GP's revelation was laughably absurd, and that is what I thought of now as I tried to ameliorate my guilt. He had proudly announced, as if producing a rabbit from a hat, that I was incredibly lucky and had permission to eat all of the food I wanted! He then struck off on the fingers of both hands all the splendid delicacies I was at liberty to gorge on: cream cakes, chocolate puddings, chip butties, cheesy pizza, jam doughnuts…. His tiny eyes twinkled and his round cheeks flushed lobster red as he listed these treats with gusto. It was so simple to him and abundantly clear that we were worlds apart. That was the day I lost faith in professionals and acknowledged the fallibility of human beings.

I was jostled to my senses by a fierce clenching of my right shoulder. I felt my body spasmodically react and I swatted the fist that had enclosed the top of my arm.

"Jeff, you're gunna have t' come over'n have a look 'ere."

*

The game was up and our escape had been foiled. The sight of two near skeletal girls cowering in a cubbyhole was enough to arouse the suspicion of these unsuspecting train wardens. In my defence, I remained headstrong to the very last in my outright refusal to provide details of where we belonged to. Millie eventually coughed up the information, scared into submission by the more burly man's assertion that he would call the police and have us banged up in the cells until morning. I numbly became willing to let myself fall into the hands of whatever would unfold. My tightrope had been snipped in the middle, this episode completed, and I was to plummet into whatever misery would come next.

After irresolutely skulking into the back of the car, we took off along unknown roads, the two men, Jeff and the burly bloke, chattering away about Millie and me distastefully. I couldn't care less and feigned deafness, choosing to watch the hills and meadows lope past out of the window, the lush greens and exuberant yellows dancing extravagantly before my dreary eyes. We seemed to be travelling for ages and it suddenly occurred to me that we must have done rather well and got quite far from the clinic. The car rattled around corners, along verges and up hills and I felt a swell of pride at having accomplished an almost successful getaway. After a while, we swerved into a built-up area and I instantly recognised the visage of the houses, down-trodden into discontent. We were but ten minutes from our final destination and our

151

doom. Remarkably, the car took the left rather than the right turning and Millie and I exchanged a knowing glance and the first smile since this journey began. Reaching Food Farm was stalled for a while longer as Jeff and the burly man swore at us and each other in frustration. When asked for directions from the burly bloke driving the vehicle I played dumb. Millie and I could have our little victory.

*

"I'm so angry with you I could give you both a plate full of food!" Our greeting from Mother Teresa was less than welcoming.   It was the reversal of the punishment I'd been threatened with as a child, that if I misbehaved I'd be sent to bed without any dinner. She hurried us inside to give us a closer examination, all the while praising the Lord for our safe return and chiding us for the colossal worry we had caused. We were ushered, unsurprisingly, into the Brown Kitchen and forced to sit one opposite the other whilst Mother Teresa got us a glass of blackcurrant squash each. I eyed Millie suspiciously, for we were never given anything but water – or orange juice at breakfast – to drink.

It was ten past five in the morning. Mother Teresa persisted with her Hallelujahs and Praise the Lords before pronouncing that it was rather too late for anything other than sleep. This show of leniency was akin to putting damp skin too close to an appliance and being electrified by static; an unexpected, but not unpleasant, shock. The pious old woman showed a

softer, more sympathetic side to her usual wrath of God harshness, and led Millie and I to the mattress cupboard. It went without saying that we were back on Total.

*

The veil of sleep partially lifted, the full extent of my retribution dawned on me. It wasn't just Total Supervision, it was also the five days in pyjamas sanction for having run away. This was meant to act as a deterrent to trying to escape, but it was really just another way the staff could assert dominance over us through mortification. We may as well have had placards slung around our necks saying 'Failed Escapee'.

"Wakey wakey!" Kaye's voice was like an ear-splitting foghorn tearing through the classroom to be answered by a unified groan.

I reluctantly opened my eyes to see an unprecedented six members of staff assembled in the doorway. We ordinarily would only ever see one or two at once in the morning, as the third and possible fourth member would be stationed in the kitchen preparing breakfast. Mother Teresa and Julie remained from the night shift, which was unusual, and filling the spaces around them were Rosie, Helen, the Tarantula and of course Kaye. Natasha and Kaye had smiles tickling the edges of their lips, but Helen and Rosie's faces were set as if in stone.

"We hear it's been an eventful night," Natasha approached, a grin opening up to expose her white teeth that gleamed at me. I could tell she was mildly amused at the news of our escapade, probably glad that we had returned safe and sound. Helen and Rosie were staring daggers at me and I knew that it was me they held accountable.

"You're back!" Layla, in a burst of ebullience, hauled herself up out of her sleeping bag and lunged over to hug both Millie and I in turn. Helen narrowed her eyes at her, clearly not deeming this the occasion for celebration.

"Come on girls, up you get!" Rosie started to promenade between the rows of mattresses, her face pinched sternly in a glower.

"That includes you Leanne," Helen remarked venomously. "Though you and Millicent are not to change into your clothes this morning, as I'm sure you're aware."

I inadvertently sighed, exhaling a huff to which Helen came up to my face and spat, "What's with the attitude? You've only got yourselves to blame."

I caught Millie's eye and she was very carefully shaking her head at me, warning me off so I decided to keep schtum. I wouldn't rise to Helen's provocation. Instead, Millie and I kept apart as we tidied our mattresses away, not wanting to increase the ire of certain nurses. As the night staff finished

their conversation with the Tarantula and Rosie, Kaye had installed herself at the door of the toilet ready to supervise the first lot of bladder emptying of the day.

I didn't know what day it was and on the way to breakfast I couldn't control my yawning. Millie looked exhausted too, violet smears beneath each eye and her bed head unattended to. We sat down next to each other and Helen immediately piped up in a raised, supercilious voice, "No, thank you girls, would you like to sit at separate ends of the table please?"

"No thank you Helen," I said, matter of fact, and a bubble of laughter rippled around the Brown Kitchen. Millie stared at me, awestruck, and I imagined that this must be my proudest moment to date, the day I finally stood up to somebody I loathed.

The Tarantula intervened, clearly sensing that I was due to cause unnecessary trouble. "Millie, why don't you go and sit over there." She pointed across to the spot next to Clara. Millie, with the most fleeting of looks at me, ambled over and deposited herself on the uncomfortable wooden bench opposite. Natasha uttered a 'thank you' before giving me an ambiguous stare that either intended to warn me that I ought to be careful, or to congratulate me for putting my foot down. Maybe it was all in my own head and she meant nothing by it, I was so overcome with fatigue. I was so tired, in fact, that I ate all of my breakfast as I was 'supposed to', i.e. No separating, no smearing,

no squeezing, and I sat obediently at the table until I was told I could move.

I immersed myself in my schoolwork that morning, just to block out everything around me. I was angry that I was back here and annoyed with myself that I'd even ran away in the first place. I felt so hideously hopeless that I wanted some reprieve from my own head. I re-read my revision notes, seeking refuge in *The Lord of the Flies* and the poetry of William Blake. Millie was busy constructing another collage of cadaverous women and actual cadavers – I really didn't know where she got these images from! - and Jocelyn was pretending to do her maths work. I ignored them, I turned my back on everyone in that instant and just focused, focused, focused. If I didn't have to think about them or this place for just a little while, perhaps I wouldn't have to feel like me.

My self-imposed trance was relatively short-lived. Bethan bounded over like the Easter Bunny, her eyes sparking in wonder, and pushed my notes to one side. "So, where did you go? What did you do? I wanna know everything!"

Layla, Fliss and Clara crawled out of the woodwork then, their eager faces expecting a thrilling story. I made a cursory scan of the room, ensuring it hadn't been infiltrated by any staff other than Kaye who was dozing off by the door as Loretta and Marcella were keeping the patients in order.

"It wasn't that adventurous," I said, "and it wasn't successful."

"What do you mean it wasn't successful?" Bethan asked, her naïve face still aglow with fascination.

"Well, we ended up back here, didn't we?"

Chapter 10

"Lea, your family are here!"

We were due to set off on an outing away from the clinic. It had been debated whether I would be allowed off site because of my recent disappearing act, but luck must have been shining on me that weekend. I'd been impatient to see my parents and siblings as I'd missed out on last weekend's visit as a consequence of running away and I couldn't wait to see them. We'd only spoken on the phone and the disappointment in all of their voices due to my exploits was blatantly detectable. Disappointment was worse than anger. I'd let everyone down yet again.

Leonard and Leonie shot into view, wielding chocolate bars from the huge foreboding cupboard. They had clearly commandeered a member of staff on the way to meet me. Sometimes I questioned their motives for visiting. Mum and dad followed, warm smiles adorning their faces. That all-familiar stab of shame as I confronted the people whose lives I had disrupted, my stupid antics reducing their trust though miraculously not their love. The palimpsest of suffering and deceit rushed back to me, the lies I'd told, my deviousness, the dinners cooked for me with care slipped sneakily in the dustbin, the bags of vomit I'd hidden about my bedroom and the 14lbs in weights I'd secretly carried around my legs and ankles to dupe them at weigh ins. The Evil Man had speculated back then that I was "too clever for my

own good." Here I was now, too stupid to know what was good for me or any one else.

"Where would you like to go before we have lunch?" My mum asked. Obviously there was a 'catch' to going out, lunch being it. The staff had already made me up a packed lunch, bulging with fat, undoubtedly mayonnaise and lard would be overflowing the packaging. My dad reeled off a number of local places we could visit, but this trip was already tainted by the prospect of food. Eating out with my family should have been an enjoyable occasion, yet I was taunted by the knowledge that they'd have dainty little snacks, healthy options, small amounts, and I'd have this monstrous binge to undertake. I nodded noncommittally at the destinations my dad suggested, though my mind was tormented by the meal ahead and whether or not a possibility for deviousness would present itself. The decisions were made around me and I cocooned myself with the sounds of their voices, just praying for the day to go well and without a fuss or spectacle.

As the five of us piled into the car, it was comforting to be back experiencing a sense of normality. Again, I was crammed in the middle between Leonard and Leonie. My mum glanced behind and reminded me to fasten my seatbelt and my dad steered us away from the clinic and out to potential freedom. Trees and houses sped past; the sun hiding behind a cluster of clouds, stalling the radiance that today was promised. None of us mentioned my escape, meaning there was another elephant in the car besides me, the

weight of it bearing down oppressively in our refusal to acknowledge it. When the car juddered to a stop, my dad sprinted off to pay for the car park, and then we were off on an expedition to please the variegated tastes of each of us. We all enjoyed Madame Tussauds, though my morbid curiosity was more drawn to the Chamber of Horrors, as was Leonard's, though I couldn't help but compare myself to every waxwork model I came across. I couldn't dispel this obsession to measure myself up against everyone to prove that Food Farm really was fattening me up beyond absurdity. We ambled through the shopping centre afterwards and every person I encountered I made a cursory estimation of their weight and dress size – I thought I was being particularly clever, though my mum didn't miss a thing and kept reassuring me time and again that I was still thin. Her words fell on deaf ears. I could tell that Leonie and Leonard were becoming tired of my preoccupations.

As we ate, mum's eyes were on me like a hawk's and there was no opportunity to commit any indiscretion. Bull-headed as ever, I announced that I wasn't eating the chocolate bar because nobody else had to have a chocolate bar with their lunch. Despite a debate arising in which it was pointed out repeatedly who was and who was not of sound mind, the chocolate bar was left uneaten. My mum checked the rest of the packaging afterwards to ensure that I hadn't left anything hidden. Resentment started to rear its ugly head. I tried to subdue it but it rested like a phantom on the edge of the scene, blighting the remainder of the day. The sun never emerged from its cavern of

clouds and I was returned to Food Farm in time for tea.

"How was your trip?" Joce asked as soon as my family had gone.

"It was all right, I guess."

"Not great, huh?"

"It felt," I struggled for the right word, "strained. Uncomfortable, unnatural, almost."

"I'm not surprised," Joce remarked knowingly.

"What do you mean?"

"It's the first time you've left the clinic with them and it's probably the first time you've all been out as a family in God-knows how long."

"You're lucky," Millie chipped in, "If me and my family were let out together it would be like World War Three! At least you and your parents don't want to kill each other!"

"Just you wait until you go for your meal out," said Joce gravely.

"I thought that *was* a meal out," I said.

"No, silly, a meal out at a restaurant. You can guarantee it will be TGI Fridays too, as recommended by the nurses."

"Yep, of course it will be!" Millie added.

My lack of understanding must have been transparent, for Joce and Millie both rolled their eyes as if to say, 'well, what are you like.'

"TGI Fridays do mammoth portions. That's why the staff always recommends your parents take you there. And of course your parents only want the best for you and they believe that the best is what the nurses recommend." Joce grinned, pleased with her assessment.

"Don't I get a say in where we go?" I asked.

"You're joking, right?"

"What happens if we refuse to go?" I asked, dreading what the response would be.

"I don't know. Nobody has ever refused to go out for a meal in the time that I've been here." The way Jocelyn said it seemed to make the consequences sound unimaginable and beyond comprehension. If I'd been so filled with grim foreboding about lunch out today, that was nothing compared to the cloying sense of dread I now had for the future meal I was to come up against.

"I shouldn't worry Lea, "Millie soothed, "you've got a while for that yet. Besides, the portions can't really be any bigger than the ones we get here, can they?" She smiled her placatory smile in a bid to settle my nerves. It worked to an extent, but although I pushed my trepidation to the depths of my mind, it had still taken up residence.

*

Trips away from the clinic became frequent and opened up the delicious possibility of escape. The stalwart rebellion was still an inherent and intrinsic part of me, even though my conscience would now tug me in the opposite direction. I was constantly looking for a way out, even if not a permanent one. I was far from happy and that peace and contentment I so craved was something I would spend my life searching for, even if it meant going to the ends of the earth to find it. There was an excursion to a local theme park and whereas I revelled in thrill-seeking and adventure as the 'old me', it failed to impact on me at all. There is a photo taken of me on one of the rides which embodies my indifference to everything. I'm sitting alone in a carriage of a large rotating octopus, my face ashen and blank, eyes staring through the camera like those of a dead person's. It was a kind of death, I suppose, looking back. Hindsight is a powerful thing and in retrospect I can see that I didn't just want to escape from Food Farm, I was desperate to escape from myself.

163

Other trips away I would accompany the others on included the cinema, which was always some film I had little to nil interest in but would go along anyway for the hell of it; some kind of Pottery Shed where we painted crockery of our choosing, which I greatly enjoyed, committed to quietude and losing myself for a few hours in the task of painting a giraffe onto a ceramic mug; the park, which was a short minibus journey away, but was a change of scenery, nonetheless, and had the added bonus of swings which we hoped could help tone our legs. My favourite place I visited in all the time I spent at Food Farm was Camden Market. It was everything I wanted and much more than I expected. It was busy in the lively, amenable way rather than being claustrophobic and the whole place was awash with vibrant colours. It resembled one big party more than anything else and for once I had been invited. I was lulled along with the music, drifting on the breeze and on instinct as my sight was ambushed by beautiful lucidity. I was beguiled by a kaleidoscope as Bethan and Robyn twirled round me trailing a rainbow of scarves behind them, and Tanya and Fliss stood hurling juggling balls through the air. Joce and Emily were dancing round clutching jewellery that glistened in the light whilst Layla splurged all her money on the smallest but most colourful dream-catchers to send back to her old friends in Australia. The sun was a red hot plate burning in the sky, invoking positivity, the festival spirit upon us all. Even the nurses would be in a better mood when we were here. I was warmed from within, optimism cooking in the roots of my soul, as the 'old me' was resurrected for a time.

On one occasion, having no money, the nurse Rachel held out her hand and pressed a little hand carved giraffe into my palm. Touched, I thanked her and asked why.

"You've seemed sad lately but as I watched you paint that giraffe on the mug the other week you looked happy - I saw this and thought it might make you smile." Rachel patted my shoulder comfortingly and I hugged her, overcome with emotion. "Just don't tell the others." She winked, gave my shoulder another small pat and then we continued to walk into the gently throbbing mass of vibrancy. I couldn't wait to show Millie when I got back. She was still refusing to be included and hadn't yet been on any of the trips. I'd given up asking her to come with me, and on the minibus journeys I generally sat in a row on my own.

"But why did she get you it?" Millie asked, intrigued.

"I don't know. She said I'd seemed sad."

"Next time you go, try and get her to buy an elephant carving for me."

"Next time, why don't you come with us?" I asked.

The decision was made for her as Millie was forced to come along next time. I felt as if I'd initiated it somehow and apologised profusely.

"What are you sorry for? It's not your fault the nurses have no respect for our decisions. Anyway,

it's because I'm on Total that I've been forced to come – they haven't got enough staff to supervise the Totals at Camden and me all alone at Food Farm. They're just making their own lives easier."

As usual, Millie had a point. In her characteristically derisive way, she was right.

*

You could tell the difference between the pukers and the non-pukers. It was in their walk. I noticed it mostly when people had finished their post-meal, for their walk was more a lunge – a purposeful surge towards a pre-determined goal. They didn't languish in a comfortable stroll or enjoy a carefree saunter, it was a brisk, precise clip clop clip clop, head thrust forward, arms swinging with momentum, and eyes set with grim indomitability. That must have been the same walk I'd inadvertently adopted and had walked the night I blocked the plughole.

As I was still on Total I had to endure the ignobility of shower supervision. It was incredible really how we only had a bath at home, and I used to marvel at the water, creating waves by moving my legs slowly and sometimes quickly, observing the little eddies and ripples that popped up as if by magic. I wouldn't dream of having a bath here, under such close and indecent scrutiny of another human being; I couldn't bear the humiliation of being sprawled out, naked and vulnerable, under the pincer-like glare of one of them, like a lamb to the slaughter or a patient on an

operating table. It gave me the creeps just thinking about it. The shower was the more modest option because at least there was a translucent shower curtain that put my mind at ease and I could turn my back on the member of staff, feigning ignorance to their presence. Unless I was showering under the supervision of Denise of course; Denise who would make ill-advised comments about the toe-ring I was wearing or would try to engage me in conversations about my family. 'Uncomfortable' doesn't go far enough to sum up how she made me feel whilst I was trying to go about my normal ablutions.

Luckily this evening - the same day Rachel had given me the wooden giraffe - I had Julie taking me for my shower. I'd jumped at the chance, as usual, beating the likes of Andrea, Anne, Bethan, Emily, Marilyn and even Millie (ruthlessness overtook friendship in this instance, I'm afraid, and Millie and I both understood and accepted this fact). I retrieved my belongings from my room in a hasty scrabbling together of items, and led Julie along the corridor to the Green Bathroom. Julie had her obligatory magazine with her – *Woman's Own* today – however, she had become more vigilant of late, mainly because one or two of us had been pushing the boundaries a little too far. She had started to take random intervals from her reading to peer round the door to quickly check what we were doing, and I don't think I'd helped by a recent purge down the toilet accompanied by the obvious flush of the chain. She'd shot up like a jack in the box, head craned round the

door, wearing an expression of betrayal. I'd taken that as a warning not to be so cocky in future.

This evening, I waited for Julie to nestle down into a position that looked comfy before springing into action. It had been just over an hour since our evening meal was over, meaning this should be a relatively easy expulsion. I turned the shower on full and got undressed, quickly climbing into the freezing water that hadn't had time to warm up. Bending over I committed myself to the usual routine, jabbing my elbows fiercely into my ribs and thrusting the contents up and outwards. I didn't notice anything was wrong until it was too late. The putrid conglomeration of undigested food, stomach acid and goo were swirling around on a lake of water – nothing was being filtered through the plug hole. I jabbed my fingers in the yucky swamp in a desperate attempt to try and force it all down, but to no avail. I was struck by absolute panic and in that moment I was truly at a loss for what to do. Motionless in the shower, water falling in sheets over my eyes, I finished emptying my stomach before continuing the frenzied swirling of detritus and gunk down the clogged plughole. The water level was swelling and it was apparent that nothing was being drained. In a second of insanity I released a strange, subhuman sound, which had Julie's ear at the door in an instant.

"Everything all right in there hon?"

"The shower's filling up!" I exclaimed, "I don't know what's happening!" I manoeuvred myself to the side,

slipping one leg out just enough so that I could grab a towel, for I knew that Julie was due to approach. Wrapping the towel around me, I decided that my best bet was to just play dumb. I knew nothing, the plughole just erupted before my eyes. Act like a gobsmacked idiot.

"Well, what on earth!" Julie gasped at the rising water level, turned the shower off, and beckoned me to get completely out. She gave me a searching look, to which I played the innocent fool.

"I honestly don't know, the drain must be blocked, you know?"

"Hmmm," Julie mused, and I felt my act was working. There was no sign of the water decreasing, bits of vomit floated atop the thick, grey water.

"It just started coming up out of the plughole! I didn't know what was happening!" I pulled a face to add credence to my story and convey my outright horror. "Ugh! I dread to think how old all that puke is that came up out of there, makes me feel ill!"

"Hmmm," Julie reiterated, more convinced this time. "You get dried and dressed, Lea, I'll go and get someone and have them take a look at this mess."

"What do you think they'll say?" I asked, still nervous that I'd be seen through.

"Girls have been throwing up down these drains for years, it was bound to happen sooner or later." My shoulders relaxed as if caressed by an experienced masseur, my relief was that palpable. "It's just unfortunate you were in the firing line."

I quickly got dried and dressed into my pyjamas and before I knew it a small crowd had gathered outside the door. Julie had returned with Kaye and Rosie in tow, Bethan and Alicia were loitering to see what all the fuss was about and I caught Millie's knowing stare as she followed Larissa up the corridor for her shower. My story held out, only Millie and I knowing what really clogged the drain in the Green Bathroom. My duplicity should have earned me an Oscar. Not only did I get away with it, but I was afforded unnecessary sympathy for being subjected to such a revolting incident. The only drawback was that the Green Bathroom was now out of bounds for the indefinite future.

*

Unwilling to submit to that daunting world of adulthood, I was a late bloomer. I played with Barbie dolls up until age 12 and was reluctant to get fitted for my first bra. I still had a favourite cuddly dog that slept on my pillow and sat guarding my bed through the day. Whilst most girls had been eagerly anticipating the start of their period, heralding it as a sign that they were becoming a woman, I dreaded it with a passion, lamenting the erosion of youth. I didn't want to grow up in any way at all. It wasn't

just the physical changes I was petrified of, (though admittedly that was a formidable foreboding that dominated my thoughts), it encompassed everything: the responsibilities and expectations implicit in adulthood as well as the uncertainty of the future that stretched ahead like a dark and narrowing tunnel. It made me want to crawl back to the sanctuary of my mother's womb and never see the light of day again. I was so filled with fear; I was surprised that people couldn't see it billowing out of me like waves of gas or whorls of vapour.

I generally avoided things associated with the adult world, although my first ever drinking binge was the event that precipitated hospitalisation, psychiatric appointments and basically everything that followed. That had been my one-off bid to behave normally, to 'fit in' with my peers and try to enjoy myself, though it went horribly wrong. To cut a long story short, my malnourished body wasn't equipped to cope with a ridiculous quantity of alcohol. Unconscious and on a drip in hospital, my 'condition' came to light and my diagnosis prompted the downward spiral.

The first time I smoked a cigarette was at Food Farm and I was amused by the irony of being sent to a place to get healthy only to adopt another bad habit. It was in Fliss and Clara's room one night. Actually, it was on the roof of the clinic, which we could access from their bedroom window. I was surprised by Fliss and Clara's room as it was so feminine, the duvets and curtains all Laura Ashley floral prints, a musky pink carpet tying all the pastel shades together. Fliss and

Clara didn't strike me at all as girly girls. Fliss was naturally athletic and even at her target weight she was super-slim, just one long strip of sinew wrapped up in Adidas, her blonde hair piled on top of her head in an economical bun. Clara was a complete and utter tomboy, adventure-seeking and untidy, she was always losing things and getting her hands dirty. Clara caught me rudely gawking at the décor.

"I didn't choose the room, y'know."

"Sorry, I didn't mean to." I didn't mean to be what? Nosey? Rude? I *was* being nosey *and* judgemental. "It just wasn't what I expected, that's all."

"This is supposed to be the best room in the house," announced Fliss mock-proudly. "Not that it makes any difference."

"Well, they hadn't realised that it had the best smoking area in the house," chipped in Clara, moving over to the window that was right next to her bed. As she clambered over the duvet to swing the window open, I noticed how the soles of her feet were filthy. Nobody was allowed to wear shoes in Food Farm; another anti-escape measure.

"Is that as far as it opens?" I asked.

"Yep," Clara said, turning round.

"Shouldn't we wait for the others?" Fliss asked.

"Nah, it'll be all right. We'll just have a quick one and they can join us later." Clara smeared her shaggy hair out of her eyes with the back of her hand. She clocked the questioning look Fliss was giving her and added knowingly, "All the staff will be busy in hand-over or with the Totals."

"But we usually have someone to keep a look-out."

"We'll be fine. We'll be quick."

Fliss bit her bottom lip, "All right, if you say so."

"Great! You can climb out first Lea."

"You'll pop out of there quicker than us," Fliss joked.

Fortunately we tended towards bleak humour and would bemoan our weight gain, noticed via our developing struggle to shimmy through the narrow gap in the window. What was initially a casual plop through the opening became an increasingly unflattering battle to flap and fidget and force our way through. Being able to climb back in would then pose a gamble; there was more likelihood of being caught because it would take longer to squeeze back up in time before a nurse would come to do night checks.

I didn't particularly like smoking, but it gave me a thrill. I looked forward to our clandestine meetings on the roof, the forbidden cigarettes representing a kind of salvation in a world where all our control had

been stolen. Millie would often join us – we would typically reserve a bathroom for each other in preparation for the end of the other's supervision time – but we tended not to bother if Holly would be there, although we could just about tolerate Alicia. Layla, Tanya and Robyn would often accompany us and the only two agreeable patients of the Blue Kitchen, Collette and Suzanne, who came for the same buzz of breaking the rules that I relished.

Not once were we caught on the roof, except for one fateful evening.

Chapter 11

I felt like rejoicing when I eventually came off Total
Supervision following our escape. It had been nearly
two weeks since we'd absconded and although most
patients get Total for a week, we had to endure it for
longer; no explanation or reason was provided.
Millie was put straight onto a two hour post-meal,
whereas I was back on Day Supervision, being
relinquished from staff captivity every evening at
9pm. I was simultaneously jubilant and livid.

"But why?" I harangued the Tarantula who delivered
this ambivalent news.

"Why what? Aren't you just glad you're off Total?"

"I am glad, but how come Millie's on a two hour post
meal and I'm still being supervised all day? It
doesn't make any sense."

"Oh Lea," the Tarantula patronised me, "Are you
having issues with fairness again? You and Millie are
not inseparable, you know, and you're not the same."

"But - "

"No buts. If I had a quid for every time you
butted….."

"Well - "

"The decision's final, Lea. Now, sit down and do some studying or something." She wafted a non-existent smell about in front of her and wandered off, clearly growing irritated with my insistence.

It was Thursday and I'd survived weigh-in without the ability or the need for tanking. Total Supervision makes it literally impossible to water load, however, having been transformed into an actual sloth on Total, it was almost as impossible to lose weight too. I was cruising along my prescribed line like a hulking barge. I registered that I was absentmindedly swinging my legs under cover of the classroom table, as if that could combust some energy. It was probably the most I'd exerted myself in days, the only part of me seeing any exercise being my digestive system.

I had no idea where Millie was. It felt strange not watching her construct some kind of macabre collage as I studied. Joce had given up the pretence of trying to learn and was effectively dismissed from the classroom to enjoy the summer sunshine in the garden. She had advised me that morning that a suntan made your figure appear slimmer and had then flounced off to try and achieve a golden glow, before I could question her. Sitting alone in an avalanche of books, writing paper and highlighter pens, I wondered if I'd bitten off more than I could chew. My loneliness coaxed out my self-loathing and with it came, hand-in-hand, my low self-esteem. My egotism cowered with my stubbornness, leaving me reeling from the terrifying prospect of failure. I was

due to sit my exams in less than a week's time and I felt far from prepared. I caught a glimpse of Andrea and Casey, sitting to my far right. Casey had her nose in a book and Andrea was perusing a set of handwritten notes. The only other patient to be sitting exams was Alicia, I swung my gaze to where she was sitting, laughing insouciantly with Holly and two girls from the Blue Kitchen. Alicia was either clever enough to pass her exams without the need to study, or she was too dumb to realise that that's what she should be doing. Holly caught me looking in her direction and I looked away too quickly, as if guilty of doing something I shouldn't. The morning dragged on and I felt like I was struggling through a dense forest. The more I read, the less information I took in. Time just seemed to stand still and I stagnated within it.

I'd done reasonably well back at college in my mock exams, - taken not long before I was institutionalised - passing all of them. However, I'd misread one of the English questions, making a huge misdemeanour which cost me the A grade I was hoping for. Instead of answering one of the questions in detail from the proposed three, I panicked and hastily answered all of them. Scrimping on description and evidence from the pieces we had to reference had compromised the content of my answers and I was justifiably marked down for having not read the question correctly in the first place. I was vexed by my own incompetence and re-lived the exam repeatedly in my own head, wishing vainly that I could have done things differently. *If only* is the most soul destroying axiom,

made more powerful in its over-use. I was mortified, but as I calmed down, I realised that my error was really a blessing in disguise, warning me to be cautious and avoid making the same mistake again. The people who consoled me over this error all blamed my anorexia, stating that I wasn't having enough nutrition to think straight. I knew this was preposterous. My anxiety was to blame, not my eating habits. I was ridiculously nervous before, during and after each and every mock exam, although my panic was heightened as I sat down to do my English paper. It seemed as if every single fibre of my being had been stretched beyond capacity, the cells in my skin bulging to breaking point. My heart was not only beating, but was spinning, and my head thumped like an ominous accelerated death march. I could hardly concentrate; I felt I was drowning in a mire of turbulence. I wondered how sitting my GCSE's in an eating disorder clinic could possibly offer me any serenity.

There was an air of tranquillity about the place this morning and oddly that set me on edge. With 30 patients inhabiting Food Farm at present – all of which being adolescent girls – you would expect much more commotion. I tried to remember the names of everyone. Even though I'd been here for 68 days it was problematic putting names to faces, especially when (and I don't intend to sound nasty here) appearances changed rapidly and, at times, dramatically in a short space of time. I reeled off the names tentatively on my fingers, pleased for a temporary distraction from my revision. Millie, Joce,

Layla, Clara, Fliss, Bethan, Holly, Alicia, Casey, Andrea, Anne…Those are all the ones that come straight to mind…Robyn, Laura, Emily who was lovely, but it was disturbing how much she enjoyed regurgitating her food, just to taste the reflux…Tanya, Elle, Ruby…Marilyn…Collette, Suzanna – very sporty and never smiled….I was starting to waver now…Mandy – she had perfectly manicured hands and was always in full make-up, her lipstick too dark for her complexion… Lauren….It wasn't easy trying to remember the patients from the Blue Kitchen as they were frequently away from the clinic doing 'normal' things. I often forgot they were my age as they gave the impression of being so much more mature than me. They marched about with an air of sophistication and superiority because they had an ounce of independence and responsibility….Sometimes I believed that they were better than me, they all were better than me….Kelsey and Kayley….I was running out of names I remembered, as well as fingers to count on…Nicole's heart-shaped face floated into my mind and I had the name to match it to…that was 24, 25 including myself….Tara, Kim – Slim Kim, I recalled now…there was a second Laura as well who I always forgot…and a second Clara – the Clara with the eyebrows!… Sam and Sarah…I counted back through and I had 30. I'd managed to kill two minutes and temporarily suppress my unease.

I'd jinxed it; it was as if my bemoaning the quietude had somehow conjured her. Making a mental note of the two empty beds, made up neatly in the one

remaining available room, had in some spooky way precipitated the arrival of the new girl. She wasn't the archetypal anorexic either in that she was bright, bonny and came bouncing into the Sky Lounge that evening as if all of her wishes had been granted. Although slim, her body wasn't ravaged by the disease like Marilyn's had been; she still had cute little dimples in her cheeks and her arms and legs didn't resemble strings of spaghetti. She was dressed head to toe in bright pink, with a Liverpool football shirt underneath and was annoyingly loquacious; her dense Scouse accent was not a problem, however, the incessant flapping of her mouth *was*, for she never shut up. I'd naturally recoiled from her from the offset. Bold, bright and brash, her presence jarred on me. Things got worse as she introduced herself with my own name. She was a name thief! Although she spelt hers differently, Leighanne still preferred the shortened nickname Leigh.

"Wow, that's great, we're like name-sisters!" She shrieked with sheer delight at the revelation. "I can't believe it! Wow, it's so lovely here, don't you think, Lea-Lea? How long have you been here? Ooooh we're just gonna have the bestest time!"

That was it, I thought, I would have to run away again!

*

Perched on the roof in the twilight, I watched Millie and Fliss blow 'O' shaped whorls of smoke into the

gloom. Clara was diligently keeping watch on the inside of the window, though she still took drags from the cigarette Fliss was smoking, pouring the smoke out through the gap, expelling it into the misty darkness. We enjoyed the silence, making the most of the dissociation. Stars twinkled in the sky like precious jewels, thousands of them, as if the glitter from Art Therapy had been spilled over a black cloth. This moment encapsulated all of my contentment for the day. I heard an animal making a lowing sound in the distance and the wind tenderly caressed the trees. I spent my day striving towards this snapshot juncture, this side-step out of myself for a fleeting point in time. Sometimes we would just lounge on the roof mutely, speculating internally, and other times we would talk, postulate, joke, moan, laugh, or even cry. I merely liked the sensation of being beyond – beyond the four walls, beyond the rules and even to feel beyond myself for just a snippet of a second.

"What do you think of the new girl?" Clara asked, stretching out of the window as she passed the cigarette back to Fliss.

Fliss rolled her eyes and Millie tried to stifle a laugh. Their eyes all fixed on me.

"She's, erm, lively," I said, aiming for indifference.

"She doesn't even look that ill," Fliss said, flicking a stray piece of hair out of her eyes. "This place will destroy her."

"What do you mean?" Millie asked, evidently perplexed.

"She'll only pick up bad habits here." Fliss handed the cigarette back to Clara.

"She'll learn from the patients here how to be 'more anorexic'," Clara added, blowing a smoke bubble proudly.

"That's a shame," I said steadily. Although I didn't particularly like this Leighanne, I wouldn't wish anything bad upon her.

"Why did her parents send her here then? She doesn't seem that sick." Millie sounded genuinely incredulous at the thought of her parents being so naïve as to send their own daughter to her demise.

"They aren't to know that, Millie. As far as they're concerned, they're only doing the best for her by sending her here. I bet they read about this place online or have seen glowing reports of it on the TV. Everyone believes what they see or hear about this place being some kind of 'wonder clinic'." Fliss stubbed her cigarette into the dust and moved towards the window.

"So, do you think Leighanne will actually get worse here?" I asked, concern bubbling like lava inside me.

"It's possible," Fliss retorted, hoisting herself up and readying herself for the big squeeze.

"If she wasn't already anorexic before she arrived, she more than likely will be when she leaves," Clara stated.

"But how? She'll still have to gain a kilo a week like the rest of us and reach her target weight" said Millie.

"It's all in the mindset," Fliss explained. "She'll pick up the tricks and food issues from everyone else. She may only be a minor case at the moment, but seeing how patients behave in here and how they try to get away with stuff, she'll become worse. She seems jolly at the moment, but once she gets broken by this place and the people in it, she's in for a rough ride."

"It's not a good idea bunching us all together really," Clara shrugged, helping Millie up through the chasm.

I considered this and it made me despondent, the thought that our disease could be propagated by us; like prisons constituting academies of crime, patients unknowingly showcased anorexia's deviousness for others to mimic its habits and tricks. Leighanne had seemed alien to us with her exemplary happiness in a place where misery was so abundant. We were essentially broken individuals; each of us damaged in one way or another. I thought about little Anne, so bereft of self-confidence that I'd never heard her utter a single word; and Casey and Andrea, both acting as the other's shadow, petrified of being unfettered and

without a safety net. Even Holly's bravado was a farce masking her own deep rooted insecurities. We were all riddled with something – or things, plural - that had prompted us to be this way. I loathed every single thing about myself - that was my problem. I was useless. Unfortunately, I didn't predict there being any cure for that. I was a hopeless case.

I took one final inhalation before plunging the butt into my right forearm. A searing white-hot heat was followed by a crackle and a sizzle and the smell of singed flesh infiltrated the cool night air. A neat ivory stamp matched the others that had accumulated in an arbitrary and morbid dot-to-dot along my arm. I tossed the fag end to the corner in the once orderly pile that was growing ever larger and more unruly. I let my senses swallow the night one last time before turning to go inside. The sounds of a cat fight somewhere not too far away, the smells of the air, laden with moisture, and the overwhelming enveloping darkness; it was so enticing to stay out here forever, to closet myself away in the pitch black night and estrange myself from the rest of it.

"Come on Lea, what's taking you so long? I think someone's coming!"

Breathing a momentous, crestfallen sigh I transported the instant of splendour within me as I hauled myself up through the ever-tightening window.

*

Roused by the usual padding thuds, anyone would have thought I'd be used to the early morning wake-up call by now. I strangled the moan that threatened to rumble from the back of my throat and turned my body over away from the wall. A bleary eye opened to note the time – 6:42am – before abruptly snapping shut again. Millie must have registered my movement.

"Sorry," she whispered, "did I wake you?"

I didn't bother to qualify that with an answer. Millie exercised voraciously every morning and evening without fail. In spite of her light-footedness so as not to alert the staff, Millie and I were closely juxtaposed so that only a miracle could prevent me from hearing her thumping star jumps and energetic zig zags.

I dragged myself up onto my elbow and tried peeling back both eyelids this time. It was exhausting just watching Millie, especially this early in the day. As if reading my thoughts, Millie slowed.

"What? I have to get it all in before 7 o'clock." I accepted this as her justification for the ruckus.

"No worries, Millie, I think I actually slept through most of it this time."

"I still started at the usual time."

"6am? Then yes, I did, yippee!" My sarcasm was lost on Millie who was too preoccupied with counting her jumps to care.

I'd never really got the exercise bug, not to the extent that most of the girls here had it. Admittedly, I would always take the stairs rather than opting for the lift and I would get off the bus several stops too soon, but that was as far as my compulsion to burn calories went. There was a bout of insomnia where I would monotonously patrol the living room at home at four in the morning, doing laps of the coffee table for hours on end, though somehow, as I watched Millie working up a sweat, that didn't count.

I tried to anticipate what fresh horrors would be dished up for us today, what unsavoury palavers we'd be forced to undergo. In spite of the regimentation of Food Farm, it was easy to forget what day it was; they all merged into one big meringue-like fog. I remembered the indignity of weigh-in yesterday, indicating that today must be Friday. Breakfast would be croissants as opposed to muffins. On the downside, croissants have more calories and can't be squeezed, though at least they weren't drowned in butter and were easier to smuggle.

Millie was waning. I'd warned her about the drawbacks of not warming up or cooling down properly; it was little wonder her legs persistently ached. I checked the time, 6:51 – only a couple of lunges and thrusts before she would collapse into a heap on her bed. It beggared belief how she could

start the day all hot and sweaty, though the alarming amount of deodorant she fired into the room could asphyxiate us both on a daily basis. After a full-throttle work-out, Millie invariably left the room to be sick. I once questioned her urge to vomit up acrid bile, for that's all that could possibly be lining her stomach first thing in the morning.

Millie had shrugged nonchalantly, her woe begotten eyes downcast.

"Why do any of us do the things we do?" Her laconic answer resonated with me in its ludicrous reasonableness.

"Isn't it just acid you're puking up though?" I cringed, recalling the profound burning sensation that claws its way upwards through the throat a couple of hours post meal.

"Probably," Millie shrugged again. "I just *need* to do it. I can't explain why, it's like I *have* to empty myself out before I can think straight."

I swerved my tongue around my gum-line, the texture of my teeth rough and ragged as harshly beaten rocks at the seaside. Cavities shaped corroded caverns which my gums heaved over, angry, bulbous and red. I didn't want to contemplate the extent of Millie's dental degeneration, no wonder she rarely smiled.

We experienced the typical hustle and bustle to get into the Brown Kitchen this morning. The seating

area was set to be rammed now that there was an extra mouth to feed. I felt my eyes narrow as Leighanne entered the room, swaying breezily as if butter wouldn't melt – of course, butter *does* melt, especially as it slides down your wrists, soaking the sleeves of your sweatshirt, threatening to give you away. For some reason my fists were puckered at my sides and I relaxed them immediately, appalled that someone could inexplicably irk me so. I plonked myself down beside Millie, and ensured the gap the other side was so small as to prohibit anybody else sitting there. Rachel started pouring out the cereal. It was like Groundhog Day: Joan was lining up croissants on a baking tray with the tender loving care of a mother tucking her babies into bed. Denise strutted up and down the aisle between the two tables with the dark, attentive eyes of a snake. She looked lethal as she patrolled the kitchen this morning, though wizened and without make-up, her grey roots unmasked by the unforgiving lighting. Denise generally did the evening shifts and clearly wasn't accustomed to early starts.

"Where's Jocelyn?" Rachel asked, counting heads around the room. "And there's someone else missing."

"There's three of them with Helen: Jocelyn, Bethan and Suzanna." Denise deliberately mouthed the words 'Spot Check' and I flinched.

"Ahhh!" Rachel continued filling the bowls and my stomach lurched, just as it always did. Breakfast was

my least favourable meal, mainly because it was so gargantuan. It was a horrendous fullness that I failed to recover from all through the day, and a pervading guilt that I could not ignore.

"Remember Lea, no separating please," Rachel said lightly, handing me the bowl of Hell. I swirled my spoon around, gathering what appeared to be an equal measure of muesli, flakes and milk, before tipping it all off when her back was turned. I liked Rachel, yes, but it didn't mean I'd eat my cereal like a performing seal for her.

"I can't bloody believe it! Why?!! How dare you!!" It was Joce's posh voice, irate and growing louder as she advanced towards the kitchen. We all turned in unison to see her in the doorway, face aflame, countenance infuriated. She hugged her ubiquitary brown cardigan around her, hair sticking out in all directions, her feet bare. For a split second she looked so fragile and childlike. She caught my eye and I gave her a conciliatory smile, shuffling closer to Millie to make space on the bench for her. Joce's face hardened so I jutted out my bottom lip, enlarging my eyes, imitating a bereft infant. She bobbed her head dismissively from side to side and walked slowly over, looking at nobody, yet a grin was trying to break through her icy exterior. She slumped down clumsily in the gap to my right.

"What happened?" I asked, impatience prickled the tone of my voice.

"I'm back on Total. I got spot-checked and I failed."

"By how much?"

"I'm in big trouble," Joce frowned. "I'm nine pounds less than I was at weigh in yesterday."

The only plausible explanation was that Joce was a serial tanker too. The other burning question was how did she lose weight. I'd resolved to ask her after we left the kitchen.

Not only was she on Total Supervision but also on 3,800 calories in order to fast-track her weight. I felt sorry for her as there was no chance of Joce getting her discharge date brought forward now. She's been deluding herself in her belief that her dad was going to come and rescue her – we could all see it, apart from Joce herself. As she slurped her soggy cereal, I genuinely pitied her, she looked so shrivelled and sunken, her wan face tired and lined, wisps of her unkempt hair stuck to it. I was originally inspired by Jocelyn, but now I could only feel sympathy for her. It was amazing, the extent of my fondness for these friends at given times – Joce and Millie mainly - these broken human beings.

Lunch time came and went in a mess of mashed potato, over-fried chicken and runner beans slimed in butter. My achievement of the day was convincing the teacher I needed to retrieve some books from my room and having Loretta escort me to conceal my CD player downstairs. That afternoon I curled up in the

corner under the Sky Lounge window and listened to Therapy? To be honest, 'Troublegum' was the best therapy I ever managed to get. Tea time was something fishy – it was almost always salmon or tuna or something smelly. It's a good job Food Farm didn't have a dog because its nose would constantly be drawn to my pockets and sleeves, arousing suspicion. I listened to music, curled up in the corner, willing myself to stay awake, warning off digestion.

I'd numbed myself to a position of indifference regarding my exams. It was as if I'd pricked an aggravated boil, for weeks of tumescent anxiety had suddenly imploded and I floated, blasé, amidst the debris of my hopes and dreams. I think I'd exhausted myself through the obsessive reading and re-reading of notes, my juddered scrawl indelibly tattooed on my retinas. The unintelligible swirl of letters had become an endless pattern, a mindless coagulation of shapes and marks, resembling nothing more than a nonsensical doodle in my mind. I felt that, in spite of my diligence, I'd retained little and I consoled myself with the grim reality that it probably wouldn't matter anyway. There was a sense of pointlessness surrounding my goals, like crows blackening my horizon, pecking away at my future. I couldn't envision a career; my life ended here, with this stinking place. Who would possibly want to employ me? Surely my incarceration here and the stint in a psychiatric unit would have blighted any gleaming possibilities my future might hold. In my view, there was nothing the matter with me. I wasn't crazy; I merely had an aversion to eating. I wish I could say

that I had an affinity with the other patients here, that I at least had some common ground or could say that I fitted in. But I wasn't like any of these girls. I was a cat amongst the pigeons. The incident with the rabbit proved that.

Food Farm had a pet rabbit, the over-sized lop-eared bunny aptly named Lunch. He was adorable, with silky grey fur, large padded feet and one of those noses that incessantly sniffed. He reminded me of a cuddly toy my parents had given me one Easter when I was little. Lunch lived outside in the hutch surrounded by the luxurious garden. The fact that even this rabbit was marginally overweight lent credibility to the argument that the staff were feeders, people addicted to pumping others with food and fascinated by their consequent enlargement. Anyway, it was Lunch's tragic death – and the outrageous reaction to it - that made me question the morality of the other girls. It was announced after our evening meal that Lunch had been killed by a fox (in this suburban area, visits from foxes, badgers and other elements of wildlife was a regular occurrence) as someone had unwittingly left the rabbit's hutch open. I was shook with utter desolation, so upset that I could barely hold myself together. However, my grief was not shared. The Brown Kitchen erupted with howls of laughter, the girls trying to out-do each other with jokes at Lunch's expense. It was horrific and beyond belief. I fled from the room in tears, appalled and aghast but most of all wracked with sorrow at the violent and unnecessary loss of Lunch's life. Even Millie – my alleged kindred spirit - joined

in with the mocking and sniggering. I could never look at her in quite the same way again and I lost faith in humanity that fateful evening. Rarely have I felt so despicably and painfully alone.

The evening came around fast. Although I loathed the days wasted in this place, they elapsed surprisingly quickly, along with my visible ribcage. I sat counting down the minutes till my sanction ended, whittling the anxious last hour away by ferociously biting my fingernails and pulling at my eyebrows. I was essentially wishing my life away in one way or another. I sat on the windowsill, (there was no fear that I would topple to my death as the key to this window had been removed), legs pulled up to my chest, overlooking the verdant garden that represented freedom. The clock hands moved slovenly and seemed to slow down under my heavy gaze. I willed the clock to speed up so I could be out on the roof with Millie, Clara, Fliss and whoever else was available to join us. The rain had been plummeting in sheets for the majority of the day, but I could not hear a sound now as I pressed my ear to the glass. Darkness had smothered everything, making it impossible to detect the happenings beyond the window, yet the stillness put me at peace and filled me with hope. It was during the silence and the calm that I could focus and as I listened I could almost smell the outdoors, the sodden fronds hanging like dewy tassels, the gentle drip-dripping of the water pearls and the plip-plopping as they sloshed gently into puddles. The smell of matrix, of nature repairing

itself; a good storm clears the air and often paves the way for change.

I cast my eyes in Jocelyn's direction. She was curled up on the sofa in a patchwork blanket, seemingly asleep. All day she had ostracised herself, created a little nest on the settee, like a dying cat making a niche before it expires, where she slept and shut the lot of us out. I could hardly complain; that was my fundamental coping mechanism when I needed it – escape. I'd offered her my CD player but she'd politely refused, stating that she couldn't stand the sort of music that I listened to. I wasn't offended as I packed the CD player back into my bag, turning my back on Joce. Sometimes we all needed a bit of isolation, especially in a place like this with the omnipresent propensity to go stir crazy if we couldn't obtain a slice of space.

Chapter 12

"Not like that!" Poison Ivy's abrasive cackle cut through the air. Clara, Bethan and Holly looked up in alarm.

"What do you mean?" Alicia mewled.

"Give it here." Poison Ivy snatched the make-up compact from Alicia. Her name was Ivy, but Millie and I added the prefix because of her toxicity. Alicia nervously licked her lips, reluctant to let on that her feelings had been hurt.

"You're gonna make a right mess with it if you do it that way," Poison Ivy blurted out, demonstrating the correct way to blot powder blush. She held the brush up before the four pairs of star-struck eyes, "See?"

Ivy was an amateur actress who wore away the hours of our supervision time regaling us with tales of her alleged showbiz lifestyle. So far she had only had walk-on parts in a couple of low-profile films; however, there was a highly sought-after role in a soap opera lined up for her sometime in the near future. If I had to hear her crow on about it just one more time I think I would rip my own ears off.

"Ah, yes! That's much better!" Alicia cooed admiringly. The girls tumbled over themselves in their efforts to compliment Poison Ivy and gain her favour. To be perfectly honest, I couldn't tolerate this painted up, preening, pouting individual. The fact that

she worked here as a carer was laughable, for the only person she cared about was herself. Whenever she arrived, Ivy would prance up and down in her shiny too-high heels, like a goddess that we were all meant to bow down to, false eyelashes fluttering against her coloured-in eyelids, dark eyes gloating with malice and self-seeking. If the girls didn't idolise her they were afraid of her, intimidated by her co-ordinated outfits and stifling swathe of scent. I chose to ignore her and this infuriated someone as self-obsessed as Poison Ivy.

"Leanne, would you like to sit down please?" She asked in a blatant imitation of Helen.

"Not really," I said, "thank you." I couldn't help but be rude to her and I didn't know why. She really riled me up.

Adopting a sterner tone of voice this time, "Could you sit down Leanne?" Her eyes glared menacingly at me and I casually slumped to the floor. I'd probably pay for my deference later on. Her gaze lingered on me for a few seconds more than was comfortable before she leapt back into performing for her overawed sycophants.

"You should at least try with her." The other carer, Karen, tried to keep a straight face. It was difficult to take her seriously when she was of the exact same opinion as me.

"Who, Poison Ivy? Why?"

"You shouldn't call her that either." Karen swallowed a laugh.

"She is poison. Look at her." She was tottering about, re-enacting a scene from a 'bit-part' she'd had. "You can't tell me that she's a good influence. She's vindictive as well." I hadn't forgiven her for the time she almost let Marilyn plunge to her death out of the Sky Lounge window. Ivy had been too engrossed with impressing the patients with her French manicure, letting them rummage in her make-up bag under beady-eyed scrutiny. She failed to notice that Marilyn had both legs dangling from the window sill! It was Joce, Millie, Fliss and I who had managed to haul the trembling beanpole back through, encouraging her with affectionate words and cuddles. The incident had been hushed up so as not to spark alarm, although I knew it was to avoid any controversy being aimed at Poison Ivy. As usual she was more concerned with protecting herself than with consoling this poor suicidal waif.

Karen was completing a work placement here, so wasn't actually a fully fledged member of staff. Poison Ivy consequently liked to belittle her using subtle and spiteful tactics, which obviously weren't unnoticed by me. I liked Karen and for some obscure reason she had acquired a fondness for me, seeing something in me that I couldn't conceive of. I think she appreciated my dry sense of humour, coupled with the fact that I studied hard. Karen often cursed my anorexia, informing me that I could have a bright future ahead of me if only I got well. That was easier

said than done and Karen's ability to sympathise with me was better than pity.

"How's your revision going?" Karen changed the subject. Casey and Andrea had had their notes confiscated by the nurses last night due to obsessive compulsive studying. The two of them were obsessive in myriad areas of daily life; you only had to look at their red-raw hands to see the tell-tale signs of compulsive washing. Their angry rants at the removal of their revision tools had driven me to distraction last night. Joce had refused to get out of bed this morning and Marilyn had been re-fitted with the tube. It was a typical day of tantrums and tirades at Food Farm. I was certain that it was the prevalence of girls that caused such pandemonium and I longed for an influx of male patients - not in the romantic, love-interest way that Alicia and the others envisaged but to help diffuse the impossibly frenetic atmosphere.
Truthfully, I had almost given up on studying; I just couldn't concentrate any more.

"It's going nowhere," I moaned.

"Why's that?" Karen asked conspiratorially, before mouthing *Is it because of you-know-who?*

"No…and yes, a little." I guess Andrea and Casey were accountable to some extent for my depleted motivation. I explained to Karen then how I was feeling and how I was stagnating because no information was actually being retained by my stupid

brain. I admitted that I was so close to actually throwing in the towel.

"No, don't do that Lea!" She'd warned. "Just think how far you've come, surely you don't want to just throw it away."

"Of course not," I retorted. "I just feel so hopeless right now. It's like one, long never-ending struggle."

"Are you talking about your exams here or your anorexia?" Karen asked philosophically, cocking her head intelligently to one side. If she were a breed of dog, she'd be a Golden Retriever, I thought then, weighing up her smartness and loyalty packaged with her neatly kept blonde hair.

Conversation switched to revision strategies and mainly consisted of reassurance that I was remembering what I learned, I just didn't think that I was. Apparently, I should be able to recall a vast amount of knowledge when faced with the pressure of having to do so. I had to just have faith in myself. I'd never possessed the ability of self-belief, always fearing the worst and being wracked with anxiety. I alternated between failure and self-loathing, like a pendulum swinging back and forth, making no progress.

*

It wasn't easy to confide in someone, least of all someone who was in an uncompromising position on the bedroom floor.

"But do you really think that?" I asked Millie, whose legs were stretched back over her head as if she was about to attempt a backward roll.

"Of course," came her muffled reply. "The amount of studying you've done, you'll sweep the board."

I sighed for about the millionth time, restlessness overtaking me in waves.

"I don't know what to do; I don't know what I should be doing." Perhaps this sense of inertia had become my new problem. Because my control over eating had been unintentionally relinquished, I had substituted a new fixation in its place. Who was I to know? I was a parasite feeding off my own insecurities, a snake eating its tail and going round and round into an eternal, infernal void.

"Come on Lea, you've studied so much you're probably better than all the teachers put together!"

Millie's flippancy wasn't assuaging my turbulence. I truly felt that she wasn't taking my exams seriously. In fact, how could she be when she had rejected the opportunity of taking her own? My fingers twitched as I contemplated having another look at my notes. My head throbbed and all I wanted was to collapse

into nothingness, but the preoccupation preyed upon me like an organ grinder.

"Leave it for tonight Lea," Millie muttered, as if seeing right through me. "You're shattered, get some rest."

I resisted the temptation to 'but'.

"I mean it, Lea." My friend's face looked at me with genuine tenderness and I was taken aback, as Millie's tools were ordinarily wry jokes punctuated with sarcasm. It was rare to behold her softer side in its full splendour. Millie was the girl who would borrow my knickers when all of hers were in the washing basket, leaving me a neatly penned note of explanation; she was also the girl who did the best impressions of the other patients and nurses, her sense of humour knowing no bounds.

My tired face dragged the corners of my mouth into a smile and I settled down into bed. As I nestled under the duvet, colours washed like an exotic sea over and under my eyelids and it sounded like I was curled inside a cowry shell, being soothed by the lullaby of the sea. I gently lapsed into my beloved realm of blankness.

*

The week of the exams passed in a stupor. One thing I can recollect is that the staff members were all much nicer to us, as if being thrust in a daunting situation

put us on a pedestal. I took more liberties that week, recklessly squandering an excessive amount of food items. My sleeves and pockets were continually bulging with secreted foodstuffs. The only way I could think straight was to foster some level of control. I grew foolhardy, a whole Satsuma rammed down my sock for a whole day; I even smeared butter through my hair.

I still went swimming on the Tuesday morning, turning my back on extra cramming time in favour of puking up breakfast at the Leisure Centre. The pressure put on me – or the pressure I put on myself – spurred my illness more and I adopted a devil-may-care attitude. I was fortunate to be such an expert in food evasion; it was a shame I couldn't get a qualification in that.

The examinations took place in the other classroom, which was essentially a glorified cupboard (incidentally, it was equal in size to the food cupboard!) This mini classroom was rarely ever used, mainly providing a more intimate space for one-to-one meetings and silent study sessions. Fortunately, the large full-length garden-facing window offset the room's claustrophobic demeanour and seeing as there were only four of us sitting GCSE's, we fitted in snugly but confidentially. In between scribbling frantically on my exam paper, I was able to appreciate the view of the garden, which seemed to extend for miles, and I allowed myself to drift away in a transient reprieve. My mind has since pulled a black mask over my experience of the exams, my only

recollections being the admirable view of summer at its finest. I can reminisce in vivid detail, marvelling at the way the sun, dazzlingly hypnotic, illuminated the lush greens of the grass, defining each single blade with pristine precision. The trees and the flowers were a euphoric caravanserai of colour, the sun gracing it all, highlighting the plethora of beauty wielded by Nature. The outdoors was abundant with movement and wonder, like an outstretched hand hauling me out of the wreckage of my misery. When I visualised the sunshine, loving the sensation of it sweeping my cheek, I felt momentarily stilled. There was a reason this was my favourite season. In summer I could feel blessed.

The perceptible relief when the GCSE's finished pushed any thoughts of prospective results right out of mind. Life returned to business as usual, which was self-explanatory considering where I was. The daily struggles of eating and trying to avoid food being the predominant factor, no leniency was extended when I got caught filling my pockets with potatoes or when I was overheard emptying my stomach in the downstairs loo. I must have held the title for the most cheese sandwich punishments administered, though I never learned my lesson; once I had gotten away with one rebellious act or another I felt it near impossible to abstain from doing it again. Even the time on Total when I got caught vomiting into the sink as I brushed my teeth, I still attempted the same brazen feat repeatedly.

It was the middle of July, I weighed a staggering 43kg, and my stay here was still indefinite. The cigarette burns to my forearms had been duly noted by the nurses, as well as the increasing amount of cuts and scratches that mingled amongst old scars. My parents hadn't been impressed with the news, but they couldn't have been as devastated as I was upon being informed that my discharge date would be 'up in the air'. I felt like crying, only I couldn't, the antidepressants having a stranglehold on my tear ducts. I couldn't function properly, I was emotionally discordant.

The nurses' idea of a celebratory post-exam barbeque was absurd, though there was no way of preventing it from going ahead. Clearly in their own best interests, a food party in honour of anorexics wasn't only ironic, it was beyond comprehension. Helen and Rosie especially felt we were being ungrateful for our lack of enthusiasm.

"You girls should think yourselves lucky that we're willing to go to all this trouble for you," Rosie asserted that morning.

"We didn't ask for the barbeque," Clara quipped.

"Don't be so rude!" Rosie bit back.

"It's true," Joce added, risen like a phoenix from the ashes of her former bedraggled self. "Why should we relish such an event?"

Joce's rhetorical question seemingly flummoxed Rosie, who delivered a cold, unrelenting stare before Nicola's voice summoned her and she sauntered off.

The weather was faultless and would be perfect for some outdoor dining, - as long as you weren't food-phobic, of course - there would be no fear of rain dashing the nurses' spirits this afternoon. Awash with golden sunlight, the garden was warm and inviting; even though I dreaded the barbecue, the sunshine hadn't failed to brighten my perspective. I hoped that perhaps the staff would be too busy enjoying themselves to notice if any food didn't make it into our mouths. It came as a welcome surprise when Helen returned from the house clutching two bags filled with bottles of wine. She walked proudly to the tables, spread neatly with peach tablecloths, and deposited the carrier bags on them. Kaye joined her, also carrying a bag of bottles and a box containing champagne glasses, the box had never been opened, the glasses were brand new. I nudged Millie tentatively and she followed my eye line.

"Looks clear now who this occasion is actually in aid of," Millie sneered.

"Indeed," I said smugly.

"What's the matter?" Alicia nuzzled in between us, suspecting gossip, and keen to hoover any shards of information up like a vacuum cleaner, ready to spit them out when the moment proved fortuitous.

"Look at that impressive stash on the table," I pointed to the wine bottles and champagne glasses.

"Oooooh! We may be in for some drunken staff! This could be a laugh!" Alicia excitedly spun off to tell someone else about this sensational revelation.

"I hope they drink so much it makes them sick," I said flatly.

"I hope all those empty calories make them fat." Millie gave me her typical deadpan expression.

The barbecue was boring. The patients were congregated around tables to ostensibly flick bits of chicken under the table and smudge remnants of chocolate gateaux into the grass with their feet. The nurses, for the most part, seemed oblivious to our antics as they relaxed with one glass, followed by another and another of wine. Helen's round cheeks flushed rosy red and her eyes became nothing more than slits in her porky white face. Kaye became convivial, her voice risen several octaves to a louder version of her usual screech, as she gesticulated wildly with her hands. At one point, Kaye managed to upturn a wine glass from over-zealously waving her arms about. That should have been the point at which the staff toned it down and brought the event to a halt, but it continued, the staff getting merrier and the girls growing increasingly listless. A few girls had scarpered at around 6:45 and the others casually made themselves scarce as and when their post-meals were up. At 8:30pm there were just me and the

Totals who remained in the garden being "monitored" by some rather tipsy members of staff. I tried to skulk away but a robust voice stalled me.

"Leanne, you're on supervision until 9 o'clock." It was Helen, looking remarkably composed. Perhaps their inebriation was no more than a figment of my imagination. I returned, irresolutely, to my seat, my brow secured in a frown. Half an hour to go then and I literally counted down the seconds on my watch. The other girls had all bandied together, though I was unfazed by my isolation, ultimately looking forward to my evening escape onto the roof. It was like watching paint dry, that final countdown to freedom, but I endured, I survived it. As I kicked the wreckage of the barbecue around in the grass – chicken bones, cake crumbs and bread and burger debris – I watched the sky change, the day's azure blue diluting into swirls of cerise, interlaced with ribbons of gold, the whole panorama paling in comparison to the striking cloudless vista of the afternoon. I adored sunsets, not only their beauty but their sense of closure. Another day withstood; another day to cross off the calendar.

*

"No, Fliss, you really shouldn't, not another!" It was Suzanna's voice, serious and disciplinarian.

A gaggle of girls could be heard as I traversed the corridor, unsure why I felt the need to be tiptoeing. I reached the door of Clara and Fliss's bedroom and

instead of casually walking in, as I would usually do, I paused, weighing up the pros and cons of knocking.

"Shut up Robyn!" Suzanna's haughty voice ordered.

"I was just saying," Robyn uttered back.

"What are we going to do?" A voice I couldn't place rose above the din.

It sounded like a den of wasps from where I stood beyond the door. Voices fought for supremacy as they all spoke over each other, talking in unison. I had no idea what was happening, though my curiosity was emboldening me to make an entrance. I knocked deliberately three times on the white wooden door. Speech was reduced to whispers at the sound of my knuckles rapping against the bark and I suddenly felt self-conscious.

"What if it's…"

"Shhhhh!"

I swallowed before announcing in a small, timid voice, "It's only me."

"Me, who?" Holly said, exasperated.

"Lea." I gently pushed the door ajar to see the room was filled with people.

"Quick, come in. And close the door!" Clara was perched on the bed, half facing out of the window.

"We don't want *them* coming in!" Holly added, giving me an icy look.

"What's going on?" I asked her.

"What's the matter, haven't you ever been invited to a party before?" Holly stoically turned away from me as if I was worth less than a piece of dirt.

Millie beckoned me over from the corner of the room. I sprinted over, my puzzlement displayed on my face. Millie merely indicated the stash of bottles at the foot of the bed, as if that was meant to explain everything. I looked around me to get an idea of who was here and who was out on the roof. Holly, Alicia, Bethan and Clara were all seated on Clara's bed by the window. Robyn, Kayley and Kesley were sprawled over Fliss's bed and Suzanna was standing with arms folded next to the wardrobe.

"Fliss, Layla and the other Laura are outside," Millie said.

It wasn't hard to tell who had been drinking and who hadn't. Holly, typically vociferous, was high as a kite and Alicia was giggling pathetically at everything that Holly said. Kayley and Kelsey were also more raucous than usual, their voices shrill and ear-splitting.

"What's happening outside?" I asked Millie.

"They're just smoking."

"What were Suzanna and Robyn arguing about when I got here?"

"Whether or not Fliss should drink the last bottle of wine." I looked at the stash of bottles, noting that all three of them were empty. "She'd already drank half a bottle. She took the last one out on the roof with her."

"Have you had any?" I asked.

"Of course not," Millie replied, semi-outraged, "all those calories!"

Apparently, Fliss and Kelsey had stolen the bottles from the feast with no trouble at all. It was intended as a private party for two or three but, of course, news travels fast in a place like this and several more patients gate-crashed once they got wind of it. Funnily enough, few of the girls were actually keen to imbibe the illicit alcohol, for the same reason that Millie was staying sober. It was a well-known fact that wine was laden with sugary calories – this even kept me off it, back then!

Without warning, a loud terrified scream flared up from outside, jarring each and every one of us to a halt. A few seconds of nervous hesitation ensued before Millie or I dared to pry, though Suzanna

rushed to oversee the scenario, Alicia and Holly snapping round her like frenetic terriers. Robyn, Kayley and Kelsey had snapped themselves up to sitting positions and were staring fretfully out of the window, whilst Bethan and Clara were exchanging worried looks.

"What's going on?" I grabbed Clara's attention and spoke with clandestine efficiency.

"It's Fliss," came the laconic reply.

"Fliss what?" Millie whispered. We both emerged from our corner, keen to assess the situation ourselves now. Kelsey had recovered her composure and joined Suzanna in trying to assert control in the matter. Holly and Alicia were ineffectually shrieking and reiterating the words stated by the Blue Kitchen girls. It was clear that something had gone wrong.

"She's just had too much to drink, that's all. We need to try and get her back inside." Laura-2 appeared at the window, her face deathly pale against the black backdrop of night, illuminated strikingly by the moonlight. Her frightened eyes betrayed the calmness of her voice. "She's not in her right mind."

I peered through the gap to see Fliss poised near the roof's edge, one hand clutching the guttering that ran down the length of the side wall up to the next floor. She was swigging from the bottle and swaying like a banshee, swinging from the flimsy plastic piping that she was virtually hanging on. Layla had a supporting

arm round her shoulder, trying to manoeuvre her away from the precarious verge. Their lips were moving but I couldn't make out what was being said.

"I'm telling you, we need to go and get help," Suzanna pronounced, the smooth contours of her face lit up in profile at the window. Her small grey eyes possessed a steely determination, however, her hands were balled up into fists and trembling at her sides.

"No! Not the nurses!" Holly implored, "We don't need them coming up here!"

"We'll sort this out," Alicia agreed, "just don't get them involved."

"Think of how much trouble there'll be if they find out."

Layla shouted a muted 'help me!" from outside and we instantaneously lunged to the window, all eight of us pressing ourselves up against the pane of glass, eyes searching the darkness, the enclosed space thick with desperation so that I could almost smell the intensity of fear. Fliss had moved away to the other side of the roof, still perilously close to the rim, her hands cupped round her face in a position of hopelessness. Layla attempted to close the gap between them but Fliss kept stepping backwards, away from her, sobbing desolately, her dull cries barely audible in the distance. Laura-2 turned and started to run towards Fliss at the same time that

Kelsey was straddling the window ledge about to shimmy to her descent.

"Nooo! Don't come here!" Fliss punctured the air with her throaty scream. "I swear I'll jump!!"

Hysteria ripped through us like a swarm and we scrambled over each other at the window trying to call out calming, soothing sentiments in an effort to placate our friend. Layla and Laura-2 stood motionless; both an equal distance from her and Kelsey was waiting just beyond the window, shivering in her thin t-shirt. Nobody dared move in case it literally sent Fliss over the edge. Eventually, Laura-2 threw caution to the wind and took a series of slow, measured steps in her direction, elevating her hands as if to prove her own innocence. I noticed that her lips were moving but her tone of voice was so gentle that her words were swept away with the breeze.

"I can't take this anymore!" Fliss bellowed, collapsing to the ground like a wounded giraffe, her long athletic legs buckling under her and her head colliding with her bony knees. She was sideways against the edge, the slight lip of the roof touching her right foot. Laura-2 increased her pace until she was knelt at her friend's side, a protective arm slung around her back hugging her away from the sheer drop. Layla and Kelsey took flight, racing to assist and it was at that moment that all our heads turned at the boom of a familiar voice.

"What on earth is going on?" It was Helen standing like a prison warden in the doorway. She had flung the door open and proceeded to surge forwards relentlessly, demonic anger flickering in her eyes. We were all in for it now. That would be the final time the roof would be used as a smoking area.

*

Fliss was fine once she had sobered up. She was more ashamed of herself than anything else and irritated to be on Total Supervision for an indeterminate amount of time. Helen and Rosie were devastated to learn that Fliss had stolen the bottles of wine, though to Fliss' credit, she took full responsibility and hadn't inculpated anybody else in the situation. Clara and Fliss were banned from outings for two weeks because it was their window that was used to breach the rules. Moreover, the window was replaced with one that wouldn't open in a way as to allow patients' egress onto the roof to smoke. The barbecue was hushed up in secrecy, largely because of the nurses' irresponsibility at having alcohol on the premises in the first place. In an effort to avoid controversy, punishments were lighter than they would ordinarily have been. Helen, Rosie and Nicola threateningly stated that we must never speak of that evening again and there would be certain repercussions should Fliss' incident be brought to light.

"You've all had a lucky escape, girls. Things could have been much worse. Consider yourselves

extremely lucky." Rosie was essentially guilt-tripping us into not saying anything, using the potential death of our friend to scare us to secrecy. To be honest, I didn't want to remember the unfortunate night that I had been paralysed by fear and plainly shaking with dread. I was truly astonished that such a tragedy had almost unravelled before my terrified eyes. Like a lot of astoundingly negative situations, I blotted it out of my memory bank for a long time, not wanting to confront what could have, *what almost* took place on that roof.

"I don't want any of you speaking of this again. Felicity is aware of the gravitas of the situation and understands how fatal it could have been." Rosie turned her head slowly and deliberately to speak to each of us in turn, checking our expressions for any sign of dissent. "If anybody has any questions about what took place, please see your key nurse about it. Is that clear?"

A swathe of affirmative nods swept around the classroom.

It seemed that the 'incident' wouldn't even be taken to our esteemed Community Meeting, a get-together of all the patients, staff on duty and the two doctors that was supposed to take place every week, but rarely even happened once a month. Community Meetings were nothing more than pointless attempts by the doctors to portray a caring, compassionate side, as if they were reaching out to us and valuing our opinions. It was complete nonsense and Joce and

I responded appropriately by filling up the question box with banalities and vulgarities. For instance, on one occasion we had scribbled down questions about the male anorexic's reproductive system, doodled crude images of bowel movement types and wrote disparaging notes that cast aspersions on the doctors' sexualities. This was all anonymous, so Joce and I were invulnerable to reproof, though it was blatantly obvious that it was either of us or both. To be honest, I'd lost the ability to care. Deeming myself a victim of this place, I was keen to persecute the doctors, who I now blamed for my being here; Joce and I would write obscene notes for the box to perpetrate insinuations and propagate untruths about them. A bitter layer encased my heart, preventing the transmission of any warmth. A blackness had been engendered within me and it thrashed about, antagonised by my condemnation. Doctor Beaver particularly exasperated me, his patronising voice and belittling judgement had rubbed me up the wrong way from the very start. I felt inclined to try and make his life just a little bit more difficult and to ensure he got at least a portion of the displeasure he deserved. He was, after all, paid a hefty salary for doing so little; he had once fallen asleep during my therapy session, my hightailing for the door curtailing his snoring. It was my penultimate session and none of the nurses believed me when I informed them that Doctor Beaver had slept through ten minutes of my counselling. Bizarrely, I was chided for making a reckless break for the door and watched even more scrupulously by the staff.

In any case, I bet that Beaver and Dicken weren't ever informed of what almost occurred that evening with Fliss. I imagine it had all been covered up so that the staff on duty at the barbecue would avoid trouble. The incident had scared the living daylights out of me. I was almost stunned to the point of submission, realising that I could not stay here any longer and this time escape wasn't a viable option. I needed to buckle up, knuckle down and do whatever was necessary to get discharged. I didn't entirely know how to bring that about, but the thing I was most certain of was that I wanted to get out of here as soon as I possibly could.

*

I returned from the ill-fated meal to be confronted by an onslaught of tenacious voices, raised several decibels in their desperation to find out how I'd got on. Joce, Millie and Layla jostled around me like a trio of over-excited kittens the minute I'd walked through the door; I hadn't even managed to make it up the flight of stairs to the Sky Lounge! I was forced to take a hasty shuffle back, my arms held up in surrender or in self-defence - I wasn't sure which - as they barraged me with questions and suppositions. "How did it go?" "Where did you go?" "What did you eat?" "Did you finish everything on your plate?" I slunk past the three of them, grateful for my small stature, and slid into the quietude of the empty Brown Kitchen. More like faithful puppies than boisterous kittens, they duly followed, their tongues finally stilled as they mulled over possible reasons for my

silence. I deposited myself heavily onto the bench and exhaled an almighty breath as if offloading the burdensome experience. In my own time, I revealed the unalleviated disaster of my customary debut at TGI Fridays.

It wasn't my choice of restaurant and that enraged me from the offset. My parents had taken the clinic's views for gospel, as expected, despite my retaliations. The Tarantula had convinced my mother that TGI Fridays was just the place to get me used to eating around other people again and the portions were on a par with those consumed in the clinic. Lies, all lies. When we got out of the car and I looked at the building –Americanised, red, white and blue – it was almost bellowing 'supersize' at me. My reticence was not aided by the size zero waitress who was accosting our table, her cheeks puckered as if sucking a lemon, her enviably long legs the width of the knife and fork handles positioned in front of me. She was so detestably chirpy too and I hated her; I felt she was brazenly flaunting her thinness and mocking me because of the amount of food I would have to engorge whilst she watched. All of my protestations about the skinny waitress were brushed away by my dad with a "don't be so ridiculous," or a "stop being silly Lea."

When my meal arrived I really thought I was about to have a breakdown. There was little wonder I hated myself so much. It was as if I'd come out of the womb faulty, I was the personification of 'wrong'. I frequently wished that I could take my brain out and

subject it to a thorough rinsing, not only for improvement but to cleanse myself of these wretched thoughts. Something inside me felt uprooted and my whole presence was under threat from an unpleasant implosion. My mum saw my quivering lip like a child's on its first day at school and came to my rescue, fearing a teary deluge, or worse, my Jekyl and Hyde transformation into a merciless tornado.

"Just try your best Leanne. That's all we ask. Take your time and just eat as much as you can manage."

One by one the chips ended up on the floor. I nibbled along one edge of the battered fish before guilefully scrunching it up underneath my napkin. I ate the peas painstakingly one at a time as I mashed the chips to a paste beneath the table. I would have been a fool to believe that my little performance had gone unnoticed and as we walked away, tears streaking my face to look like Alice Cooper, I floated above the hushed whispers at my expense. Even Leonard and Leonie were questioning my outlandish behaviour, my mum rebuking them with comments like, "it's only her first meal out, she'll do better next time."

"What a waste," was all that my brother could say and I couldn't agree more.

Chapter 13

An inordinate thrill of delight rushed through me at the sight of the red flourish, like crimson ink darkening blotting paper. I felt as if all my Christmases had come at once. It was extraordinary how something I had been so embarrassed about aged 13 and strived to keep secret was now the source of such triumphant elation. It was 6:45am and there was nobody officious to report this to. Overcome with excitement, I hurtled back to my bedroom, the words escaping from my lips the moment I'd flung open the door.

"Mille! Guess what! You'll never guess! Are you awake?!"

"Ugghh." A choked noise rattled up from beneath the duvet. I leaped onto Millie's bed, knees first, unfazed by the contortion of limbs that were resting under piles of covers unseen.

"Ouch!" Millie shrieked.

"Sorry, I was just making sure you were awake."

"Why, so you could assault me, you crazy cow!" Millie sat up, tenderly rubbing her shin, her face lit up with a crooked grin. "Come on then, Lea. What's all the fuss about?"

"It came back!" I squealed, and I cringed at having done so, realising how pathetic and puerile I must

sound. Millie offered a vague, quizzical expression, so I continued. "My period, Millie, it's come back!" Millie lunged over and enveloped me in an unexpected hug.

"Wow, that's fantastic news! Well done!" I was rather confused at Millie's choice of words, at how I 'done well' in achieving this seemingly natural body process, but I acquiesced and hugged her back. "How much more have you got left to gain?" She asked, letting me go.

"Six pounds."

"So they'll drop your target weight now then." Millie clapped her hands together with glee. I was invigorated by Millie's apparent pleasure at my happy news.

"In theory, they should," I beamed.

"That's fantastic news Lea, you must be overjoyed! It's just like Jazz."

"Yeah, well, I don't *feel* like Jazz." I rued the transformation of my body, how it rippled into curves that I'd never before had, my flesh felt spongy like dough, and the word 'succulent' came to mind, making me squirm. Millie met me with a blank look. "See this! It's disgusting!" I squeezed my bare upper arm to justify my self-deprecation, squelching the fat that bulged between my fingertips like children's

play-dough. Everything about me had become pink and squishy, round and globular.

"Don't be silly!" Millie trilled, "You're on the skinny side of normal. Look, you can still see some bones," she pointed to my wrist and I gave her a fake smile, making it clear that a wrist bone doesn't count as they are visible on practically everyone. "I've got to get to my target and I'm bigger than you already. At least you'll get your weight lowered now that your period's back."

Like a cruel joke, nobody took my pleas for a lower target weight seriously and I felt not only wronged, but duped. In my eyes it was the great betrayal, for the one 'fact' that I had relied upon had all turned out to be, in my case, a huge farce. As soon as I spotted Nicola and Denise that morning I'd bombarded them with the news and instead of congratulating me, they warned me to calm down and to not get my hopes up. Bemused but not without hope, I moved on to Rosie who was pouring out the cereal at breakfast.

"I don't want to hear about it Leanne, just go and sit down please." She shook me off, her Irish voice pulsing like a berretta, urging me step aside and shut my mouth. When I again approached Nicola, she merely stated that there was nothing to be done on a Friday morning, it would have to wait until an official weigh day. Deflated, I decided there was nothing I could do at the moment and surely someone would have to listen to me properly soon.

I'd pestered the Tarantula about it later that day and as she was my key nurse I'd assumed that she'd be my best bet. Again, I was wrong.

"Oh Lea-Lea!" (I hate it when she calls me that) "Why this great obsession?"

"It's not an obsession, it's the truth! Jazz got her target weight lowered!" I realised that I must sound like a petulant child, but I was beyond caring. I felt like I was trying to get to the bottom of some odious hypocrisy.

"So?" The Tarantula held her hands on her hips, as if to demonstrate who had the upper hand here.

I inhaled, preparing myself to speak, but stopped abruptly, letting the wasted breath seep from my lungs.

Needless to say, I went on to accrue not only the mandatory half a stone, but two extra unnecessary pounds just for the absolute Hell of it. I felt not like the beached whale, but as large as the ocean itself, a tremulous mass of uncontrollable substance. Once my hostility had subsided – and that took a while – I was overtaken by a fog of despondency that crippled me emotionally for the remainder of my incarceration.

*

The day had come and none of us truly believed it would. Joce had all of her belongings packed up and was sitting hunched over a large suitcase in the Blue Kitchen in anticipation of her father's arrival. Joce had been at her target weight for a meagre two weeks but her dad was on his way to rescue her, as he had stridently promised. I remember the day with perfect clarity, the August sun seeming to billow through the window as the shadows of the trees undulated across the white kitchen tops. The window was crammed with emerald leaves, the sunlight glistening through and between them to create a kind of splendour, the veins illuminated like a surreal ultrasound scan that both attracted and repulsed me. In spite of Jocelyn's ecstasy at being freed from this place, I felt miserable. Not only did I not want to see her leave, but I feared for her well-being. I found it too hard to pluck up the courage to dampen her parade. I bit my tongue and held my harsh appraisal in check.

"I'm really gonna miss you, y'know?" I had to say something before the tears would creep out.

"Awww Lea, I'm going to miss you too!" She still spoke like a young woman from finishing school and it made me smile. Even the time when she was at her lowest ebb, wandering around with her hair dishevelled, wearing that dreadful cardigan, she still spoke with such grace and class. Unsurprisingly, it was Joce's abhorrent cardigan that held the secret to her weight decline and the resultant spell back on Total Supervision; the gigantic pockets and crevices of this monstrous garment had devoured most of her

food so that Joce didn't have to! Joce only intimated this titillating nugget of information a week prior to our parting and she exuded the imperious blissfulness of having not disclosed this fact to anybody other than me. In fact, Joce bragged that the nurses were still tying themselves in knots trying to fathom her mystery weight loss technique.

"You swear you'll keep in touch, won't you?" I swallowed the lump that was growing in my throat.

"Of course I will! I'll look forward to hearing from you Lea and finding out about your escapades. Your letters will make an even better read than our Food Farm Handbook."

"That reminds me, who gets to keep the final copy of it? It's still in my room!"

"You keep it. After all, it was your idea in the first place." Joce and I underwent a journey of reminiscence then, remembering that night together on Total when, huddled up within a hair's breath of each other, we had formulated the embryonic 'From Stick Insect to Elephant in Six Months'. I certainly would miss Joce, for we had shared a lot of humour and heartache over the past five and a half months. The secrets we'd disclosed and the schemes we'd thought up; here was a friendship that could never be forgotten.

"What time's your dad getting here?" I asked, diverting the conversation from any potential pathways to over-sentimentality.

"He should be here any minute now. He's always late."

"Well, I'd best get back up to the Sky Lounge, before they send out a search party for me." I was aware of the tremor in my voice and wanted to make a hasty getaway before the teary flood could manifest itself.

"They'll think you've snuck off with me," Joce said, amused at the thought.

"I would have said there'd be room for me in one of your bags, but I'm not so sure now I'm at this weight!" Joce locked me in a hug.

"Take care of yourself Lea, won't you."

"I will. You make sure you look after yourself too."

"Of course! The last thing I want is to be back here on a four thousand calorie weekend! That's not my idea of a vacation at all."

I turned and walked away, the smile falling from my face. Days ago I had found out that the Sky Lounge wasn't thus named because of its location up in the sky, surrounded by leafy branches and birdsong, but because it was the only room in the clinic that had Sky TV. Another illusion shattered, I felt like my

reality was crumbling around me and nothing embodied truth anymore. Even Joce's discharge was a farce, for she wasn't well, she had not recovered. If anything, it was exactly like Fliss had stated up on the roof that evening a while back, that most patients leave here more ill than they came in, the acquired tricks of the trade impeding any progress. Food Farm had the quick-fix statistics and guaranteed weight-gain to corroborate its success, though few long-term health benefits were ever witnessed. Most patients dwindled and declined the minute the reins of their lives were handed back over to them.

Joce's image imprinted on my consciousness, the quirky pixie haircut and the quick searching eyes that peered beneath her fringe, I would never forget the severity of her jaw line, razor sharp like a model's. I bundled up all my memories of Joce – her posh, conspiratorial laugh, her wardrobe of sophisticated browns and dark blues - and carried them around with me on my own way. That was the last time I ever saw or heard from Jocelyn.

*

The day hadn't been an easy one and I was grateful when 9pm swung round and I could ensconce myself in my own room, in my own space, in my own sanctuary. After the imperative retching - however, after jacket potato for tea, it was to little avail, carbohydrates digest too irritatingly quickly – I made my way along the corridor to my room, noting the escalation of noise ever since the smoking window

had been replaced. There was a clash and a clamour of voices, tinkles of laughter and a mish-mash of divergent conversations taking place at once. Since the patients were unable to sneak onto the roof, all the socialising took place in bedrooms, without the need for the imperative hush-hush associated with being up to no good. I was stunned when I opened the door and my hand involuntarily flew up to my mouth as I gasped in astonishment. Joce's beloved cuddly Dalmatian, Lucky was resting across my patterned duvet, his polka dotted face poised in my direction as I entered the room. I stood motionless in a stalwart effort to hold myself together, to stop the glints of emotion from becoming a convulsive maelstrom.

"Are you all right, Lea?" I hadn't even registered Millie's presence, so overwhelmed by the gift of generosity from Jocelyn. I nodded, not allowing any sound to emit from my lips, else I would start to cry. Millie could sense my susceptible precariousness too, advancing to my side to pat my shoulder, in a 'there, there' moment as I caressed the Dalmatian's head, reading the letter that Joce had left to accompany Lucky. In her paradoxically elegant and jagged hand, she had succinctly penned.

Dearest Lea,

Take care of Lucky, but more importantly, take care of you.

Much love
Joce x

It was a piece of note paper torn neatly from her unused exercise book, the red margin skirting the left hand side, her note composed precisely in the centre of the page in black biro. Her name was signed at the bottom with a flourish, the large, grandiose 'J' swirling interminably and the italicised letter 'e' joining up to the solitary kiss at the denouement. I was surprised that she hadn't written more and I instantly felt ashamed at being so ungrateful. What more had there been to say? What else could she possibly have to write? Admittedly, I was jealous at her being granted reprieve from Food Farm, but that sentiment certainly paled in comparison to how much I was going to miss her.

"Do you think she'll be ok?" Millie asked, swirling a strand of her trademark mermaid hair around her thumb and forefinger. I held my breath for a couple of seconds, hesitating.

"I hope so Millie. I really hope so."

Chapter 14

"There's two for you this morning Lea."

Two envelopes dropped into my lap as I sat cross-legged on the sofa in the Brown Kitchen. Funnily enough, I never did ascend into the trustworthy ranks of the Blue Kitchen; I remained one of the shifty-looking quiet ones that had to be watched out for. I was cocooned between Millie and a newer admission called Katey, who had debunked a couple of weeks ago.

I considered how this place resembled a conveyor belt, pumping us in, stuffing us up and spitting us back out into society without even a thought as to what went on inside our heads; our grey matter and emotional well-being remained at the bottom of the priority list, un-prodded, un-penetrated and, for all intents and purposes, superfluous to the staff's quest to fatten us up to a 'healthy weight'. Since Joce had left, two other patients had been discharged and this new girl Katey and another called Annie had arrived to take their places. We were nothing more than cargo, coming here to dock for a while and piled with baggage before being shipped off to another destination, the daunting task of managing that weight our own responsibility.

Inevitably, Marilyn started to fill out, her jagged planes and angles being smoothed over by softer contours, tissue repairing the fissures and padding over her bones. Her figure swelled to present

covetable curves and although she would never be a shapely Monroe she still eternally aspired - like the rest of us - to be Twiggy. Marilyn came to epitomise the grim reality that no body was exempt from the Food Farm regime.

A flicker of maroon at the periphery of my vision as Katey lurched her face around to stare at me, her ponytail flicking from side to side like its namesake.

"Aren't you gonna open them then?" Katey asked, aghast, her pupils like fine black points in her rich hazel eyes.

"It's unlike Lea to not tear her letters open like a wild animal," Millie teased, "what's gotten into you?"

I ignored that statement, unwilling to unleash the truth just yet. My gaze specifically honed on Millie, I shredded the envelopes like a feral beast, entertained by the reverberation of laughter, like water droplets ricocheting off stainless steel, as Millie and Katey appreciated my charade.

"Who's it from? Who's it from?" Katey chirped and at times I could see why others found her annoying. Millie arched an eyebrow in mutual understanding.

"Hang on a second…" already knew who they were from, I'd judged the handwriting immediately. The small lilac envelope was from Leonie and I had already predicted the contents of it, meaning I would have to keep it secret from the others. The A3

231

envelope was undeniably a card. It was adorned with a picture of an owl brandishing a bundle of colourful balloons, the word 'Congratulations' in embossed silver above his head. Inside was a lovely note from Mrs Pringle who congratulated me on my GCSE results and expressed that she was looking forward to seeing me return to study my A Levels.

It had seemed a long time since the blood, sweat and tears of exams, and the relief was palpable when I had received my results, realising that I had done better than expected. Two A*s in English Language and English Literature were the pinnacle of my accomplishment, an A in Art sealing my satisfaction. In all I had obtained eight GCSE's at a grade C or above. I couldn't believe it initially and, as sceptical of ever, I pondered whether this was another wicked joke calculated by someone at the clinic; an evil attempt by someone to lift me up before pulling the rug out from beneath my feet. As the news began to sink in and I could accept that I had genuinely done well and against all the odds, I felt I could afford to contemplate a future beyond the chocolate bars of this prison cell.

"That's really nice Lea, well done!" Millie said, after reading the note inside the card. I'd secreted my sister's letter in my pocket, reluctant to have my real news be revealed prematurely.

"Your teacher's called Mrs Pringle?" Katey uttered, "she'd fit in well here – Pringles, like the crisps."

"I had a teacher at High School called Mrs Bakewell as well actually," I declared. "And she was the Cookery teacher as well!"

"You're making that up!" Katey exclaimed.

"No I'm not, I mean it!" I nodded vigorously.

"My Head of Year was called Mr Crumble," Millie added, "and there was a dinner lady called Miss Frooty. She took a lot of stick for her name, poor woman!"

"I'm not surprised," Katey grinned.

"There's just no avoiding food," I said.

Over the past few weeks I had withstood another three meals out, each one an improvement upon the last. I had grown to understand that this place operated in a similar way to school; as well as the cliques that were determined by popularity, the staff 'favourites', the groups of misfits and the individual outcasts, we were rewarded for our good behaviour; our ability to gain weight and adopt conformist eating habits were tantamount to getting praise on a report card. Moreover, I could foresee that towing the line was my ticket out of here.

The Tarantula and Helen had harangued my parents with the usual spiel prior to leaving the building for my second restaurant meal. They ascertained the value of dining at TGI Fridays, emphasising the

nutritional value of the food and asserting that the portion sizes were just what I had to learn to deal with if I ever hoped to survive in the 'real world.' I think their words had bludgeoned my mum and dad into indignation, for the minute we'd got into the car my mum turned to me.

"There's no way we're going to that place again."

The tension fell from my face, making me feel years younger, and my shoulders lost their rigidity. I marvelled at my parents' abnormal deviation from the ethos of Food Farm. My dad was driving, staring straight ahead, although I noticed the distinct nod of his head at my mum's words.

"The food was rubbish in that place and the service wasn't up to much either," he remarked, still focused on the road ahead.

"Mc Donald's! Mc Donald's!" Leonie chorused mirthfully.

"Mc Donald's isn't any better either," my mum said.

"The food's all made of plastic," my dad stated, "we'll find a nice little pub somewhere."

"I can have a beer then," Leonard declared, brightening up - he had been forced to postpone yet another weekend with his mates in order to come and applaud me for finishing a meal.

My dad pulled in to the car park of a friendly-looking family restaurant and instead of feeling fraught with nerves, I was relaxed and open-minded. My stomach wasn't knotting itself in horror as we walked inside the large rustic double doors either, and I was able to take in my surroundings in a leisurely way. There was a little outdoor play area to my left as we entered, a slide, three swings and a miniature climbing frame and I recollected how, in the past, I would have charged towards it with childish impetuosity, oblivious to the stricken glances that I drew my way. Uninhibited and unabashed I would have leaped upon the play things with delight, Leonard and Leonie taking my lead and joining in the ambush. How different things had become as we plodded cumbersomely through the entrance. It was with a heavy heart that I understood the cause of our dejection was me. My anorexia had been a noose tightening about all five of our necks, restricting our lives and sucking the joy out of us. Watching the ashen countenances of my mother and father – the sheer exhaustion that streaked their once glowing faces – and the ennui of my two siblings, the full extent of my self-absorption suddenly dawned on me with crippling clarity.

A clean plate marked the end of the meal and I had surprised even myself. Admittedly, the portion was not as horrendous as the gluttonous serving at the other restaurant and I felt more at ease in these muted, cosier surroundings. The following expedition was another success, and the radiance crept back into my parent's cheeks. Leonard became more animated

also, more comfortable by my more conventional conduct. Leonie was as lovely and encouraging as ever, reminding me that the more food I ate, the sooner I'd be back home with them all. The fourth and final meal out was another TGI Test and although I failed to vacuum up everything on my plate, I refused to succumb to my old ways. The floor beneath my feet was clean and tidy once the meal was over, even if I did leave half a plate of chips behind on the table.

There was a perpetual shift in my mood over these couple of weeks. I couldn't bring myself to look in the mirror yet - that was still quite a way away – and I struggled to comprehend any qualities that I possessed. Nonetheless, hate was becoming too strong a word to describe how I felt towards myself. I was beginning to accept the unconditional value deposited on my by others and I learned to accept their love and concern for me in a way that I had never been capable of before. No longer blighted by such a yearning to self-destruct, I was alternately humbled by the care afforded to me by my faithful network of family and close friends. This newfound sense of cohesion was the bungee cord that held me aloft so that I wouldn't hit rock bottom again. Bruised but not battered, I started to appreciate the life I had and which still awaited me once I got out of this place. There was a future enriched with opportunities, everyone kept telling me, I just had to get out there and seize it. I owed it not only to myself to start living my life again, but to all those others

who had supported me, believed in me and who had very nearly grieved for me.

Chapter 15

The weather was abysmal that day and I should have felt upbeat, but the molten grey sky cast a dark shadow over my disposition. The clouds had been threatening precipitation all morning and, after lunch, the heavens finally opened, drowning me in melancholy. I was leaving today. It was my last day and I should have been rejoicing. However, I was overthrown by an unfathomable perception of grief, of loss, of eventuality and I couldn't rally my spirits to conquer such negative feelings. Deep down and in spite of my pertinacity, I was a sappy sod, burdened by sensibilities and driven by emotional fervency. I struggled to keep my feelings in check – unable to understand how I felt something or why most of the time. Piling on three and a half stone sure helped to upset my emotional balance as well as impair my physicality. I'd been appalled that since my hormones had 'changed' again, I was once more peppered with acne. I struggled to accept my new body, complete with lumps and bumps which were difficult to ignore – I could *feel* the difference without having to use my eyes to deduce the extravagant changes in a mirror. For the first time in my life I had thighs that swelled beyond the boundaries of my quadriceps and my gargantuan hips volumised my entire bodily circumference. I no longer had the figure of a child, but I was not in possession of an adult mind.

Some things changed, yet I was still flailing in a dark and terrifying vortex. The only thing, I guess, that I

could glean from my experiences was that the worst was over. I'd confronted my fear – my punishment for my anorexia was to be installed in a place like this – and I was set to be ejected out the other side to continue with my life. My emotions fluctuated like the weather and I remained equally as unpredictable. Inexplicable sadness could catch me off guard, yet I had the good fortune to be able to experience and appreciate happiness as and when it appeared. For the most part though I remained an incredibly restless individual and I was at pains to find something to quieten the ferocity of my nerves.

I'd x'ed off the days counting down to my discharge with the zeal of a child preparing for their annual visit from Santa. The only thing that had pulled me into line was the sincere promise that I could leave on the 22nd September, all being well – *all* indicating me in this instance. I had to demonstrate blind faith in this instance, as, sceptical as ever, reason dictated that there must be another trick up the nurses' sleeves. I felt certain I was set to be made a fool of.

We were all assembled in the classroom, four walls rife with so many memories. The tree extending beneath the large window, beyond the pale blue patterned curtains would assist my dogged pursuit of sanguinity. I would recount the vestiges of mealtimes strewn about that tree – the Food Tree it was secretly referred to - as most of the patients were responsible for slinging something or other out of the window to decorate its branches. There were half-eaten sandwiches, bits of potato, mouldering fruit, all sorts

of discarded foodstuffs stranded in that tree. Desperation had coerced us into flinging the remnants from our pockets or wherever we could conceal anything from our plates, out of that beguiling window to be swallowed by ambiguity. Remembering the Food Tree always raised a smile, more so because it remained undiscovered and, as a result, represented another conquest.

School had started for the new term and I had a moment of déjà vu as I spotted Clara and Holly going to any lengths to evade work. Robyn and Bethan were misbehaving as usual, foraging in the forbidden cupboard for colourful supplies. Millie was still devising grisly concoctions, juxtaposing gaudy and repellent images, only she was sitting at a table facing Leighanne, in a dour parody of how I used to be seated opposite; in a bleak way, I had already been replaced by the name thief. Katey and Layla sat either side, Layla was making origami boxes and Katey was doing as little as humanly possible. My anxiety levels peaked as I had expected my parents ten minutes ago so I took pains to distract myself by observing the schoolroom dramatics.

My bags were neatly packed up in my room; all was in order and everything was in its place, contrasting sharply with my mind which was in complete disarray. It was difficult to imagine life beyond this place now, my future uncertain and my own to fulfil. I felt as if I had somehow redeemed myself, my keys to freedom handed back to me. I was excited and unnerved by the prospect of being in the driving seat,

navigating the unknown roads that snaked treacherously ahead.

Millie had commented how empty and devoid of colour the bedroom looked with all of my belongings packed away. My menagerie of stuffed toys was gone, including Lucky, who was lounging over the handles of my grey suitcase, his head lolling longingly towards the door. The multi-coloured dream catcher that I'd bought from Camden Market was no longer gracing the window and my bedside table was free of the organised clutter that had previously been displayed on it: the tangle of bead bracelets, pile of postcards and letters, and the small group of animal ornaments that watched over me as I slept. I'd carefully stripped the three large posters that hung above my headboard; one large iconic black and white image of Kurt Cobain, cradling his left-handed guitar, whilst blowing a captivating smoke cloud from his lips, a trio of dolphins leaping gracefully in an arc amidst a lilac backdrop, and a tattered poster of the Manic Street Preachers, their clothes emblazoned with spray painted slogans, circa 'Generation Terrorists'. Millie said she would miss the hum of my music blaring from my headphones as I dozed in bed, though I guessed that was her way of reassuring me that I wouldn't be forgotten. She wasn't a particular fan of my music and, similarly, I couldn't stand her dance tracks, the pulsing, pummelling noise that she exercised to day in and day out. I realised now that I would miss that music, it represented Millie and the close bond we had shared. Every time I heard a particular tune for years

afterwards it would call to mind my darkly effervescent mermaid-haired friend. Like Joce, Millie also had a special place carved in my heart and I had memories I would cherish with such fondness for the rest of my life.

I had been irrevocably altered as a result of my subjugation in an eating disorder clinic for nearly six months and it wasn't easy to explain how or why. I had been indelibly marked – mentally tattooed or emotionally scarred – because I had an intrinsic link to this place and these other patients, a bond that would be with me, un-severable, for the rest of my days. Anorexia still had a stranglehold over me, that I was sure of, and I doubted it would ever fully relinquish its power over me; like old friends, we stuck together literally through thick and thin. My illness remained the comfortable glove I sought refuge in and our loyalty was certainly reciprocated. I believe that the way out is through and, in order to develop, we must endure situations that test us. My confinement at Food Farm is testament to that theory. Despite the laughs and sense of camaraderie I'd shared, I had encountered the toughest chapter of my youth and perhaps even my entire lifetime. I wouldn't be walking out into a gorgeous sunset or facing the glamorous happy ended as promised in the movies and in many ways nothing had changed. I balked at clichés that referred to life being 'a bed of roses' or the 'grass being greener on the other side' because change took effort and willingness. If I had realised anything in my sojourn it was that change for the better had to start from within.

Staring intently at a tiny wren that had landed on the windowsill, I hadn't a clue who I would become and what would shape my future, but at least I had hope, and that meant everything.

EPILOGUE

My past resembles a dreamscape; an unhinged montage of images, textures, feelings, and colours, sensations and memories tumbling over one another, colliding, competing for dominance. History washes over me like flotsam on a beach, debris informing my existence, the pulchritudinous wreckage of my life never fully laid to rest.

Millie wrote to me for several months following my departure, her microscopic handwriting mimicking her hollow whisper. We still referred to the patients and staff by the dog-breed nicknames we had assigned them. On my last day I had given Millie the Food Farm Handbook that Joce and I had humorously composed, pre-empting her to augment her own thoughts and notions to it. In the first bout of letters, Millie would conjure some wicked anecdotes for 'From Stick Insect to Elephant in Six Months'. We even joked about publishing the document. But, inevitably our correspondence disintegrated and now, like Joce and the others, she is untraceable.

I have no idea what happened to the plethora of girls who did time in that clinic. The only former inmate I've encountered out and about is Clara, sparkling with health, three vivacious children keeping her on her toes. I heard rumours circulating Leighanne - she was committed to an adult psychiatric ward, that she had gone downhill and lost an unbelievable amount of weight, even reports that she had died, but the validity of all this 'gossip' is questionable. There was another

'report' of an attempted suicide at the clinic a few years after I left, but I chose not to tie myself up in speculation that did not concern me.

At first, I tried to maintain various friendships I'd established but the vivacity of living took over, sweeping me off into a myriad other endeavours. I had to accept that some things were gone – relationships lost albeit not forgotten - and that some ties are better shed in order to move forwards. If I have learned anything, it is that the purpose of life is to live it unabashedly, relishing each and every moment, and, slowly but surely, I am able to take the rough with the smooth. I will never forget or regret the events that have brought me to this point, for all experiences are crucial in my personal variegated tapestry.

Whatever I have enjoyed or endured, whether I have beheld pleasure or been afflicted with pain, all fragments have accumulated to make me the person I am today, for without darkness, there cannot be light.

47443263R00139